"*I hope your friend appreciates the danger he's put you in.*

"I wouldn't be surprised if you run out of clothes this weekend, because, personally, I plan to have a glass of Perrier on hand at all times just in case you get out of line."

Jed could hardly believe it. A sly smile, a teasing tone, and his hormones were going haywire. He couldn't let her roll over him this way. He'd be damned if he was going to spend the entire weekend ducking water.

"There's something you need to understand," he said. "My character may be a jerk, but he doesn't *know* he's a jerk. He thinks he's irresistible to women. If you throw a drink at him again, he'll assume you're interested, haul you over his shoulder and march you up to his room."

"How very fascinating! And what would he do once we got there?"

"You're a beautiful woman, Ellie. Thorpe may be a jerk, but he knows the difference between a lump of coal and a priceless diamond. He would make love to you as sensitively and as passionately as he could."

Dear Reader,

Spellbinder! That's what we're striving for. The editors at Silhouette are determined to capture your imagination and win your heart with every single book we publish. Each month, six Special Editions are chosen with *you* in mind.

Our authors are our inspiration. Writers such as Nora Roberts, Tracy Sinclair, Kathleen Eagle, Carole Halson and Linda Howard—to name but a few—are masters at creating endearing characters and heartrending love stories. Their characters are everyday people—just like you and me—whose lives have been touched by love, whose dreams and desires suddenly come true!

So find a cozy, quiet place to read, and create your own special moment with a Silhouette Special Edition.

Sincerely,

The Editors
SILHOUETTE BOOKS

SE-RL-3

BROOKE HASTINGS
Double Jeopardy

Silhouette Special Edition

Published by Silhouette Books New York

America's Publisher of Contemporary Romance

For Uncle Alvin,
who always has kind words about my books.

SILHOUETTE BOOKS
300 East 42nd St., New York, N.Y. 10017

Copyright © 1986 by Deborah Gordon

ISBN: 0-373-09349-7

First Silhouette Books printing December 1986

America's Publisher of Contemporary Romance

Printed in the U.S.A.

Books by Brooke Hastings

Silhouette Romance

Silhouette Special Edition

Silhouette Intimate Moments

BROOKE HASTINGS

is a transplanted Easterner who lives in California with her husband and two children. A full-time writer, she won the Romance Writers of Americas's Golden Medallion Award for her Silhouette Romance, *Winner Take All*. She especially enjoys doing the background research for her books and finds it a real challenge to come up with new plot twists and unique characters for her stories.

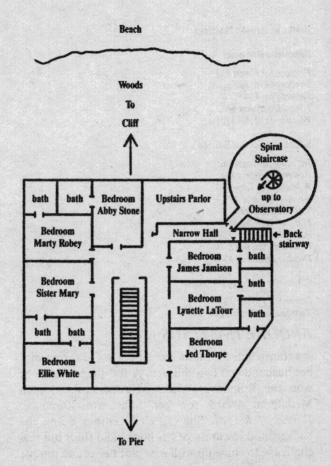

**SECOND STORY–TIPTON HOUSE,
RAVEN'S ISLAND**

Chapter One

It was one of the most beautiful dining rooms Ellie had ever seen. The fabric on the walls looked like silk damask and the rug was worn enough to be a genuine Aubusson. A crystal chandelier of labyrinthine intricacy was hanging above a gleaming mahogany table. Seven chairs were arranged around the table, their backs and seats upholstered in antique brocade. It was only early afternoon, but by this evening one of those seven seats would be filled by a murderer.

Not a real murderer, of course. He—or she—would be no more real than the silk, crystal and brocade probably were. Ellie had come to this splendid mansion on an island off the coast of Massachusetts to take part in a mystery-adventure game called Death on Raven's Island. She would be acting out a role and trying to solve a crime. Everything here was make-believe, but still, the house was so eerily silent that real murder didn't seem out of the question.

Nobody had even answered her knock on the front door. The boatman who had ferried her to Raven's Island over choppy, wind-whipped seas had finally pushed it open and let her inside. Then he'd returned to his launch, leaving Ellie alone in the hall.

Shaking off her edginess, she carried her suitcase and portable computer to the foot of the staircase and walked into the front parlor. Its furnishings were as understated and elegant as those in the dining room. Skulduggery Enterprises, the company that was running the game, certainly was thorough. The house was supposed to be a luxurious but dangerous vacation retreat, and that was exactly how it looked. The fact that it was on an island added to the sensation of isolation and impending doom. Outside, the wind had come up and the surf was pounding against the shore. Huge trees surrounded the place, making a cloudy day seem even gloomier. It was such a gothically creepy setting that Ellie began to believe that Skulduggery Enterprises had even ordered up the weather.

She walked to the front window, wondering if she were totally alone here. If the seas got much rougher, the short trip from the mainland would become downright unsafe. The other guests might never make it. The thought of being stranded here all night made her shudder.

The disquieting stillness was broken by the sound of a discreet cough. Ellie nearly jumped out of her skin. She hadn't heard anyone come into the room.

She jerked around to find a man in formal attire standing no more than six feet away. He was fairly young, probably under thirty, and looked as if he'd escaped from the pages of an Agatha Christie mystery novel. Obviously he was the butler here.

According to the information packet she'd received, the butler was an employee of Skulduggery Enterprises. He was supposed to help the game run smoothly and take care of any problems or emergencies that might arise. Ellie was relieved to see him.

"Good afternoon, miss," he said with a polite bow of his head. He might have looked like a genuine English butler but his accent was more Bostonian than British. "Please accept my apologies for the delay in greeting you. On behalf of Mr. Tipton, welcome to Raven's Island and Tipton House."

"Thank you." Ellie had no idea whether it was proper to introduce oneself to a butler, but told herself this was the Commonwealth of Massachusetts and not Edwardian England. "I'm Ellie—White." She'd almost used her real last name, Landau, instead of the name of the character she was playing. She chided herself for the near slip.

The key to solving any mystery was to gather as much information as possible, so she decided to ask about the mysterious man who owned this place, T. T. Tipton. "When will Mr. Tipton be joining us?"

"I'm afraid he won't be, miss," the butler answered. "He was called away on business. Nonetheless, every provision has been made to ensure that your stay will be a pleasant one."

"I'm sure it will be," Ellie said, wondering what other surprises lay in store. "I take it you're Mr. Tipton's butler?"

He nodded. "Yes, miss. My name is Scott."

Although Scott was the picture of dignity and propriety, he couldn't quite suppress the twinkle in his eye. He was having a good time and it showed.

Egged on by the twinkle, Ellie proceeded to break the cardinal rule of the whole game: *Stay in character at all times.* Maybe she had a streak of larceny in her, because she saw nothing wrong in skirting the rules a little if she thought she could get away with it.

"Let me make sure I understand this," she said. "You're an employee of Skulduggery Enterprises but you're also acting out a role in the game. You might even be the murderer." She paused, then asked mischievously, "Did the butler do it, Scott?"

Scott drew himself to his full height. "That would be unforgivably trite, Miss White, and I assure you that nothing about your stay here will be trite. I really must ask you to remember that you're Ellie White, and that you've come here to vacation. No murder has taken place yet. You have no idea that a murder is *about* to take place. You must make a greater effort to stay in character."

Suitably chastened by this sternly delivered lecture, Ellie changed the subject to how beautiful the house was. Scott agreed that the place was magnificent and then gestured toward the doorway. "If you would follow me, I'll show you to your room."

They made their way to the foot of the steps, where Scott picked up Ellie's belongings and led the way upstairs. A protective wooden railing surrounded the staircase opening on the second floor. Ellie counted eight doors off the hall, all of them closed.

Scott led her to the room in the right front corner of the house and opened the door so she could precede him inside. He set her computer on the dresser and slid her suitcase onto a luggage rack. "I hope you'll enjoy your vacation, miss. If you require any assistance, please don't hesitate to ring." He pointed out the velvet pull cord by the door and turned to leave.

There was no phone in the room, no electric clock, no radio or television set. If it hadn't been for the electric lights, Ellie might have imagined she'd gone back in time. The feeling she'd had downstairs, of being isolated and vulnerable, came back all over again.

"Just a moment, Scott," she said. "Has anyone else arrived yet?"

"You're the third of our seven guests, miss. Mlle LaTour and Mr. Thorpe are on the island also."

"In the house?"

"I'm afraid I have no idea. Mr. Tipton wishes you to treat his home as your own during your stay, so you're certainly free to search for them." Scott took another couple of steps toward the door, then stopped and turned around. "Do be careful, though. Raven's Island can be a dangerous place."

"Dangerous how?" Ellie asked quickly.

"There's quite an undertow at the east end of the island, where the beach is," he answered. "We've had reports of sharks in the surrounding waters. The steps leading down from the cliff above the beach can be slippery and treacherous when the weather is damp, as it is today, and the cliff itself is less secure than it looks." He hesitated, looking sober and a little nervous. "Accidents have happened here, most unfortunate accidents. Now, you really must excuse me."

Ellie let him go. She knew there hadn't been accidents here, unfortunate or otherwise, just as there were no sharks or undertow in the waters offshore. Scott's warning had been part of the game. Still, looking out the window at the darkening sky, it was easy to forget all that, easy to imagine the danger was real.

She searched the area in front of the house for signs of life. She could make out the pebbled path she'd taken to get to the house, but nobody was walking on it. A boardwalk and dock, both deserted, lay at the foot of the path. A small boat with an outboard motor was tied up at the pier, bobbing up and down in the water, but the sleek little launch that had brought her to Raven's Island was gone now.

Given the day's cool dampness, Ellie had no desire to tramp around outside. She'd been working at an exhausting pace for the past couple of weeks and was too tired to do anything strenuous. She turned away from the window and looked longingly at the bed.

A moment later she was straightening her shoulders and marching to the closet. She'd agreed to come here and play the role of Ellie White in return for a free vacation, and the least she could do was get into the spirit of the game. First she would review the materials she'd received and then she would explore the house.

She hung up her coat and took a large manila envelope out of her suitcase. Sitting down in an armchair, she opened the envelope, removed its contents and reread the letter on top.

Dear Ms. Landau:

You have been recommended to Skulduggery Enterprises as a candidate to pretest one of our solve-a-mystery adventure games, Death on Raven's Island. In case you haven't heard of our company and its products, I'll explain how our games work. Each participant—seven in the case of Death on Raven's Island—will receive a detailed packet about a character he or she is to play. In your particular case, the character will be a modest but intrepid saleswoman in a Boston department store who has won a free vacation on Raven's Island.

At this point, let me assure you that in fact as well as fiction, the island is a gem. You will have a private bedroom and bath in a splendid old mansion. Your meals will be prepared by a French-trained chef. Although the ocean is rather cold for swimming, the beach is lovely and secluded. The island is an ideal place to walk, to birdwatch, or simply to read and relax.

Unfortunately for your character, the idyllic peacefulness of Raven's Island will be interrupted by sudden and unexpected violence during her stay. One or more of her fellow guests will die. Is it an accident? Is it murder? Who is responsible for the tragedy that will strike?

The most entertaining part of your visit, and your real challenge, will be to figure out the answers. The clues available to you will be sufficient to solve the mystery. However, it is only fair to warn you that in the process, your character will subject herself to the gravest danger.

Skulduggery Enterprises prides itself on its creativity and attention to detail. We do not offer any of our games to the general public until it has been pretested with a group of carefully selected volunteers. In return for your participation, you will receive a stimulating vacation at no cost whatsoever. We ask only that you play the game fairly and to the best of your ability, and that you fill out an evaluation form upon your return.

Death on Raven's Island will be played on July 11 to 14 on Raven's Island, which is off the coast of Massachusetts near the town of Magnolia. We hope you will want to participate. You may reply in the enclosed postage-paid envelope or contact our office directly by phone.

Sincerely,
Brent Beattie, President

Ellie had been intrigued. She wasn't a mystery buff, but she read detective stories every now and then and enjoyed television shows like the old *Columbo* and the more recent *Murder, She Wrote*. It was a challenge to match her wits against a clever writer and try to reason out the identity of a killer.

In a way, solving mysteries was part of her job. She was a management consultant, hired by companies to analyze their problems and recommend solutions. One of the first things she'd learned was that records were often contradictory and people didn't always cooperate. Uncovering the truth could be difficult, but that was part of what made her work so interesting.

Although Death on Raven's Island had sounded like fun, she wasn't sure she could get away. After two slow years, her

business had recently picked up. She had a pair of cases
nearing completion and a third she'd barely begun. Her
newest client, Cludds Haberdashers, had been very patient
thus far, but they'd hired her back in April. She couldn't
expect them to wait around indefinitely.

What she'd seen so far of their records had left her shaking her head in dismay. They were such a mess that a master detective would have had trouble making sense of them.
The company had been founded in the 1790s. For most of
its nearly two hundred years, the owners had acted as
though time had stood still. Then, the previous fall, they'd
abruptly decided to computerize. The result was total chaos.
It was little wonder they'd turned to a management consultant to straighten things out.

In the end, Ellie had checked Skulduggery Enterprises out
with acquaintances in the business community and then decided to accept their offer. The company had a reputation
for delivering exactly what it promised: luxurious accommodations, an intriguing challenge and a delightful respite
from the demands of everyday life. The more she'd heard,
the more enthusiastic she was about going to Raven's Island.

She'd mailed in her acceptance and then thrown herself
into finishing her two oldest cases. It had taken more fif-
teen-hour days than she cared to think about, but she'd
managed it. As for Cludds, she'd put in a couple of days of
preliminary study and planned to continue her work here on
Raven's Island. After all the delays, she wanted to make the
company into a model of corporate efficiency.

She put aside Brent Beattie's introductory letter and
picked up the letter beneath it. It gave her instructions about
getting to Raven's Island and explained the game in further
detail. Both the butler and the cook, it noted, would be employees of Skulduggery Enterprises as well as participants
in the game. She could count on them to help her if any
genuine problems arose, but otherwise she was to stay in

character at all times. The admonition was underscored and italicized.

Her fellow players? She should remember that one of them would commit a murder. He, or she, could be expected to lie baldly, but everyone else would be required to tell the truth.

Clues? They would take the form of either physical objects or stories in magazines and newspapers. Everything she would need to solve the mystery could be found in the house or on the grounds.

Other rules? She could explore anywhere on the island, and anywhere in the house with the exception of the kitchen wing and the third floor. If she wanted to keep the other players from rifling her possessions, she should make sure to lock her door. She might know some of her fellow players in real life, since people so often recommended their friends and business acquaintances for these games, but she should try not to show it. Finally, each player would be given a black folder containing background information about his or her character. Under no circumstances was she to look in anybody else's folder.

The final item in the manila envelope was the black folder itself, which had a white label reading ELLIE WHITE affixed to the front. Although Ellie had studied it at home, she knew she should review it before the rest of the players arrived. She could do that later, before dinner, but now she was eager to explore. The house was as quiet as ever, so it was the perfect time to take a thorough look around.

She placed everything in the top drawer of her dresser and let herself out of her room. Her first stop was the next bedroom down the hall. She gave a soft knock on the door, failed to get an answer, and turned the knob. Something about this house made her expect skeletons to drop down from the ceiling at any moment, but the room beyond was an ordinary bedroom. The decor was feminine and airy, indicating that a woman would soon move in, but there were no cosmetics in the bathroom or clothes in the closet. The intended occupant hadn't arrived yet.

Ellie continued down the hallway, tracing a path that would eventually take her back to her own room. The third bedroom, with its masculine four-poster bed and blue-and-gray color scheme, was as lifeless as the second. At that point she called out, "Is anybody around?" but there was no answer. She was obviously alone up here, so why did she feel as if somebody was going to sneak up behind her with a lead pipe and clobber her over the head? She'd probably played too many games of Clue as a child.

She checked out the fourth room, another bedroom, and crept along to the fifth. The door was slightly ajar. Ellie was about to push it open when she heard a low howling sound from inside, almost like a baby crying. After so much eerie silence, the noise was enough to make her heart start racing.

More unnerved than she wanted to admit, she gave the door a push and peeked into the room beyond. It wasn't a bedroom, but a charming parlor. Not a soul was in sight.

Before she could take more than three or four steps inside, a large object came flying across her path, seemingly out of nowhere. Ellie took a startled step backward, her heart pounding faster than ever. The object in question, a coal-black cat with a Siamese's triangular head and crossed blue eyes, gave her a bored stare and strolled to the sofa. He'd apparently been sitting on a chest just out of Ellie's line of sight.

Feeling like an overimaginative idiot, she went over to sit beside him. The silver ID tag on his jeweled collar gave his name, Lucifer, and a phone number to call in case he got lost, but there was no owner's name or address. Skulduggery Enterprises really did think of everything. After all, what self-respecting creepy mansion would have been complete without a black cat to spook the human inhabitants?

She scratched Lucifer's ears until he rejected any further attentions and then she left the parlor. She had two choices at that point. She could either continue along the main hallway and check out the remaining three rooms, or she could make a detour down a dark, narrow passageway that ended in a pair of closed doors.

After her nerve-racking encounter with Lucifer, she wasn't about to creep into any mysterious hallways or open any ominous-looking doors. She decided to stick to the main hallway, at least for the time being. Two of her fellow guests were somewhere on the island, so two of those bedrooms had to contain somebody's possessions.

The first room was empty, but a woman had moved into the second, leaving three pieces of luggage on her bed. Ellie was a little hesitant about poking through her belongings, but rules were rules. The woman had left her door unlocked, all but inviting others to snoop.

Whoever she was, she had plenty of money. The suitcases were made of soft, fragrant leather and contained beautiful, expensive clothing. Checking the bathroom, Ellie found a silk robe hanging on the door and a bottle of designer perfume on the vanity.

Back in the bedroom, she noticed a fashion magazine on the night table, and, sitting nearby, a slim black folder with a gummed label affixed to the front. It was identical to her own folder except that the name Lynette LaTour was typed on the label.

Although Ellie was dying to peek inside, she sternly resisted temptation. It wasn't only a question of obeying the rules, but of knowing she would gain an unfair advantage by reading about Lynette LaTour. After all, Lynette might be the murderer. It was fine to bend the rules by trying to wangle information out of the butler, but she never would have ruined the game by looking in somebody else's folder.

It suddenly struck her that Lynette LaTour might, at that very moment, be in *her* room, going through *her* things, because she'd forgotten to lock her door. Some detective she was! Lynette was obviously off with Mr. Thorpe, but in the future she would have to be more careful.

There was only one room left to explore, the one directly opposite her own. She quietly slipped inside, closing the door behind her so nobody could see what she was up to. Thorpe had taken the time to unpack before going out; an empty suitcase sat open on the luggage rack. Otherwise the room was spotless. He was obviously a very neat person.

Ellie started toward the closet, only to be stopped in her tracks by a sound coming from inside the bathroom. Someone had set a bottle or can on the marble-topped vanity. Did she have time to get out of the room or should she duck into the closet? She took too long to decide. Only moments later the doorknob turned and the door was pushed open. The man who emerged from the bathroom was wearing a towel around his waist and nothing else. It was obvious that he'd just come out of the shower.

As a management consultant, Ellie had quickly learned to be crisp and professional at all times. Her youth and sex could be liabilities in her work. Men often refused to take her seriously. She coped with their skepticism by adopting a no-nonsense style that said she was smarter and tougher than any other kid on the block. She had learned to hide her insecurities.

Now, confronting a half-naked man whose room she'd just invaded, the lessons of the past automatically took over. To look at her, nobody would have guessed that her knees felt shaky and her pulse rate had jumped. Nobody would have known that she was reacting to the man in front of her in a way that both amazed and confused her. Outwardly, at least, she was the picture of aplomb.

And inwardly? The man's masculinity had hit her like a Mack truck. She'd always insisted that intelligence was the most important attribute a man could possess, but it wasn't a genius-level IQ that had sent her body into sensual shock.

It was a six-foot frame and the muscular chest and arms of a professional athlete. It was broad shoulders and flat stomach and dark brown hair that was damp and appealingly tousled. It was a pair of light blue eyes, wide with surprise. It was high cheekbones and thin lips that might have looked sinuously dangerous on a less astonished face. It was raw, erotic maleness, and Ellie, whose strong sense of sexual morality was sadly out of step with the times, had her hands full pretending not to notice.

Still, her voice was remarkably steady when she greeted him. It just went to prove the value of practice. "Mr. Thorpe, I presume?"

His eyes traveled down her body, starting with the long, dark hair she hadn't bothered to braid and jerking to her cashmere sweater and close-fitting jeans. It was too quick an appraisal to be insulting or lascivious. Ellie had the feeling he hadn't wanted to stare but couldn't help himself. It wasn't every day you walked out of your private bathroom to find a total stranger standing in your bedroom.

Just before he spoke, she noticed something else about the man. His cheeks were noticeably flushed under his suntan. She would have put it down to the heat of the shower if he hadn't looked so startled. "Uh, yes," he said. "That's right. Are you—you must be Ellie White."

Ellie gave him her best professional smile. "Yes. How did you know?"

He took a moment to answer. "The butler described the other characters—I mean the other guests."

"I see." Ellie walked up to him and offered her hand. "It's nice to meet you."

She knew she was playing with dynamite the moment he grasped her hand. Her physical response was immediate and intense. She couldn't understand why. She never reacted this way to men. It was like something out of a soap opera.

He finally seemed to get his surprise under control as he released her hand. Much to her relief, he took a few steps backward. "Do you mind if I ask you what you're doing in my room?" he said.

"Not at all. I was about to search it." Ellie paused, then added baldly, "Of course, I didn't know you were in here. I suppose I'll have to come back after you leave."

He smiled at her audacity, displaying even, white teeth that were as gorgeous as the rest of him. The fact that the smile was a little frazzled only made it that much more attractive. "Hey, listen, don't leave on my account. If you're going to search the place anyway..." He suddenly stopped talking and looked downward, as if he'd remembered what he was—or wasn't—wearing. "I guess I should put some clothes on."

"By all means," Ellie said. She didn't know what she was going to do if he started changing right in front of her. Probably bolt out the door, thereby ruining the spectacular performance she'd just given.

He pulled what he needed out of the dresser and closed the drawer. Ellie stood motionless as he turned around and headed back to the bathroom. If he'd ever looked her way, he would have seen the incredible relief on her face, but he didn't. She sank to the bed the moment the door was closed.

Jed Thornhill had the feeling he'd been ambushed, hog-tied and hung up to twist in the wind. His business associates would have laughed their heads off if they could have seen him just now. He was supposed to be as tough as nails, a corporate raider whose expanding empire was the envy of half of Boston. He was supposed to be sharp, politically astute and downright intimidating, at least according to his press clippings. And what had just happened? A woman no more than five-and-a-half feet tall had turned him into a tongue-tied blob of putty. True, he wasn't nearly as confident with women as he was in his business dealings, but he didn't generally act like an embarrassed teenager, either.

He hung up his towel and pulled on his briefs and jeans. He didn't have to look in a mirror to know that Ellie Landau had knocked him sideways. He could feel his response to her in every inch of his body. One look, and *pow*! It was like slamming into a wall. God, she was lovely!

He hadn't expected that. He'd heard she was a walking computer. He'd heard that she dressed like a man, thought like a man and acted like a man. Nobody had mentioned the long, wavy hair, the amused green eyes and the lissome body that curved in all the right places. Nobody had warned him that he wouldn't be able to talk to her without also wanting to touch her.

He gave himself a lecture as he buttoned up his shirt. He had to remember why he was here. A good friend of his, Lynn Cludd, had been having problems with the company she'd inherited from her late husband. Jed had come a long way by trusting his gut instincts, and his gut instincts had eventually told him that somebody was stealing from her. Granted, it hadn't looked that way at first. The decline in profits had been steady but undramatic. It was only the past few months' figures that were really bad.

Lynn had accused him of having an overactive imagination, but she'd also been willing to humor him. Always game, she'd cheerfully gone along with what he'd begun to think was the nuttiest scheme since some hapless con man in California had tried to sell Death Valley to a group of Arabs who turned out to be undercover FBI agents.

Lynn would identify the likely crooks, all of whom would be invited to take part in one of Skulduggery Enterprises' mystery-adventure games. Besides Lynn, Jed knew only one of the invitees—her late husband's son, Marty Cludd. Still, by watching how everyone played the game, he thought he could get a handle on who might be capable of embezzlement. Lynn, who was acting the role of Lynette LaTour, would be keeping an eye out as well. The weekend hadn't been hard to arrange—not for Jed, who happened to own Skulduggery Enterprises.

As much as he hated to admit it, Ellie Landau had just jumped to the top of his list. She'd been hired by Lynn's attorney in April but had done virtually no work yet. She was a computer expert with access to Cludds's accounts. Most damning of all, the dramatic downturn in Cludds's profits had coincided exactly with Ellie's involvement in the company's affairs. And just now, he'd seen for himself how unflappable she could be. Not only had she stared him down; she'd made him feel almost guilty for daring to disturb her while she was searching his room. A suspicious personality if ever he'd met one, but he was trying to keep an open mind. Her brazenness could have been sheer bravado.

Jed sighed and picked up his comb. At the moment, Lynn's declining profits were the least of his problems. He was supposed to portray a homicidal maniac named Jared Thorpe this weekend. Bruce Scott, who had written the script and was playing the role of the butler, had come up with a brilliant but unpleasant strategy for hiding Thorpe's murderous intentions. Thorpe would pass himself off as a wealthy playboy. He would pretend to be a conceited male chauvinist who believed that every woman in the world was dying to get into his bed. Nobody would suspect that someone with the brains of a toad and the manners of a gorilla would be clever enough to plan and carry out a complicated series of murders.

Between looking for a real-life crook and pretending to kill everyone in sight, Jed was going to have his hands full this weekend. Even worse, he was going to have to act as obnoxious and slimy as he could. It went against the grain and Scotty knew it. That was probably why he kept reminding Jed how important it was to play Thorpe well.

Jed was from a very old and proper New England family. He was sure that the first four words out of his mouth must have been mama, dada, please and thank-you. Politeness had been bred into him. He could be very, very tough in business negotiations and single-minded about acquiring a company he wanted, but he never yelled, he never cursed people out and he never demeaned his opponents.

Scotty had told him to relax and enjoy the weekend—it could be fun to play a lout. Besides, everyone would understand it was only a role Jed was acting out. He set down his comb and tucked in his shirt, feeling like a general about to charge into battle.

Ellie sat on the bed for about thirty seconds and then told herself to show a little spirit and finish what she'd started. Thorpe's clothes were expensive—custom-made suits, silk ties and private-label sportswear from the best New England stores. His attaché case, which was sitting on the night table, was made of leather and embossed in gold with what she assumed were his real initials—J.L.T. She would have opened it up and checked out its contents, but it was locked. J.L.T. wasn't a pauper; that much was obvious.

She'd just closed the last of his drawers when he walked out of the bathroom. He came closer than he had any business coming and proceeded to look her up and down as slowly and thoroughly as a Thoroughbred breeder might inspect a filly on the auction block. "I see you couldn't bear to leave," he said. "Like every other woman I've met, you find the combination of money and good looks irresistible. Tell me about yourself. Why should I be interested in you?"

Ellie's mouth almost dropped open in astonishment. The man in front of her had nothing in common with the one she'd just met. He was an egotistical jerk who was treating her like a slab of meat. What had happened to the flustered, delightfully human fellow who'd been embarrassed to be caught half-naked?

She suddenly figured out the answer. The first man she'd met had been too startled to stay in character. He'd had to get his clothes on and remind himself about the game before he could start playing his role correctly. Ellie almost congratulated him on being a wonderful actor, but then remembered that she was supposed to be acting, too.

She gave him an icy look and backed away. "I wouldn't think of expecting you to be interested in me. I'm only an ordinary salesclerk at Filene's. And you, Mr. Thorpe? What do you do for a living?"

"Call me Jed," he answered. "It's short for Jared. And I don't do anything for a living. I don't have to."

So he was supposed to be independently wealthy. Ellie probed for more information. "Tell me, Mr. Thorpe—"

"Jed," he interrupted.

"Mr. Thorpe," Ellie repeated firmly. "What brings you to Raven's Island?"

"I believe in looking a place over before I buy it." He gave her a lecherous smile. "The same is true with a woman. In your case, I happen to like what I see. I hope your room isn't too far away."

"It's directly across the hall—not that you'll ever get inside it," Ellie sniffed. "But we were talking about your investments."

He was quick to correct her. "We were talking about you and me. Your talents are wasted at Filene's. They belong in my bed."

He was being so outrageous that Ellie didn't know whether to laugh at him or kick him. She did neither, because Ellie White was supposed to be a street-smart young woman who had made her own way in the world since the age of eighteen. She wouldn't have been flustered by a jerk like Thorpe.

Unfortunately, it was going to be hard to portray the cool and controlled Miss White with a man as attractive as Jed. Ellie was constantly tempted to react personally. Trying to ignore both his sex appeal and his chauvinist propositions, she continued as though he'd never spoken. "So you're thinking of buying Raven's Island. Are you acquainted with T. T. Tipton, our absent host?''

He told her they were old friends. She could tell he was about to proposition her again, but they were interrupted by a knock on the door. Without waiting for a response, the person outside called, "Jed? Are you decent? Can I come in?''

The woman had a husky voice with a slight Boston accent. "Sure," Jed answered, "but there's someone—''

But the woman had already opened the door. She looked at Ellie and grimaced. "Oh, Lord, I've really blown it. I'm sorry. Can we start all over again?''

A moment later she was back outside. This time, the speech that followed her knock was delivered with a lilting French accent. "Monsieur Thorpe? It is Lynette. I am bored to tears. You must come out and rescue me.''

Jed opened the door and invited her inside. "It would be my pleasure to rescue you, my dear, but I prefer to perform my heroics in the bedroom.'' He caressed her backside, earning himself a bewildered look, and then turned to Ellie. "This is Lynette LaTour. Her father is a diplomat with the UN in New York. She's a student in Cambridge. Lynette, this is Ellie White. She works at Filene's.''

Lynette shook Ellie's hand and then slipped her arm through Jed's. She was a beautiful woman, tall and slender with a full bust and narrow waist. Her peaches-and-cream complexion was flawless, and her platinum hair hadn't come out of any bottle. Obviously, she and Jed were friends in real life, but not intimate friends—at least, not yet. His lover wouldn't have worried about whether he was decent or asked permission to enter his room.

"It's a pleasure to meet you, in more ways than one,'' Ellie said to her. "You seem to have a far greater interest in Mr. Thorpe than I do. I'm more than happy to give you a clear field. I'll be going now, but I'm sure I'll see you again at dinner.''

"Maybe and maybe not," Jed drawled. "We might be too busy to make it."

Ellie rolled her eyes and quoted from *Hamlet*: "A consummation devoutly to be wished." She closed the door securely as she let herself out of the room, mostly because she wanted to eavesdrop. You never knew what you might pick up.

Lynette was the first one to speak. "I don't think she likes you, and little wonder. Now I know why you were so close-mouthed about your character. He's a complete idiot."

"At least he's not boring," Jed replied. "Where have you been?"

"Walking around outside. I like it here." Lynette paused. "You know, Lynette LaTour is supposed to be a real sexpot. I think she's going to find you irresistible."

"Then she has lousy taste. Come on, let's go downstairs. I want to try out the harpsichord."

Ellie scurried back to her room. It was a good thing she hadn't locked her door because if she had, she never would have made it inside in time. So Jed was a musician. She looked forward to hearing him play.

She took out the folder marked ELLIE WHITE but was too restless to concentrate on it. After only five minutes she walked to the window and stared out at the sky. The clouds were darker than ever.

She was about to turn away when she noticed the launch approaching the pier. It wasn't long before a figure emerged from below. Ellie kept watching, curious about the latest arrival. She could tell it was a woman by the way the boatman helped her out of the launch. The two of them started up the path.

They were halfway to the house before Ellie made out the black and white veil on the woman's head. She was a nun, of all things. A nun wasn't likely to murder anybody, but then, neither was a womanizing boob like Jed Thorpe. Ellie left her room and made her way to the top of the stairs, eager to meet the woman.

Chapter Two

The nun could have come straight from Central Casting. Her skin was free of makeup and her features were plain but appealing. She was probably about forty, but it was hard to tell with nuns. In any event, she had such a perky bounce to her step and such a cheerful smile that Ellie found it impossible not to smile back.

Scott, who was carrying her suitcase, stood to the side while the two women introduced themselves. Ellie went first, giving her name and mentioning which room she was in. "How lovely," the nun answered. "We'll be neighbors. Scott was telling me I'm right next door." As the two of them shook hands, she continued, "My name is Sister Mary Mc—oh, dear, I almost used my real last name. For the life of me I can't remember what my character is called. I'll have to look it up and repeat it until I know it cold." She bit her lip and gave Scott a contrite look. "I wasn't supposed to say that, was I!"

The twinkle was back in his eye. "I think we'll all manage to forgive you. In the future you might refer to yourself simply as 'Sister Mary.' That would eliminate the problem."

"Thank you, that's wonderful advice," she said. "I'll do exactly that."

"Very good, Sister. Would you care to get settled in your room now?"

"Indeed I would. It's been a long day." Sister Mary winked at Ellie and continued in a stage whisper, "Isn't he marvelous? Just like something from *Masterpiece Theatre.* I can't wait to meet the others, especially if they're as good as he is."

Although Scott didn't comment, Ellie could see he was amused by Sister Mary's compliment. He showed her to her room, informed her and Ellie that cocktails would be served in the parlor at five and dinner in the dining room at six, and took his leave.

While Sister Mary unpacked, she and Ellie exchanged background information. Sister Mary was a teacher in a Boston-area high school who was now on her summer break. Her health had been poor that year, and her principal had suggested that a few days on Raven's Island might help her recoup her strength. The island's owner, T. T. Tipton, happened to be a friend of the bishop, and he occasionally offered the place to members of the religious community for free.

When Sister Mary yawned and sat down, Ellie said she would look forward to seeing her again at dinner and suggested she get some rest.

"At cocktails," Sister Mary corrected. "I do love a little nip before my meals. Helps the digestion, you know."

"Then I'll see you in the parlor," Ellie agreed. Maybe a "little nip" helped the digestion, but it didn't do much for one's mental acuity. Personally, she planned to abstain.

As soon as she was back in her room, she took out her black folder and slipped into bed. She was too comfortable to stay awake for long, but later, after she woke up, she studied Ellie White until she knew the character backward and forward—her childhood, her school days, her various jobs, the names of her boyfriends, where she liked to vacation and even how she spent her free time.

Some of those facts would probably prove important in the game, but it was far too early to say which ones. At the moment, Ellie's chief concern was to meet the three remaining players. Since it was almost four o'clock, she assumed they must have arrived.

So she wouldn't have to return to her room later, she changed for dinner, putting on a silk skirt and matching blouse. Then she locked her door with the skeleton key she'd found on the night table and went off to look for the other guests.

Sister Mary was still resting—at least her door was still closed—but the next door down the hall was wide open. A blond-haired man about thirty years old was standing in front of the dresser mirror, straightening his tie.

He spotted Ellie at the same moment as she spotted him, and gave her a big grin. "Slow down, beautiful. We're supposed to be relaxing, remember?"

Ellie walked into the room. With his azure eyes, dark, even tan and perfect features, the man reminded her of a model in an ad for suntan oil. She regarded him with a sort of detached appreciation, as if he were a beautiful statue. Despite his dazzling good looks, there wasn't even a hint of the erotic spark she'd felt with Jed.

He studied her right back, smiling all the while. Ellie wasn't physically attracted to him, but she somehow felt drawn to him. He was like her secretary's new puppy— happy, lively and harmless.

She'd no sooner introduced herself than he reached out to caress her. She was telling herself that appearances could be deceiving when she realized she'd been right about him after all. He wanted to examine her necklace, not make a pass at her.

"That's a lovely piece," he said, lightly fingering the diamond-encrusted pearls. "Exquisite workmanship. Is it a family heirloom?"

It was, but the fictional Ellie White didn't come from the kind of family that would have passed such a necklace down through the generations. Determined to stay in character, she said, "I found it in an antique shop during my last vacation. It cost me a fortune but I had to have it." She paused, then reminded him, "You haven't told me your name yet, or what you do."

"Marty Robey," he answered. "I'm a jewel thief. If I were you, I'd lock my door at night."

Ellie smiled and brushed away his hand. If Sister Mary made a wonderful nun, Marty made an even better jewel thief. He had a slender, athletic build and was only about an inch taller than she was. She could easily picture him dressed all in black, dancing over the rooftops of buildings.

"You must be singularly unsuccessful if you go around warning off all your potential victims," she pointed out.

"On the contrary, I'm extremely successful—or was. I'm retired now—living off my ill-gotten gains. And you?"

"I'm a salesclerk at Filene's. The downtown Boston store."

"You? A salesclerk?" He shook his head, laughing at the idea. "My God, what an atrocious piece of casting. Beattie must be sorry he ever sold out. He's lost control of his own operation."

Marty's reference had been to Brent Beattie, the president of Skulduggery Enterprises. He shouldn't have mentioned Beattie or the game—he'd broken the rule about staying in character—but Ellie wasn't going to scold him for it. She was too curious about what he'd meant.

"Who did he sell out to?" she asked. "And why?"

"To a big conglomerate and for the usual reason," he answered with a shrug. "He wanted more capital to expand his operation."

Marty's explanation made sense, but why had he laughed at the idea of Ellie's being a salesclerk? Did he know for a fact that she wasn't? "Why couldn't I work at Filene's?" she asked.

"Too little makeup and perfume," he replied. "Too much education and too many brains. Frankly, you terrify me, but I realize I've just violated that ridiculous sheet of rules we've all been given. Stay in character and all that. Tell me, have you been through the house yet?"

He almost seemed to know who she was. "Have we met?" she demanded. "Did you read about me in the paper?" There had been a short profile of her in the Boston *Times* about three months before.

He clucked his tongue and took her by the arm. "Now *you're* violating the rules, but all right, I'll confess. I know some of the people at Skulduggery Enterprises. One of them happened to mention you. Why don't we start our tour with the observatory? The view up there is wonderful."

Ellie stayed right where she was. "I'm sure it is, but if you know who I really am, it's only fair that I should know who *you* really are." She gave him a flirtatious look. "Come on, Marty, you wouldn't want me to get so curious about the real you that I can't concentrate on the game, now would you?"

"From what I've heard, there's not much danger of that happening," he said with a laugh. "Given how clever you're supposed to be, why don't you figure out who I really am?"

Ellie knew when she was being teased. Marty wasn't going to give her any answers, but then, his real identity didn't matter. Only his character, Marty Robey, mattered.

She gave up asking questions and allowed him to shepherd her into the narrow passageway she'd skipped on her earlier tour of the house. He opened the door on the left,

which led to a round room that was entirely empty except
for the spiral staircase in its center. Ellie had noticed a high
turret rising behind the back of the house as she'd walked up
the path from the launch. The observatory was on the top
floor of the turret, up three flights of narrow metal steps.

The room contained maps, charts and various astronom-
ical instruments. There was a sliding skylight for the telescopes, but it was closed against the inclement weather.
Windows were spaced at regular intervals along the circular
wall, allowing the sightseer to view every part of the island.
Despite the low, cold fog that was rolling in, Ellie could
make out the mainland to the west. Looking toward the
east, she could see a thick evergreen woods, and beyond it,
a sharply pitched field that ended in a sheer cliff. The ocean
looked so gray and foamy, she was surprised to see the
launch slip into place at the dock.

Two people got out with the boatman—a man and a
woman. Marty fetched a couple of pairs of binoculars so he
and Ellie could take a closer look. The woman, who was
probably in her sixties, was a total stranger to Ellie, but she
recognized the man at once. His name was James Emerson, Jr., and he was the attorney for Cludds Haberdashers,
her client with the horrendous records. In fact, he was the
only person connected to the company whom Ellie had met.

He had explained the situation when he hired her. One of
Cludds's owners was a recently bereaved widow and the
other lived in Europe. For the time being, Emerson was
handling most of their business affairs. Ellie had asked for
some financial records and explained that her work for other
clients might tie her up at first. He'd been very understanding about the possibility of a delay.

She wasn't surprised to see somebody she knew. Emerson had probably recommended her for the game. She
would have to thank him, but not when anybody could
overhear them. Skulduggery Enterprises had instructed

players who knew each other to act like strangers, and she would certainly try to do that.

Marty showed her the various telescopes, then suggested a quick look at the mansion's third floor. Ellie reminded him about the rules—the third floor was out-of-bounds—but he simply grinned. "If they're determined to keep us away, they'll have locked all the doors. What do you want to bet they're open?"

"I never bet against something I hope will happen," she said. "If you want the truth, I'm as willing to snoop as you are."

They took the spiral staircase to the third floor, found that the door was indeed unlocked, and emerged into a narrow passageway identical to the one on the floor below. The first three rooms along the hall contained furnishings and props and the others housed the staff. Since they didn't want to be caught where they didn't belong, they didn't do more than glance around.

A minute later, back in the narrow passageway, Marty pointed to the door next to the tower-room entrance and asked Ellie if she knew where it went. She shook her head. He opened it up, discovering a back staircase that was obviously to be used solely by the staff. He and Ellie looked at each other, smiled, and headed down the steps.

They opened the bottom door to find a large, modern kitchen where a young woman wearing jeans and a T-shirt was standing at a professional stove. She was the cook, obviously, and like Scott, an employee of Skulduggery Enterprises. Not surprisingly, she didn't take kindly to having her domain invaded. She gave Marty an exasperated look, reminded him the kitchen was off-limits and ordered him to leave.

"That's the trouble with the hired help these days," he grumbled. "You don't know your place anymore."

She put her hands on her hips. "Out, Marty, and don't you dare come back."

"Is that any way to greet a man who's traveled thousands of miles to take part in your idiotic game?" He was every inch the harmless puppy now, right down to the wounded look on his face. "Really, Rebecca, I expected better from you. After all, you haven't seen me in over a year, since we had dinner together in Paris."

Marty had said he knew *some* of the people at Skulduggery Enterprises, but Ellie was beginning to think he knew them all. In any event, he was too amiable to stay angry with for long. Rebecca forgave him and kissed him hello, saying, "My character is named Rebecca Hill, Marty. Try to remember that." She placed a hand on his chest and pushed. "Now scoot!"

"Meet Ellie White," he answered, allowing himself to be propelled backward.

"I'm sorry I can't be more friendly," Rebecca said to Ellie, "but you shouldn't be in here. I'd be grateful if you could help keep Marty in line. I don't think he's taking this seriously."

"I never take anything seriously," he said, and then, when Rebecca glared at him in mock irritation, promised, "Okay, I'll be good. I swear it!"

Rebecca dismissed him with a stern, "See that you are," but Ellie suspected it was hopeless. Marty was an unregenerate cutup.

Out in the hallway, Ellie picked up the sound of harpsichord music and realized it was coming from the room on their right. She hesitated in front of the closed door, but Marty didn't stand on ceremony. He barged right in.

Jed was doing the playing, with Lynette sitting on a couch near the door. The next few seconds were remarkable. Marty, who was as extroverted and easygoing as any man Ellie had met, looked at Lynette and stiffened. Lynette, who was hardly the type to blush, reddened and dropped her eyes.

The two of them obviously knew each other, and unless Ellie missed her guess, their past relationship had been anything but casual. Jed, meanwhile, was so wrapped up in his music that he never noticed the strong undercurrents in the room.

He didn't look up from the keyboard until he was finished with his piece. "You play beautifully, Mr. Thorpe," Ellie said. Her voice was softer than it should have been, given Ellie White's low opinion of Jed Thorpe's morals. She couldn't be snippy to a man who could create such lovely music.

"It's a beautiful instrument," he answered, sounding distracted. "I only hope the climate-control system in this room does its job and protects it from the damp salt air."

The reply had come from the charming man in the bath towel rather than the chauvinist lout. Jed seemed to realize his mistake at once because he added, "The harpsichord isn't the only instrument I play beautifully. A woman's body is also a type of instrument. I assure you, my dear, that I could play yours exquisitely."

"I'll take your word for it," Ellie retorted. His egotistical boast should have broken the spell cast by his playing, but it didn't. She suddenly pictured his hands caressing her body as expertly as they'd caressed the keyboard, and hastily looked away. She never had thoughts like that—never. To have them about a man she barely knew was absurd.

She covered her embarrassment by rushing to introduce everyone. By the time Jed walked over to shake Marty's hand, she had launched into an explanation of what each of them did for a living. Then she realized she was babbling, and snapped her mouth shut.

Marty seemed to be his old self again, relaxed and smiling. Marty being Marty, Ellie wasn't surprised when he broke his promise to the cook and blithely stepped out of character. His cheerful "You're looking better, Jed" announced to everyone in earshot that he and Jed knew each other in real life. Jed's answering "Thank you so much, Marty!" had a distinct edge to it.

Lynette had gotten up by then and was walking over to join them. Like Marty, she seemed to have recovered from her earlier embarrassment. She looked him over with a roguish eye and remarked that Raven's Island was becoming more and more interesting with each new male arrival. Marty's answering smile was a little frayed at the edges, but he managed a flowery thank you—in perfect French, no less.

"Perhaps I should transfer my affections to Monsieur Robey," Lynette added to Jed. "His eyes, I think, do not wander as much as yours."

"Nor as much as yours, my dear Lynette." Jed's gaze settled on Ellie. "I'm going upstairs to change for dinner. Feel free to join me. You can help me straighten my tie— among other things."

"The help you need has nothing to do with your tie," Ellie answered. "Frankly, I'm more interested in seeing the rest of the house than in spending any time with you." She marched out of the music room, her head held high. Maybe she shouldn't have abandoned Marty, but if she hadn't gotten out fast, she would have burst out laughing. Where did Jed come up with those lines of his? Were they provided in his black folder?

She let herself into the room next door, an artist's studio. In front of a large picture window there were several easels, one of them holding a painting of the sea. Ellie smiled when she noticed the shark's fin in the water. It was probably supposed to be the ocean off Raven's Island.

Scott and Marty were standing together in the hallway when she came out, with Scott doing the talking and Marty looking guilty. Ellie doubted his remorse would last. He was having too good a time breaking all the rules to suddenly start obeying them.

She continued on her tour of the house, passing a large ballroom and an elegant powder room before coming to a glassed-in veranda. It ran the length of the north side of the building and was already set up for the next morning's breakfast. The final room on the ground floor was a cherry-paneled library. At first Ellie thought the books on the floor-to-ceiling shelves were stage props, but they turned out to be real. The collection included every conceivable kind of title, with the emphasis on mysteries. Some newspapers were sitting on the coffee table and there was a stack of magazines on an end table.

Ellie remembered that the second letter from Skulduggery Enterprises had mentioned clues in the form of newspaper and magazine articles. She picked up the top magazine, a *National Geographic*, and sat down to thumb through it. There were articles about ancient Chinese artifacts, the coast of Maine and a gorilla who used sign language, but nothing rang a bell. In the meantime, her fellow guests were making their way downstairs. Setting aside the magazine, she told herself she couldn't expect to recognize clues when she didn't even know what crime would be committed. She was better off going to the parlor and studying her fellow guests.

Jed was standing with Lynette when Ellie arrived, but he excused himself as soon as he noticed her and made his way over to greet her. Lynette accepted an hors d'oeuvre from Scott and joined Sister Mary and Marty Robey. Marty smiled when he saw her coming, but Ellie got the same feeling she'd gotten in the music room. Something about Lynette made Marty uncomfortable.

Ellie could understand that, because Jed had a similar effect on *her*. He looked wonderful no matter what he was wearing, but a suit and tie added an aura of power. She knew he was rich by the cost of his clothes, but he carried himself with a self-confidence that said he wasn't just some millionaire's brat—he was successful in his own right. Ellie had the feeling he would be a dangerous man to fight, and on some primitive level she respected that and responded to it.

"Ah, the prudish little salesgirl joins us at last," he said to her. "I was beginning to think I'd scared you off. Is there anyone you haven't met?"

"Only those two." She gestured toward James Emerson, Cludds's attorney, and the woman he'd come onto the island with. Jed took her arm to lead her over, not bothering to ask her permission. She might have been annoyed by his sheer presumption if it hadn't been for the excitement of having him touch her. Unsettled by her own reaction, she took back her arm as soon as she could.

Emerson's companion smiled uncertainly as Jed and Ellie approached, but the lawyer frowned in obvious puzzlement. Ellie realized he was surprised to see her. If she hadn't been selected to play Death on Raven's Island on the recommendation of James Emerson, what was she doing here? Had one of her other clients suggested her for the game?

Jed began the introductions with Emerson's companion, who, as a woman and the senior member of the foursome, was entitled to be addressed first. Not only did he have impeccable manners; there was something unmistakably patrician about him. Ellie had lived in Boston long enough to recognize the patina that exclusive prep schools and colleges conferred. Jed wasn't only rich and successful; he was well-connected.

"Mrs. Stone," he said, "permit me to present Miss Ellie White, who works at Filene's. Ellie, this is Mrs. Stone, a retired nurse."

Mrs. Stone extended a timid hand. With her gray hair and drab gray dress, she reminded Ellie of a frightened little mouse. "My patients always called me Abby. That's short for—for Abigail."

The woman seemed so nervous that Ellie felt obligated to reassure her. "It's very nice to meet you, Abby. Maybe you can tell me about your favorite patients during dinner."

Abby nodded but didn't say anything. She looked as though Ellie had suggested an interrogation rather than a casual conversation.

"And this is Dr. James Jamison, a surgeon," Jed went on, referring to James Emerson.

Ellie couldn't help but chuckle at the character's occupation. "I should have known there would be a doctor in the game," she remarked as they shook hands. "There always is in mystery stories, isn't there?"

He smiled and nodded, then plucked a handkerchief out of his pocket and sneezed into it. Now that Ellie thought about it, his hand had felt a little warm and clammy. "Are you sure you're feeling all right?" she asked. "You don't look at all well, Mr. Emerson."

He'd no sooner said he was fine than Jed was putting his arm around Ellie's shoulders and telling her she needed a drink. As he hauled her toward the bar, he murmured, "Mr. Emerson? And here I thought you never slipped out of character."

His warm breath and husky tone did funny things to her sense of balance. She hadn't even realized she'd used Emerson's real name. Jed's presence seemed to have a disastrous effect on her concentration.

Before she had the wit to answer, he raised his voice and continued, "Just what I like, a woman with the milk of human kindness flowing through her veins. I knew you weren't as cold as you pretended to be. Now all you have to do is expend some of that feminine warmth on someone who can fully appreciate it—me."

The real Ellie Landau was a curious mixture of innocence and sophistication. A childhood chess prodigy and adolescent computer whiz, she'd finished high school a year early, breezed through college and gone on to do graduate work in computer science. She'd planned to complete her doctorate and teach in a university, but something she hadn't understood had made her take a different road. Although she wasn't an impulsive person, she'd suddenly decided to leave school and take a job as an analyst with a management consulting firm.

Two years later she'd gone into business for herself. Potential clients were skeptical at first. She'd never been a corporate executive. She didn't even have a master's degree in business administration. How could she presume to tell them how to become more efficient when she had so little practical experience?

The next few years had been tough ones, filled with hustling for cases and bargain-basement fees. She supported herself doing free-lance computer programming and reminded herself that her trust funds would eventually provide a safety net. It was ironic, but she'd come into the money just when she no longer needed it, at about the same time as her business had finally taken off.

People said she had an uncanny talent for figuring out what was wrong with a company and knowing how to fix it, but the truth was less mysterious. Her secret was old-fashioned hard work. She didn't hesitate to ask questions, even to the point of politely badgering people. She insisted on complete and detailed information, no matter how sensitive or secret it was supposed to be. She used her computer expertise to test out possible recommendations, a process that could add weeks or even months to her work. It wasn't easy to stand her ground when clients got impatient or annoyed, but she knew that thoroughness produced the best results. She could only hope they would forgive her when they saw her final report.

When it came to business, Ellie was confident about her abilities, but in her private life... The fact was, she didn't have much of a private life. Her older sister, Carol, said men were afraid of her. According to Carol, who had a doting

husband and three children, men wanted women to look up
to them. They wanted admiration, support, and in certain
extreme cases, simpering adoration. Far from gazing wor-
shipfully, Ellie was always telling men what they were doing
wrong. She was always analyzing their problems and telling
them how to improve. With her expensive business suits, her
careful professionalism and her computer printouts, she
could have intimidated King Kong.

She met dozens of men through her work, but few of
them had asked her out. Those who did ran into an obsta-
cle even more daunting than Ellie's career: she believed that
love and marriage should precede physical intimacy. A lot
of people paid lip service to commitment and fidelity, but
Ellie really believed in those things.

Some men thought she was joking; others were astonished or angry. Carol kept telling her to stall them or manipulate them rather than being so honest the moment they
pressured her to sleep with them, but Ellie couldn't bring
herself to do it. She wasn't going to apologize for her values, no matter how antiquated they were in the fast-track
world she moved in. And she wasn't going to pretend she
might ever go to bed with a man she didn't love and plan to
marry.

Still, like most people, she had her share of doubts and
fears. She wondered if she was repressed. She worried that
she would never fall in love. She couldn't understand why
she hadn't been more tempted to give in, especially to dates
who were attractive and successful and could have had their
pick of women. One of those dates had labeled her frigid
and another had called her a tease, and in her worst moments she was sure they were right. She was twenty-six. It
wasn't normal to be a virgin at twenty-six—at least not in
Cambridge.

It hadn't really occurred to her that her stay on Raven's
Island might involve anything more than trying to solve a
crime, but now, standing in Jed's embrace, she felt con-

fused and unsure of herself. Why did he have to keep touching her? And why had he just looked at her as though even a triple-locked door wouldn't keep him out of her room that night? It was an act, wasn't it? Of course it was. He was obviously trying to distract her. If she wasted her time worrying about what he was up to, she would never be the one to solve the mystery. He would.

She firmly reminded herself that Thorpe, Jed's character, was an utter lout. Ellie White, her own character, had brains enough to recognize that and act accordingly. Somehow she had to pull herself together and concentrate on the game. She'd always been competitive, and nobody, not even Jed, was going to knock her out of the running this soon.

She would have been astonished to learn that Jed, far from trying to distract her, was cursing himself for being an infatuated idiot. Every time he tangled with Ellie Landau, he lost. Upstairs in his bedroom, down in the music room, here in the parlor—she always got in the final, crushing word. He would look at her face, listen to her voice, and turn into quivering Jell-O. Without the slightest effort, she could make him forget about Thorpe, forget about the game and forget about the fact that she might be a crook.

Most appalling of all, nothing seemed to faze her. Her mind was always clicking away, measuring and analyzing everything. If he didn't watch his step, she was going to realize Thorpe was the murderer and unmask him. The game would be over and they'd all go home. Jed would have arranged this whole weekend for nothing.

He promised himself then and there that he wouldn't slip up again. No more besotted comments about the climate-control system in the music room. No more whispering in Ellie's ear or fantasizing about the places he would have liked to kiss. He had to convince her and everyone else that he was a conceited dolt whose only concern was seducing every woman in sight.

When she stiffened and pulled away, he tightened his grip so she couldn't escape. He had the satisfaction of seeing uncertainty flicker across her face, but it was replaced almost at once by fastidious distaste. "You're being exceedingly tiresome," she said. "If I were you, I'd stick to Miss LaTour. She seems to find you more amusing than I do."

"You need to loosen up," he answered, pulling her toward the bar. "A glass or two of wine should do it."

"I don't suppose it's ever occurred to you that women are perfectly capable of deciding what they *need* without male help," she retorted. "I don't want a drink, but I'll have a Perrier. And you can take your arm off my shoulders. I'm also perfectly capable of walking to the bar without your steering me there."

He shook his head, plastering a look of utter pity on his face. "Ellie—Ellie—what am I going to do with you? You don't have to play hard to get. After all, I'm rich, sophisticated and handsome. Both of us know you're thrilled I've even noticed you."

"On the contrary, you're an egotistical chauvinist with the morals of a common alley cat. If you're rich it must be family money, because I've seen no indication that you're bright enough to have earned it on your own."

Jed managed a confident smile, but he was thinking that Ellie was even more formidable than he'd realized. Not only was she brazen; she was in total control of her emotions. No matter what he dished out, she always managed to top him. It was a new experience, and not an especially pleasant one.

Out of the corner of his eye, he noticed Scotty give a reproving shake of his head. The message was perfectly clear: Jed was blowing the characterization. If he wanted everyone to dismiss Thorpe as a womanizing idiot, he would have to come on stronger.

Given his upbringing, the prospect should have been distasteful. He was surprised to realize it wasn't. The more he saw of Ellie Landau, the more she got under his skin. For once—just once—*he* wanted to come out on top.

He took his arm away, but only to open a bottle of Perrier. "Your insults don't fool me, sweetheart. It's obvious you're attracted to me. Naturally you feel threatened by my attentions, given our respective stations in life." He dropped some ice cubes into a highball glass and poured out the sparkling water. Moving closer, he went on in his oiliest voice, "I can be a very generous man, Ellie. All it takes is the right kind of woman."

Ellie picked up her glass and took a sip of Perrier. She'd never felt so confused in her life. She was enjoying Jed's performance and the challenge of flinging back answers, but she was also beginning to simmer. Game or no game, she didn't like the chauvinistic way he was talking to her. He had trapped her between the bar and his body, and she didn't like that, either. He was being too physically aggressive. It made her nervous.

Don't let your emotions get involved in this, she silently told herself. *He's probably hoping you'll run to your room and hide there all weekend.* "And is Lynette LaTour the right kind of woman?" she demanded aloud. "Does *she* appreciate being molested at a public gathering?"

"We were talking about you," he answered. "You have a beautiful body. You should show it off. I'd like to buy you something filmy and clinging, take you someplace where dozens of men will see you and want you, and then bring you back to my house and enjoy what none of them can have."

Ellie could feel herself redden. Nobody had ever spoken to her that way before, especially not in public. Jed's back was to everyone else in the room so they couldn't see the way he was staring, but that husky voice of his carried much too well. People were beginning to notice.

She wasn't only simmering by now; she'd begun to take Jed's comments personally. Why was he doing this to her?

Did he get a kick out of embarrassing her? Did he want her to lose her temper? Well, she wasn't going to do it. She never lost her temper in public.

She gave him a look that was pure, icy disdain and said, "I'm finding it a trial to even stand here and talk to you, much less contemplate spending the night with you. Now, if you'll excuse me—"

"Sure I will, for the moment. I know your type perfectly. You act like a self-righteous little puritan, but underneath..." He backed up a step. "Let's put it this way: one word from me and you'll be knocking on my door tonight."

Ellie had heard enough. The man was going to get the tongue-lashing he deserved. "Only to kill you," she said coldly. "You're the most obnoxious, egotistical jerk I've ever met, and—"

"And you find me irresistible." His smile was so smug she longed to slap it off his face. "Admit it, Ellie. You've pictured us together from the moment we met. Before the weekend is over you'll be begging me to make love to you."

That did it. Ellie told herself Jed could have made a saint lose patience with him. The game went straight out of her mind. So did her determination to stay calm and controlled. The man was a perfect jackass who deserved whatever he got.

Without a moment's hesitation, she raised her glass and poured its contents over his head. Out of the corner of her eye, she saw the previously stone-faced Scott bite his lip to keep from laughing, and pull the bell cord. Jed was so totally astonished by her attack that he stood rooted to the floor, blinking away the liquid as it dribbled down his face.

His shoulders absorbed most of the soda, with the remainder splashing to the floor and beading up on the thick coat of wax. "How careless of me!" Ellie drawled, and then added to Scott, "I'm so sorry about the floor. I hope it won't damage the wood."

"Think nothing of it, Miss White. These little accidents do happen, but we'll have it cleaned up in no time." Scott looked at Jed, snickered, and then asked blandly, "Might I take your jacket, sir?"

"By all means." Jed didn't look especially angry, just disgruntled. Oddly enough the object of his bad temper seemed to be Scott, not Ellie.

The butler was helping him off with his jacket when Rebecca came hurrying into the room. She took one look at the mess on the floor and pulled off her apron to mop it up. Jed walked out of the room a moment later, with Scott not far behind.

Drinks were refilled and conversations were resumed. Ellie started to talk to Sister Mary, but her mind wasn't on the nun's cheerful chatter. She was beginning to regret what she'd done. Jed hadn't made a scene. In fact, he hadn't said a single angry word. It took a certain amount of class to display such calm resignation when one was showered with a glass of Perrier. Jed—the real Jed—probably had class to burn. But, my God, why had he pushed her so hard?

Five minutes later she'd made up her mind. She wasn't going to get any answers by standing here in the parlor. She and Jed needed to talk.

Chapter Three

Ellie had almost reached Jed's room when she heard a burst of laughter from inside and realized he wasn't alone. She figured that if snooping was permitted, eavesdropping had to be too, and pressed her ear to the door.

"Me? You're blaming it on me?" The speaker was Scott, but he'd dropped the snooty accent. "Hell, Jed, you're lucky she didn't do something worse, given the things you were saying. Why did you goad her that way?"

"You have the nerve to ask me that? After all your lectures about what a chauvinist jerk the guy is and how important it is to play him that way? And after the look you gave me downstairs?" Jed cursed with eloquent succinctness. "Thanks a lot, Scotty. Remind me to return the favor someday."

"You don't owe me a thing," Scott said magnanimously. "It's reward enough to see one of my creations brought to life so perfectly. Thorpe is even more obnoxious than the guy I modeled him after. Although I have to admit, I didn't think Ellie would have such a volatile temper. She seems so controlled, I thought it would take an atom bomb to get that much of a reaction from her.''

"You and me both. But don't pretend you would have acted any different if you'd known. You probably would have badgered me into making Thorpe twice as bad, just for the pleasure of seeing me get creamed.''

"Could be," Scott said. "Nobody likes their landlord. By the way, you don't have to worry about your jacket. I showed it to Rebecca. She says it'll be fine.''

"You must have been relieved. Now you won't have to buy me a new suit." There was a brief silence. "Here, take the tie, too, and ask Rebecca if it's salvageable. It was a gift from my mother. If the stains don't come out, *you* can explain what happened.''

Scotty started to laugh. "Oh, God, Jed, not your mother. You wouldn't do that to me, not when I've worked all these months to convince her what a respectable guy I am.''

"You want to bet?''

"You're a hard man.''

Now Jed laughed. "Not hard, just afraid of my mother. You might as well take the shoes while you're at it and see what you can do about the water spots.''

"Certainly, sir." Scott was back in character, talking in his snootiest tones. "Will you require anything else?''

"Maybe an umbrella and a bulletproof vest," Jed replied. "Now get out of here before I raise your rent.''

Ellie scurried back to the top of the steps. By the time Scott opened the door she was strolling down the hall, looking as if she'd just arrived. It kept her options open about whether to reveal what she'd overheard.

"I thought I'd have a word with Mr. Thorpe," she said. "Is he in his room?''

"Yes, miss. He was just changing his clothes.''

Ellie didn't miss the laugher in Scott's eyes. "Should I wait a few minutes before I go in, or is he decent?''

"That's a matter of opinion, miss." Scott permitted himself a small chuckle. "Those who have come out on the short end of their business dealings with him might question his decency, but most people consider him an admirable gentleman." With a dignified nod, he continued on his way.

Scott hadn't been talking about Thorpe, but about Jed Whoever-he-was, the real person. Since it wasn't like Scott to step out of character to praise somebody, he must have felt guilty about getting a friend assaulted. Ellie was feeling a little guilty herself by then. It would have been more adult to have told Jed off or simply walked away.

He answered her knock with a muffled, "Yeah, come in." He'd evidently expected Scott again or perhaps Lynette, because he gave Ellie a surprised look as she opened his door. He'd changed into a different pair of slacks and was pulling on a fresh shirt.

She ignored his bare chest as best she could and got straight to the point. "I'm sorry about pouring my drink over your head, but you went too far with making Thorpe obnoxious. You really got under my skin. You're too convincing an actor for your own good."

He stood there with his shirt half-open and a knowing smile on his face. "I understand exactly why you did it. You wanted to pique my interest—to arouse my passion. You'll be glad to know you've succeeded completely."

Not Thorpe again! Ellie could have groaned aloud. What had she done to deserve this? "Look, can you forget about staying in character for a minute and talk to me straight?" she asked. "We need to reach an understanding."

"What's to understand? You're in my room, aren't you? If you remember, I predicted you would show up."

She folded her arms across her chest and prayed for patience. "I'm here to talk, not to swoon at your feet. I'm sure you realize that."

"Actions speak louder than words." He started toward her, a patented Thorpe leer on his face. "We don't have to wait till tonight, sweetheart. You can have me here and now if you're really that desperate."

After the lines Jed had used downstairs, he would have had to come on to Ellie like the hero in an X-rated movie to get a rise out of her. Half-exasperated, half-amused, she said, "You're totally impossible, Jed. What will it take to make you stop?"

"Stop what? Stop wanting you?" He took another couple of steps in her direction, stalking her now.

At that point, Ellie realized she was wasting her breath talking. Jed wasn't going to step out of character unless she forced him into it. So much for the effectiveness of acting adult and controlled.

She dashed into his bathroom and poured herself a glass of water. She was holding it high above her head when she came back out. "If I were you, I wouldn't press my luck," she said. She wiggled the glass in a menacing way. "Do we understand each other?"

Jed knew when he was licked, but told himself it was only a temporary setback. He should have realized Ellie had eavesdropped on his conversation with Scotty. She couldn't have heard anything damaging, but still, he would have to be more prudent from now on.

Despite the drenching he'd just received, he'd finally gained the upper hand with her. She'd been so aggravated downstairs, she'd forgotten he was even acting. Although she'd made a quick recovery since then, the momentum was still on his side. All he had to do was keep it there.

Unfortunately, he had no idea how to do that. Ellie's guard was up. She'd be tough to provoke and even tougher to ambush. He could only wing it and hope for the best.

"So you listen at doorways, do you?" he drawled. "I'll have to be more careful about what I say."

"That's always a sound policy," she agreed. "If I remember correctly, Scotty asked you why you pushed me so hard. You never gave him an answer."

"It wasn't a real question. He was trying to needle me. He wrote the script and he talked me into playing Thorpe. He knew I was only acting out a role."

"But you didn't have to go so far," she complained.

Jed decided to tell her the truth, or at least part of the truth. "I didn't realize how much it annoyed you—until you poured your drink over my head, that is. I assumed you weren't taking me seriously."

She looked at the floor for a moment, visibly perturbed. "I wasn't, not at first, and I doubt I would again, but you kept provoking me until I forgot there was a difference between the real you and the character you were playing. I took your comments personally and I reacted personally." Her voice grew husky. "Too personally, I suppose."

Jed hadn't expected Ellie to turn feminine and vulnerable on him. It tempted him to do something disastrous, like take her in his arms and reassure her. It tempted him to forget she might be a crook. But there was one thing he couldn't forget—the defeats she inflicted every time he dropped his guard.

He forced himself to keep his distance. "Thorpe is an objectionable lout, but I agreed to play him and I have to stick to the script. If that gets me into trouble at times, there's not much I can do about it."

Ellie hadn't expected Jed to be so stubborn about toning Thorpe down, but she couldn't argue with his dedication to the game. As long as his comments weren't meant personally, she supposed she could learn to live with them. After all, she suddenly realized, she wasn't entirely defenseless. She didn't intend to drench him again, but *he* didn't have to know that.

She smiled to herself, pleased to have come up with such a perfect solution. "I hope your friend Scotty appreciates the danger he's put you in. I wouldn't be surprised if you run out of clothes this weekend, because personally, I plan to have a glass of Perrier on hand at all times, just in case you get out of line.''

Jed could hardly believe it. It was happening again. A sly smile, a teasing tone, and his hormones were going haywire. Ellie had grabbed the initiative and would no doubt subject him to a total drubbing if he didn't watch his step.

He couldn't let her roll over him this way. He'd be damned if he was going to spend the entire weekend ducking sprays of water. ''There's something you need to understand,'' he said. ''Thorpe may be a jerk, but he doesn't *know* he's a jerk. He thinks he's irresistible to women. If you throw a drink at him again, he'll assume you're inviting him to retaliate and he'll almost certainly oblige. To be specific, he'll haul you over his shoulder and march you up to his room.''

If a threat like that had come from Marty, Ellie would have laughed out loud and dared him to try it. She wasn't about to do that with Jed, though. He might have called her bluff, with results she didn't care to contemplate.

She set down her glass, acting as though she encountered men like him and situations like this every day of the week. Jed could play the Big Bad Wolf if he wanted to, but she wasn't going to flee in horror like some terrified Victorian maiden—not even if that was how she felt.

Arching an eyebrow, she said, ''How very fascinating! And what would he do once we got there?''

''You're a beautiful woman, Ellie. Thorpe may be a jerk but he knows the difference between a lump of coal and a priceless diamond. He would make love to you as sensitively and passionately as he could.''

A priceless diamond? Ellie thought in bemusement. If Jed's smoky voice was anything to go by, he'd spoken for himself as well as for Thorpe. This conversation had gotten totally out of hand. "The real Jed and the real Ellie might have something to say about that," she informed him.

"Are you asking whether the real Jed would enjoy it?" He smiled at her, letting her read the answer in his eyes.

Discretion, Ellie told herself, was the better part of valor. Although she managed a crisp retort—"The real Jed has as much chance with the real Ellie as Thorpe has with Sister Mary"—she couldn't get out of the room fast enough. The real Jed had a better chance with the real Ellie than any man she'd met. If they tangled again, *she* would choose the battlefield—and it wouldn't be within inches of a double bed.

Scott appeared in the parlor at exactly six o'clock and summoned everyone in to dinner. Ellie was seated between Marty and the doctor, directly across from Jed. She only hoped the wide table and tall centerpiece would discourage any additional propositions.

Everybody stuck to small talk at first—the weather, the newest movies, sports, their characters' backgrounds. Still, as dinner progressed, Ellie realized most of these people seemed to know each other. Sometimes an unthinking slip tipped her off, like when Lynette asked Abby whether she'd gotten around to seeing a certain movie, and sometimes it was the air of comfortable familiarity between two people.

Her fellow guests behaved as she'd come to expect. Sister Mary was chatty and warm with an impish sense of humor. Jed paid his smarmy brand of attentions to Lynette, who responded with coquettish flirting. Marty joked and teased, slipping out of character more than everybody else combined. Abby Stone, the elderly nurse with the bad case of nerves, picked at her food and said very little. The final character, Dr. James Jamison, was a double of his alter ego, Cludds's attorney James Emerson. Ellie had met Emerson once and had spoken to him on the phone several times. He was a smooth talker with a considerable amount of courtly charm. She imagined he was effective with jurors, especially female jurors.

He wasn't well, however, and as a result, his charm gradually wilted as the evening wore on. Every now and then he would cough or sneeze. His appetite lasted through two courses, then disappeared. He finally confessed to Ellie that his wife had recently gotten over the flu, and he was afraid he might have caught it.

Even before the main course, Ellie was coaxing him to have a word with Scott. If a worsening case of flu wasn't an emergency, she didn't know what was. Emerson was reluctant to spoil the game but finally conceded that Ellie might be right. After Scott had served the dessert, Emerson followed him out of the dining room. He never returned to the table.

The remaining six guests retired to the living room after dinner. A bridge table was sitting in one corner of the room and a chessboard in another, but Ellie wasn't in the mood for games. Now that she'd met her fellow guests, she wanted to think about who might be capable of murder. She headed for the couch, to warm herself in front of the fire.

Sister Mary and Marty seated themselves at the bridge table, then asked for two opponents. Lynette was willing to play, but Jed, her first choice of a partner, turned her down. He felt like playing chess, he said, not bridge. After Ellie declined as well, a reluctant Abby Stone was persuaded to join their game.

Since Ellie was the only one left, she wasn't surprised when Jed started over toward the couch. He sat down only inches away from her and rested his arm along the top of the back. Given her exit line upstairs, there was only one possible way she could react. She ignored him.

He sat there for what seemed like ages, saying nothing. Finally, when his closeness had stretched Ellie's nerves to the breaking point, he asked whether she played chess.

"Not very often," she answered, staring at the fire.

"Then I'll give you a couple of pieces. I'm very good, but I wouldn't take advantage of a novice." He couldn't have sounded any more lascivious if he'd panted in her ear. "You won't be sorry. Chess is a very erotic game."

The final sentence was vintage Thorpe, but after their skirmish upstairs Ellie could also imagine the real Jed coming up with something like that. His voice would have been teasing rather than oily, though, and probably captivating. All in all, she preferred Thorpe. He was easier to cope with.

She gave him a supercilious look. "I'm afraid not, Mr. Thorpe. Erotic games bore me." The truth was that she seldom played social chess because she was just too good. The average player couldn't compete with her.

Jed crossed his legs and made himself more comfortable. Another unsettling silence followed. Ellie could neither relax nor think, not with Jed's hand only inches from the nape of her neck. She pictured his fingers on the harpsichord, delicately stroking the keys, and swallowed hard. She couldn't just keep sitting here. One of them would have to leave.

She was about to get up when he sighed and tried again. "Please Ellie, just one game. I'm really in the mood to play. I'll even get you a glass of Perrier to keep on the table for emergencies."

"Would I need it?" Ellie asked, weakening. Jed was hard to refuse when he turned on the charm.

"No," he promised.

He looked so innocently eager that she never stood a chance. As they made their way to the chessboard, she told herself a single game wouldn't kill her. How long could it take to defeat him? She was so confident, she scarcely bothered to concentrate as they made their opening moves.

Her mind was on Death on Raven's Island, not chess. According to the rules, the murderer could be expected to lie. Had one of these six people already begun to deceive her, perhaps about who he or she really was? Could anybody be as cheerful as Sister Mary, as nervous as Abby or as slimy as Thorpe? As flirtatious as Lynette or as careless about the rules as Marty? Which of them was pretending to be something he or she wasn't?

She studied the foursome at the bridge table, hoping to learn something from their game, but the only conversation concerned the bidding. Then, just when she'd decided that watching was a waste of time, Lynette slipped off her shoe and ran her toe up Marty's calf. He stiffened and jerked his leg away, but Lynette only smiled. She hadn't been playing the flirtatious Mlle LaTour with Marty, Ellie was sure of it. She'd been chasing him for real.

Ellie was musing about their past relationship when a soft "Your move, Miss White" broke into her thoughts. Something about Jed's tone warned her to study her position thoroughly rather than making another cursory move, and once she had, she realized in astonishment that he had a solid advantage. Her natural competitiveness took over and she finally started to concentrate on chess.

Before too long she was absorbed in the game, but not so absorbed she could block out her opponent entirely. Jed studied the board with a look of passionate involvement on his face and moved his pieces with an almost sensuous grace. Ellie had been attracted to him from the start, but that had been mostly because of his looks. Now she started to feel an intellectual attraction as well. He was a talented player with a brash style similar to her own, but he was far less experienced than she was. He would have been a joy to teach.

Fortunately for her chances, she was extremely self-disciplined when it came to chess. She made a series of bold moves that threw Jed off balance and then ground away at him until she had the advantage. Jed fought valiantly, but he was less consistent than she was. After an hour of skillfully outflanking him, Ellie had him scrambling to stay alive.

He watched her capture his bishop and shook his head. "You've got me. There's no point in prolonging the agony."

She was amused by his nettled tone. "You're not used to losing, are you?"

"No. I made some costly mistakes." He frowned at the board, shaking his head in self-disgust. "You're a damn good player but you're not beyond my reach. Next time I'll give you a better game."

Ellie understood his frustration. Fighting one's hardest and dying by inches was murder on a player's ego. "Believe me, I know how you feel," she said. "I competed on the national level as a child. I learned that winning is as much a matter of experience and concentration as raw talent. You're a good player, but I have all those tournaments on my side."

Her explanation only seemed to annoy him. "You don't need tournaments to learn how to concentrate. I was distracted because I allowed myself to be. I won't make the same mistake twice. Tomorrow I'm going to win."

Wounded male ego or not, Ellie wasn't going to insult Jed's intelligence by not playing her best chess against him. "In that case," she said, "I'll make sure to watch the chessboard rather than the bridge table tomorrow—right from the first move."

Tension crackled between them. Jed was every bit as competitive as Ellie, and she had the feeling his competitiveness extended to other areas of conflict besides chess. He was looking at her as if he wanted to ease the sting of defeat by engaging in a far more elemental type of contest.

He stood up, his eyes lingering on her face. "I'll look forward to the rematch. Are you ready to go to bed?"

His choice of words notwithstanding, Ellie understood there was no double entendre intended. He was simply offering to walk her upstairs. Still, things had a way of happening in dim, deserted hallways. She felt a panicky need to put some distance between them.

"I'm ready to go to *sleep*," she answered, deliberately misinterpreting him. "In my own room and by myself, Mr. Thorpe. If you insist on accompanying me upstairs, I'll have to ring for Scott and ask him for a glass of Perrier."

He stiffened for a moment, then smiled smugly. The look was pure Thorpe. Much to Ellie's relief, he was following her lead and slipping into character. "That won't be necessary, Miss White. I'll let you run away—for now. When I decide to have you, I'll have you. Both of us know that."

"I only sleep with men who can beat me at chess," Ellie shot back. "That leaves you out." She rose from her seat and marched to the door, only picking up her pace when she was out of Jed's sight. He hadn't answered her back, but the frown on his face had told her what sort of revenge he longed to exact.

Lucifer, the black cat, followed her into her room and curled up against her legs once she'd gotten into bed. Ellie hoped he would stay all night, but he got restless after a while and scratched to be let out. She was curious about who owned him and might even have called the number on his tag, but the only available phone was in the kitchen—off-limits. She was still musing about it as she drifted off to sleep.

Ellie was a light sleeper, especially when she was away from home. The noise that awakened her was so soft that it took her a few moments to identify it—the sound of the front door opening and closing. She got out of bed and hurried to the window, curious to see who was coming or going at such an early hour. It was still quite dark out, and she had to strain to make out any details.

A tall man with thinning hair was walking toward the pier, obviously James Emerson. Scott was by his side, his hand under the attorney's arm. Scott helped him into the waiting launch, handed him his briefcase and turned to leave. As the launch pulled away from the pier, Ellie realized that Emerson hadn't taken any luggage on board. Assuming his illness had forced him to leave early, why hadn't he taken his belongings?

Intrigued, she slipped on her bathrobe and tiptoed down the hall. The house was as still as a morgue. Emerson's room was near the top of the steps, its door firmly closed. Ellie listened for signs of life, heard nothing, and turned the knob. Then she eased the door open and peeked inside the room.

What she saw there made her face go pale and her heart race in shock. Somebody was in the bed, his face turned into the pillow and his arm dangling limply over the side. An empty glass sat on the night table and various articles of clothing were scattered on the dresser and chair. Ellie almost screamed out loud, but her common sense took over just in time. None of this was real. James Emerson was very much alive, and not so sick that he hadn't made it to the waiting launch under his own steam.

She slowly crept closer. A dummy was in the bed, not a human being, but the scene was incredibly realistic all the same. Although the dummy didn't look that much like Emerson, it had the same thinning gray hair and blue eyes as he did. Ellie realized what must have happened. Scott had taken Emerson's unexpected departure and incorporated it into the game. He'd killed off Emerson's character, the doctor, rather than simply telling everyone that illness had forced him to withdraw.

Investigating further, Ellie noticed that the rug under her feet was wet, as though the water in the now empty glass on the night table had been spilled onto the floor. Perhaps both the glass and the wetness were clues—part of the game. Was the glass supposed to have been knocked over in a struggle, indicating the doctor had been murdered? It was certainly a possibility.

Ellie debated her next move. The discoverer of the "body" was probably expected to rouse the whole household with a bloodcurdling scream, but a better idea suddenly occurred to her. The dummy was too intriguing a touch not to follow up on.

Walking as quietly as she could, she opened the door to the back staircase. Every creak of the old wooden steps sounded like a clarinet blast to her sensitive ears, but the third floor was as silent as the second. Ellie slipped next door, into the turret room, to listen and wait.

When she was sure the coast was clear, she let herself into the next room down the hall, a storage room. She and Marty hadn't done more than glance inside, but now she took a thorough look around. Between the spare light of dawn and the drawn shades, the room was very dim, but she didn't dare turn on the lights. Somebody might pass by in the hall and notice the telltale strip of light under the door.

As far as Ellie could tell, there was nothing of interest in the room, even in the closets. The same was true of the second room down the hall. She was about to step outside again when the shuffle of bedroom slippers sent her scuttling backward. She pressed herself against the wall, hardly daring to breathe. The footsteps approached and then receded. A door opened and closed. Somebody, perhaps Rebecca, had just gone downstairs.

Ellie waited another minute and then checked out the hall again. It was empty. Taking a quick, sharp breath, she hurried down to the third storage room, slipped inside and closed the door. It was filled with drapes, furniture and knickknacks, none of which told her a thing. The only place left to explore was the closet. Doubly cautious now, she opened the door, stepped inside and pulled the door shut behind her. A tiny bit of light filtered in from the room beyond.

The closet was very large, and nearly pitch-black. There had to be an overhead light—all the other closets had had them—but where was the blasted string? Ellie batted the air in front of her, clumsily feeling for it. When she finally found it she gave it a quick yank, and then instinctively closed her eyes against the sudden glare.

No sooner had she opened them than she was gaping at one of the most macabre sights she had ever seen. A group of dummies was suspended from the ceiling by means of ropes around their necks. Even eerier, each of them represented one of the people staying in the house.

It wasn't hard to identify Ellie White. She had long brown hair that was braided down her back, just as Ellie's often was. She had Ellie's green eyes and a youthful, unlined face. Most unsettling of all, her throat had been slashed, the painted blood running down her neck and soaking into her blouse. The dummy gave Ellie the chills. It was like looking into her own coffin.

Studying the dummies, Ellie realized that every single person on the island was scheduled to die. Abby Stone had bruises that suggested strangulation. Marty Robey had a grizzly collection of scrapes and cuts. Sister Mary and Jed Thorpe had bullets through their heads. Rebecca Hill, the cook, was as pale as a ghost, perhaps the victim of poison. Scott and Lynette, like Ellie, had been assaulted with a knife.

It took a little while, but Ellie eventually smiled. The people who ran Skulduggery Enterprises had the most incredible imaginations. With fewer than three days left, people were going to start dropping like flies.

She turned off the light and opened the closet door, thinking she would have to be careful. She didn't want to wind up the victim of a modern-day Jack the Ripper. She was just congratulating herself on how clever she'd been when she glanced up and saw Scotty in the room, lounging against the door. The look on his face was exceedingly reproving.

"Miss White, you were told to stay off the third floor," he scolded. "You've seen something you weren't meant to see. What do you propose we do about it?"

Ellie grinned at him, unable to resist a little one-upmanship. "That all depends, Scotty. If you happen to have a knife handy, you could always dispose of me here and now."

He straightened, not in the least bit surprised by her use of his nickname. His friend Jed must have mentioned her habit of eavesdropping. "I've already told you, the butler didn't do it. Credit me with a little imagination, Ellie. I'm a better writer than that."

"So you rent an apartment from Jed, which is how he got involved in this, and you wrote the script for Death on Raven's Island," Ellie said.

"A cottage on Jed's property," Scott corrected.

"A cottage, then." Ellie began to think out loud. "There are too many dummies in that closet. If all of us are meant to die, who can the murderer be? Is it someone we haven't met yet, hiding out on the island?" She thought it over, then shook her head. "One of those dummies has to be a red herring. You didn't lock the closet because it amuses you to picture us stumbling across your phony corpses and getting more confused than ever. You're a sadist, Scotty."

"Let's just say I cover all the bases." With a grin, he opened the door and gestured toward the hallway. "After you, Miss White. I hope you'll refrain from passing on your discovery to your fellow guests."

Ellie said she wouldn't think of sharing the advantage she'd gained, and allowed Scott to chase her downstairs. Giving a yawn, she decided somebody else could discover Emerson's "body." It was early yet and she wanted to get some more sleep.

She was just about to open her door when a soft scratching noise caught her attention. It was Lucifer again, asking to be let out of Jed's room. Ellie wasn't particularly eager to open Jed's door, given her habit of catching him half-naked, but the cat gave a howl too plaintive to ignore. She took pity on him and opened the door just far enough for him to slip out.

If she'd had any brains, she would have closed it again immediately, but her curiosity got the better of her. She couldn't resist peeking inside, to make sure Jed was sleeping and not wandering around with a gun or a knife.

To her chagrin, he was wide awake, propped up against the headboard with a manila folder across his lap and a pencil in his hand. A tray holding a silver coffee carafe and two cups was sitting on the night table nearby. The second cup belonged to Lynette, who was curled up in a chair beside his bed. Both of them were dressed in sweat suits.

It looked more like a business meeting than a romantic rendezvous, but the crack of dawn was an odd time to get together. Only the night before, Ellie would have sworn that Lynette's sole interest was in Marty, but now she wasn't so sure.

She hastily closed the door, but not before meeting Jed's eyes and seeing the amusement in them. Another skirmish, another retreat. Just once, she would have liked Jed to be the one doing the retreating.

Chapter Four

Jed had reached the point where any victory over Ellie Landau, no matter how small, was an event to be heartily savored. Not only had she thrashed him at chess the night before; she'd added insult to injury by coolly announcing she only slept with men who could defeat her. It annoyed him that his thoughts had been so transparent. Why did he have to find her so appealing?

He watched her close the door, then turned to Lynn. "She eavesdrops," he said, referring to Ellie. "We should go outside to talk."

Five minutes later they were strolling through the woods, arguing about whether Ellie was a thief. Jed would have liked to explain his personal response to Ellie and how it was interfering with his objectivity, but he and Lynn didn't have that kind of relationship.

Lynn wasn't the sort of woman you confided in. She was too hard, too calculating. That was why Jed had never made love to her, despite her intelligence and beauty.

Six years ago she had married I. V. Cludd, a man more than three times her age, in the expectation that he would leave her a wealthy widow. She'd been a good wife to him, but she hadn't pretended to be devastated when he had finally died. Hypocrisy wasn't Lynn's style.

She'd come into Jed's life at a critical time. His fiancée had left him for another man and he was trying to sort out his feelings. Lynn was clever, undemanding and a lot of fun. She'd gotten him out of the office and taught him how to have a good time. His sister Rebecca said Lynn had loosened him up, and he supposed it was true. A couple of months ago he wouldn't even have taken part in a game like Death on Raven's Island, much less arranged the whole thing.

"We're never going to agree about Ellie," Lynn finally told him. "In my opinion, the only reason you suspect her is that she gets the better of you so often. You're a sore loser, Jed Thornhill."

"Maybe," he conceded. Since Lynn was right—they were never going to agree about Ellie—he moved to the next person on the list, James Emerson.

Scotty had paid a late-night visit to Jed's room the night before to tell him Emerson would be leaving the island first thing in the morning. The attorney's illness had thrown a monkey wrench into Jed's plans—he'd barely had time to meet the man, much less size him up—but there was nothing he and Scotty could do about that. Their only recourse had been to "kill off" the character prematurely.

He hadn't told Lynn that the attorney was gone. She didn't even know that Thorpe was the killer. He'd told her it was Scott, mostly because he didn't trust her to keep her mouth shut. She had a wicked sense of humor and wasn't above amusing herself by making things as difficult for him as she could.

"Emerson strikes me as a typical lawyer," he said. "Smart, careful and slick. I know he has access to your records, but is there any other reason to suspect him?"

"Only that Izzy disliked him." Lynn meant her late husband, Isidore Van Buren Cludd. "I thought it was odd that Izzy would keep him on retainer, given how he felt. He claimed it was out of loyalty to Emerson's father, who was our previous attorney; but Izzy wasn't the loyal type." She laughed. "After all, look how many wives he had."

"So you think Emerson might have been blackmailing him?"

She shrugged. "It's possible. Nobody ever accused Izzy of leading an exemplary life."

They moved on to the next suspect, Abby Cludd, the firm's bookkeeper. Abby had been I.V. Cludd's second wife, marrying him back in the 1940s. "About Abby," Jed said. "Is she always so nervous?"

"Not so much nervous as mousy or timid. Izzy always called her 'the saint.' She works like a dog, minds her own business and rarely says a word. Still, she *is* the bookkeeper, so I suppose she could have transferred money to her own account and then covered it up."

"And Rosemary McKay?" Rosemary ran the company's factory, where private-label garments were manufactured. The clothes were sold in Cludds's two local stores, in selected shops outside the Boston area, and by mail order.

"She makes a wonderful nun, doesn't she!" Lynn said.

Jed gave an appreciative smile. If Lynn hadn't told him that Rosemary had been I. V. Cludd's mistress for the past twenty years, he never would have guessed it.

"I've always had the feeling that Rosemary knows where all the skeletons are hidden," Lynn continued. "She's been around forever and she's very smart. Other than that, there's no reason to suspect her."

That left only one person, Marty Cludd. Marty was I. V. Cludd's only child. He'd been in Europe for the past six years, racing cars, but Lynn had insisted on including him. Jed had gone to prep school with Marty and couldn't picture him as a thief, but he'd bowed to Lynn's wishes and nagged him into coming to Raven's Island.

"There's no reason to suspect Marty, either," he pointed out. "He isn't disciplined enough for embezzlement. Besides, he would have to have an accomplice in the States."

He was surprised by how quickly Lynn agreed. "Marty isn't guilty. It was the only way I could think to get him over here. Why do you suppose I went along with this whole crazy scheme in the first place?"

"You and Marty..." Jed began, and then stopped, at a loss to finish the sentence.

"Me and Marty." Lynn smiled coyly. "Now you know why I put his name on my list. If you'll excuse me, darling, I'm going to take him some hot coffee and see if I can't thaw him out." She winked and sauntered off, leaving Jed to contemplate the wiliness of the female sex.

He strolled through the woods, thinking about the various suspects. It had been a game till now, this business of trying to unmask a thief, but suddenly it occurred to him that the situation might be dangerous. Somebody who would steal might also be willing to kill, if that's what it took to protect her secrets. Maybe it was the island, with its dark woods, sheer cliff and pounding surf, but his instincts told him to be careful. He would have to put the fear of God into Lynn about mentioning why he was really here. He didn't want any accidents to take place unless they were in the script.

Breakfast at Tipton House was served buffet-style on the veranda. The six surviving characters appeared one by one, making casual conversation as they served themselves from chafing dishes on the sideboard. It was a crisp, clear morning with the promise of bright sunshine, and Ellie was thinking about going to the beach. It had been ages since she'd sunbathed by the ocean.

The doctor's absence wasn't noticed immediately, but about fifteen minutes after the last guest came downstairs, Sister Mary looked around the table and remarked, "I hope Dr. Jamison isn't any sicker. Perhaps somebody should check on him."

Ellie looked at Abby. "You're a nurse. Why don't you go upstairs and see how he is?"

"But I'm not a real one," Abby said nervously. She always seemed to be afraid of something—breaking the rules, making a slip, offending a fellow guest. "What would I do if something was actually wrong?"

Ellie gave her a reassuring smile and whispered, "Abby, try to remember that nothing on this island is real. I know for a fact that he's fine, but if you want me to, I'll go upstairs with you."

The offer was accepted at once. A minute later Abby opened Emerson's door and let out a shriek that could have raised the dead. Every member of the household went dashing up the stairs. Ellie had her arm around Abby's shoulders by then and was explaining that the body was a dummy. The poor woman was so shaken up that Ellie had her hands full convincing her that Emerson had left the island earlier that morning with nothing worse than a case of flu.

Marty was the next one to reach the body, and, predictably, he didn't take the situation seriously. "The poor fellow looks dreadful," he said with a grin. "Like somebody coated him with plastic. He must have died of some horrible new disease."

He motioned to Scott, who was standing at the edge of the crowd, calmly observing the action. "Do you suppose it's contagious? Will we be quarantined here for the rest of our natural lives?"

Scott started forward, the guests smiling at Marty's comments as they silently moved aside. Since nobody had mentioned the wet patch on the rug, Ellie decided to do it. "The glass on the night table must have been full when the doctor went to bed last night, but it's empty now and the rug is soaked. I think there was a struggle here. Maybe the water was knocked over when Dr. Jamison tried to fight off his attacker."

"But there's no sign of a fight," Jed pointed out. "There are no marks on his body and no bloodstains. He was probably delirious from fever and thrashing around. He must have knocked over the glass himself."

Everyone in the room nodded in agreement. The doctor hadn't spoken of any enemies or shown any fear of a fellow guest. He'd probably died from natural causes.

Ellie kept arguing he'd been murdered and finally browbeat everyone into keeping an open mind. Maybe one of them *was* a killer. If so, perhaps a search of the house and grounds would turn up a weapon or clue.

They started with the doctor's bedroom, opening drawers and checking under furniture. When nothing interesting turned up, they went next door to Lynette's room. Ellie stayed with the group until her own room had been checked, then settled down to do some work. She would have loved to join the hunt, but Cludds had to come first. She'd promised herself she would make a good start on the case this weekend.

It was almost lunchtime when she stacked Cludds's computer printouts into a pile and returned them to her top drawer. The records were even worse than she'd thought. Some of the numbers had to be misprints. Still, her eyes were glazing over and she needed a break.

The house was empty when she got downstairs, everyone having gone outside when they'd failed to find anything of interest indoors. Ellie played on the harpsichord for a while, then went into the dining room to wait for the other guests.

They trooped in around twelve-thirty, empty-handed, ill-humored and hungry. Jed grumbled that the island was too big to search thoroughly, and that its terrain was too dangerous. "I nearly scratched myself to shreds in the scrub. One wrong move and you're over the cliff and splattered onto the rocks below. There's no way we could find something as small as a weapon, even if one existed, which it doesn't."

Ellie silently disagreed. The letter they'd all received had said the clues would be findable. Jed was too darn skeptical about everything. Her suspicions were aroused, and she started firing questions at him. She was hoping to trap him into admitting a connection with Dr. Jamison, but he swore they'd never met. Before too long the others had joined in the fun, grilling each other about their backgrounds and looking for links to the dead man.

Only Lynette stayed aloof from the conversation. She kept giving Marty proprietary looks and touches, silently suggesting she knew better ways to spend their time than by playing detective. He ignored her as best he could, at least until she started undoing the buttons on his shirt. Then he turned beet-red and whispered, "Dammit, Lynnie, behave yourself!"

By the time Scott brought in dessert, Lynette had taken as much rejection as she planned to. She stretched in a way that drew attention to her breasts and stared restlessly at the chandelier. "If I hear another word about murder, I will either scream or fall asleep! I do not see how you can ask the same stupid questions over and—*Mon Dieu!* What is that?"

Within seconds, she was climbing onto the table. Since she was wearing a thigh-length skirt and a clinging jersey top, everyone got a splendid view of her body. Marty couldn't take his eyes off her legs, but maybe that was the whole idea.

She reached into the chandelier and pulled out a small crystal bottle filled with an amber-colored liquid. After pulling out the glass stopper in its neck, she sniffed and then grimaced.

"*Mon Dieu*, the smell alone could kill an elephant. Perhaps it contains poison." She looked around the table, smiling triumphantly. "You see where all your talking has led you? *I* found the first clue! Perhaps this very poison was used to murder the doctor." She handed the bottle down to Scott and hopped off the table.

"It's odd that you of all people should find something important," Ellie said. "You had so little interest in our conversation."

"I have always been lucky. At cards, at *chemin de fer*, in love." Lynette winked at Marty.

"Or maybe you knew where the poison was all along," Ellie accused. "You began to worry about being found out, so you just happened to spot it."

"To divert suspicion from myself?" Lynette laughed. "I must say it makes sense. Here, Scott, take me to the police." She held out her wrists, as if inviting him to slap on a pair of handcuffs.

Scott permitted himself a thin smile. "If you insist, Mlle LaTour, naturally I'll take you to the mainland when I go there to inform the police about the doctor's death. The motorboat, after all, does hold two people."

The motorboat? Ellie thought. She hadn't seen any motorboat in the water when she'd watched Emerson board the launch. "It's gone," she said. "I happened to look outside earlier this morning and it wasn't there."

Scott frowned. "Are you quite sure, miss? I tied it down securely."

"She's right," Marty agreed. "We were down by the water half an hour ago and the boat was gone. It must have broken loose during the storm last night. Is there any other way to contact the mainland?"

"As you know, we have no phones here," Scott said, "but I believe we have an old two-way radio upstairs. Perhaps I can get it to work. If not, a boat is due in on Monday, to bring us fuel for our generator.''

Ellie wasn't surprised by this turn of events. Naturally, they were supposed to be stuck here, with no boat, no phone, and sharks in the surrounding waters. No sane person would hang around an island when a homicidal maniac was on the loose.

Her fellow guests were trying to act worried and failing miserably. They were having too good a time to stay in character. The only exception was Abby Stone, who seemed to be taking the whole thing seriously. She bent her head to take a bite of pie, but her fork was shaking as she raised it to her lips. Ellie decided to take her aside and tell her about the phone in the kitchen. Maybe she would be less frightened if she understood that they weren't really stranded here at all.

The beach on Raven's Island was nestled into the curve of the cliff at the eastern end, with nothing but the Atlantic Ocean for as far as the eye could see. Ellie loved the Eden-like isolation of the place, but she also recognized its potential dangers. A hungry shark, a rock from the cliff above, and the unsuspecting sunbather could become a dear departed victim.

If she hadn't known she was due to be knifed to death, she would have turned around and left. As it was, the beach's isolation was also a form of protection. There were only two ways to reach it: the rock-strewn trail that followed the island's shoreline or the flight of stone steps chiseled into the face of the cliff. If she was attacked, all she had to do was scramble up the steps or escape along the shoreline trail.

She spread down her towel and sprawled on her stomach, facing the stone steps. She could also see the trail from where she was lying and felt perfectly safe. After smoothing on some suntan oil, she took a stack of newspapers out of her tote bag. They were back issues of the Boston *Times* that she'd filched from the library.

If the papers contained clues, the technicians at Skulduggery Enterprises would have had to excise actual stories and substitute their own. Ellie was hoping she would recognize stories that had never actually appeared. She was also looking for articles about violent crimes and reports that mentioned Raven's Island.

She found her first planted item in the second paper she checked. The headline read, "Shark Kills Woman Near Raven's Island," but Ellie was sure there had been no shark attacks that summer. She assumed the story was meant to back up Scott's warning that the waters were deadly to swim in.

A few pages later she came across a profile of Rebecca Hill, the cook. Rebecca had an excellent reputation in the Boston area, so excellent that T. T. Tipton considered himself lucky to be her employer. She'd previously been the chef at an elegant inn in New Hampshire, the same state where Ellie's character had recently vacationed. She wondered if the tie-in was important.

A number of the other papers contained stories about grizzly crimes. Since Ellie usually skipped such articles, she couldn't be sure what was real and what was planted. An ax murder in Allston, body parts washing ashore off the coast of Maine, adultery and murder in a town near Raven's Island—was any of it significant? She didn't know.

Rubbing her eyes, she put the final paper aside and laced her fingers together under her chin. Between the warmth of the sun, the smell of the air and the gentle slapping of the surf, the beach was sheer heaven. Her eyelids drooped; she cradled her head in her arms. She knew she should think about what she'd read and learned, but the peacefulness of the place defeated her. It was dangerous to drop her guard, but she couldn't stay awake.

She woke with a panicky start at the sound of a hideous yell. Frightened and disoriented, she bolted to her feet and looked around. The scream had apparently come from the top of the cliff.

The next thing she knew, a body came hurtling vertically downward, bouncing from rock to needle-sharp rock. It jerked to a halt at the bottom of the cliff, about ten feet from Ellie's towel. Now she knew how Marty Robey had gotten all those bruises and scrapes. A sharp blow to the head, a violent fall, and the poor man was tomorrow's headline.

Without so much as a passing thought about sharks, Ellie dashed across the beach and ran into the sea. She kept moving until she was far enough out to see the scrub-filled terrain at the top of the cliff. Nobody was there. The murderer—assuming it *was* a murder—had disposed of Marty's body and taken off into the woods. It was already too late to follow.

Ellie had missed her chance at melodrama when she'd discovered the doctor's body, but fortune had dealt her a second opportunity. Smiling to herself, she trotted out of the water and began to shriek like a crazed hyena. "Help! Help! It's Marty Robey. He's been killed. Can anybody hear me? Oh, please, help me!"

She kept on yelling until somebody appeared on the cliff top. It was Abby, the nervous nurse, who of all Ellie's fellow guests was the least likely to have murdered anybody. Not only was she scared senseless most of the time; she was old and seemingly frail. She wouldn't have had the strength to throw Marty over the cliff.

Who had? Marty was slender and small, so it wasn't inconceivable that Sister Mary or Lynette might have sent him to his final reward. Jed could easily have done so. But Abby? She was a longshot.

Abby stared at the body in open-mouthed horror. "Dear Lord, what's happened? This is terrible, just terrible!"

"It's Marty," Ellie called up. "He's been thrown over the cliff. Can you get help?"

Abby took a step backward, lurching unsteadily. "Is he dead? He is, isn't he!" She buried her face in her hands.

At that point, Ellie realized Abby's imagination had run away with her. She climbed halfway up the steps so she wouldn't have to shout and reminded Abby it was only a game. "That's another dummy down there. Marty is probably hiding out somewhere, waiting to leave the island—just like the doctor."

"But you sounded so frightened," Abby said. "And it looks so real from up here."

"Take a closer look," Ellie suggested. "The body would be covered with blood if it was a real person."

Abby climbed down a ways and squinted at the dummy. "I can see it's not really Marty now," she said sheepishly. "It's just that he's—he's a kind of relative of mine. The thought that he might have died..." She shuddered. "I'll go get Scott. He's the proper one to handle this, don't you think?"

Ellie told her yes, he certainly was, and climbed back down the steps. She had just begun to gather up her things when Jed came into view, jogging along the shoreline trail from the south side of the island. He was dressed in running shoes, white tennis shorts and nothing else. Ellie thought he looked as good as a man could look.

As she watched him approach the "corpse," she told herself he'd shown up awfully quickly, given the length of the shoreline trail. Would Marty's murderer have taken a chance on admitting he'd been so close by? He might, if he had Jed's audacity.

He looked at the blond-haired dummy lying facedown on the rocks. "Marty Robey, I presume. Was it an accident?"

Ellie pointed to the artfully manufactured lump on his head. "I doubt it. It looks like he was struck from behind with the proverbial blunt object and then thrown down here.

Besides, he was a cat burglar. He wouldn't have lost his balance and fallen.''

Jed was feeling very pleased with himself at that moment. It hadn't been easy to pry Marty loose from Lynn and get him to the top of the cliff, but he'd done it. Abby had come along a minute later, but he'd managed to get himself and Marty out of sight before she spotted them. All he had to do now was survive the cross-examination Ellie was sure to subject him to.

Fortunately, he'd discovered her Achilles' heel. It had come to him this morning, while he was walking in the woods. Ellie was skittish with men, or perhaps only with him. She found him either threatening or distasteful, he wasn't sure which. In any case, her weakness gave him a way to ambush her.

He ran his eyes over her sleek nylon maillot and tanned, glistening skin. It was something Thorpe might have done, but that wasn't the only reason Jed did it. He enjoyed looking at Ellie Landau—too damn much, maybe.

He took a steadying breath and reminded himself to keep his emotions out of it. "I suppose that's true. Then again, maybe he saw you sunbathing and couldn't wait to join you. You'd be enough to make any man lose his balance. You should have told me you were coming here. I would have given you the most unforgettable afternoon of your life.''

Ellie was amazed by how quickly an answer sprung to her lips. It was automatic by now; an instinctive defense mechanism. "I can well believe it. It's not every day I get to fend off a pompous jerk.'' She started to walk away, but his hands shot out to circle her waist. "Mr. Thorpe, if you don't mind—''

"I do mind, if it's running away you're talking about.'' He slid his palms up her sides and brought them to rest on her shoulders. They were warm and gentle against her skin.

She tried to dismiss him with a disdainful stare, but it was hopeless. The desire in his eyes made her flush, and she couldn't hold his gaze for more than a few seconds. She wound up looking at his chest.

Her body was responding to his closeness in a disturbing, unfamiliar way. Her breasts tingled, the nipples hardening against the revealing fabric of her swimsuit. Her heart started to race and her chest felt tight. She had had no experience with this sort of thing. She didn't know if Jed was playing a game with her or not, touching her because he wanted to or because his character would have wanted to.

He kneaded her shoulders with a light but possessive touch and then wrapped his fingers around her neck, his thumbs gently stroking her throat. She started to tremble. "Maybe I've already killed James Jamison and Marty Robey. Maybe I plan to make you my next victim. I have a huge physical advantage. I could strangle you with very little effort and leave you here on the sand, or drag you into the water and drown you. You should learn to be more careful about who you're alone with."

Ellie raised her eyes, mesmerized by the quiet deadliness of his tone. His warning was strangely erotic, his gaze hypnotically seductive. She could picture him making love to her in a way that drugged her senses and then, when she least expected it, striking violently.

She looked away, physically shaken. It had to be a game. Jed was a sophisticated man. They were alone on this beach, without a soul nearby. If he had really wanted her, he would have taken her, not simply teased her. "If you were going to kill me, I'd already be dead," she said. "You wouldn't waste your time talking to me about it."

Jed looked down for a long, tense moment, struggling to keep his feelings under control. It had been a mistake to get this close to Ellie. He felt like he was in the middle of a raging brushfire. Why wasn't she telling him off and storming away? She was supposed to be afraid of him, dammit! The woman was always one step ahead of him, torturing him in ways he'd never anticipated.

You're Thorpe, he silently told himself. *Act like a jerk. Say something offensive. Don't let her get the upper hand.*

"Maybe I changed my mind the moment I saw you," he said aloud. "Maybe I decided I wanted to take you to bed before I kill you. Admit it's what you want. Why else did you open my door this morning?"

Ellie stiffened. Jed's proposition was so obnoxious and egotistical that it snapped her out of her trance and cooled her off. The fog left her brain and her heart slowed down. Suddenly, a macabre picture flashed into her mind: the simulacrum of Ellie White was hanging by its slashed neck in a third-floor closet. Its *cleanly* slashed neck, she realized. The wound had been made by a sharp knife, not something makeshift like a rock. Had she ever been in any danger?

She could be maddeningly single-minded at times, and this was one of them. Her entire attention was suddenly focused on the answer to that all-important question. A yes could trap a murderer and solve a mystery—providing she got out alive.

She placed her hands on Jed's buttocks, checking his back pockets. Her fingers continued exploring with a deft touch that was unwittingly erotic—moving lower, coming forward to his hips and belly, seeking a concealed weapon under his shorts. Her only concern was to gain information.

She gained information, all right, but not the kind she was after. She couldn't have said which came first—the realization that she'd touched Jed in an extremely intimate spot or his startled flinch and strangled, "Ellie, what do you think you're doing?"

She pulled away her hands as if they'd just touched fire. "Checking your pockets for a knife."

"My *pockets*?" he repeated.

"And, uh, under your shorts. Anyplace you could have hidden a knife." She was thoroughly rattled now. "That's how I'm murdered. My throat is cut with a knife."

"How do you know?" he demanded.

"Never mind that. I just do." Jed's hands were still resting on her neck. Finally getting a grip on herself, she joked, "If you strangle me, you'll ruin everything."

He relaxed his fingers and removed his hands. They lingered in midair, then settled on her shoulders. The two of them stared into each other's eyes, not speaking. She knew what was on his mind. The same thing was on her mind.

How would it feel if he kissed her? How would it feel if he caressed her breasts? The thoughts wouldn't stop. He would lead her back to the house and carry her to his room. He would undress her and make love to her. It would be the most exciting thing that had ever happened to her.

She was a bloody fool.

How could she be fantasizing about something she so strongly disapproved of? She knew nothing about this man, not even his real last name. They were here to play a game, and *she'd* been played for a sucker. Jed had done such a good job of distracting her that she'd never even asked him where he'd been when Marty was killed.

Her voice was coolly suspicious when she finally got it to work, but it was sheer bravado. She was still reeling from the thoughts that had been chasing through her mind.

"It's a big island," she said. "You must have been fairly close by or you wouldn't have heard me yell."

He didn't answer her right away. "I, uh, I was walking along the path." His voice was surprisingly tight.

"So you must have heard Marty cry out."

"Yes, but I was too far away to tell where he was. Then I heard you scream and realized you must be on the beach. That's when I started running." He paused and looked to his right. Abby and Scott had just come into view, walking along the shoreline trail. As far as Ellie was concerned, their timing couldn't have been better. Being alone with Jed was making her a nervous wreck.

Jed would have concurred. He didn't know which was worse, his frustration over wanting to make love to Ellie and knowing he couldn't, or his frustration over losing the latest round in their continuing battle. It was obvious that he hadn't heard the last of her questions. She'd read through the papers, and sooner or later she was going to put two and two together and figure out why people were being killed. How long could he hold her off?

Chapter Five

Raven's Island was having a disastrous effect on Ellie's self-discipline. She showered and dressed for dinner, then gave her dresser a baleful stare. She had a little time before cocktails and knew she ought to work, but she simply didn't feel like it. With a sigh, she walked to the dresser and opened the top drawer.

The folder she removed contained computer printouts from Cludds along with the notes she'd made about erratic or puzzling numbers. She opened it and then frowned, because the papers were in a perfect stack. She was neat, but not *that* neat. In fact, everything about the drawer was a little too neat. Had somebody gone through her things while she was out?

She checked out her closet and the other drawers, but only the top drawer had been disturbed. Somebody must have been looking for information about her character. Her clothes wouldn't have told them anything, but the stack of folders in the top drawer must have looked promising. The intruder must have been disappointed to find nothing but financial information on Cludds Haberdashers.

Ellie wasn't annoyed about the search—the rules specifically permitted it—but she *was* surprised. She had locked her room. How had the intruder gotten in?

Her first thought was that the skeleton keys they'd all been given might work in each other's locks. She picked up her key and crept into the hallway to check. Sister Mary was walking downstairs but didn't see her. She waited a moment and then inserted her key in Sister Mary's lock. The key slid in but wouldn't turn. Crossing the hall, she knocked on Lynette's door, got no answer, and checked to make sure it was locked. It was, but again, her key wouldn't work. Whoever had gone through her drawer was handy at break-ins, although it probably wasn't hard to jimmy a simple skeleton lock if you knew what you were doing.

Ellie knew she was never going to be able to work now. Her mind rebelled at the thought of spread sheets when it could be dealing with deceit and murder. Abby, she decided, was the logical person to begin with. She was the only one Ellie trusted.

She returned to her room just long enough to lock it— perhaps a futile exercise, given those disturbed papers—and then started down the hall. A thin-voiced "Yes?" greeted her knock on Abby's door. As usual, the woman sounded scared of her own shadow.

Ellie told her who it was and explained why she'd come. "I think we should talk. We'll never be able to figure out what's going on if we don't start comparing notes."

She heard the sound of approaching footfalls, but the door stayed firmly shut. Ellie couldn't blame Abby for being cautious. Everyone was being cautious now; Marty's death had them seeing murderers behind every door and tree.

Forty-five minutes before, Jed and Scott had carried Marty's body up to the house and stashed it in Marty's room. Then Scott had called a meeting to discuss the situation. By the time it was over, Ellie was more suspicious of Jed than ever. He'd dismissed the idea that Marty might have been murdered, saying the cliff was slippery and unstable. Marty must have plunged over by accident, sustaining the bump on his head in the process.

As for the doctor, Jed pointed out that nobody knew what was in the crystal bottle. Even if it was poison, there was no reason to think it had been used on the doctor. The bottle had been almost full. The doctor had obviously died of natural causes.

Lynette had been the first to disagree, especially about Marty Robey. First the doctor's death, and then Marty's—it was too much of a coincidence to accept. Since the remaining guests had been scattered around the house and grounds at the time, each of them by himself, nobody had an alibi. They could agree on only one thing—it would be prudent to avoid being alone with a fellow guest in the future.

"I can't let you in," Abby insisted. "You can talk to me through the door if you like."

"Abby, be sensible," Ellie coaxed. "You must have heard Marty call out. I started screaming only seconds later. I wouldn't have had time to kill him, run down the steps and then call for help. The steps are too steep and there are too many of them."

There was a long silence. Ellie was about to try again when she heard a key turning in the lock. A moment later Abby opened the door.

Ellie walked past her and sat down by the window. Abby closed the door but remained where she was, clutching the doorknob, ready to flee at a moment's notice.

Ellie acted as natural as she could, hoping to calm the woman down. "I've been turning this over in my mind, and I think the first thing we need to establish is whether there's a connection between the two of us. For example, do you ever shop in Filene's? I'm supposed to work there."

"If I do," Abby replied, "it doesn't say so in my folder."

Ellie listed some of the other places they might have met, but Abby kept shaking her head. When Ellie ran out of ideas, Abby timidly asked whether Ellie had ever been in the hospital. The answer was no.

Ellie tried a different tack. "Maybe one of us has a connection with someone who died. Last night Dr. Jamison mentioned that he generally performed surgery at Beth Israel. Is that where you worked?"

"No, I was at Mass. General. I retired six months ago and I live on a pension now."

"Then how could you afford a vacation on Raven's Island?" Ellie asked.

"It was a gift," Abby answered. "An anonymous gift from the parents of one of the children I nursed. They wrote that they wanted to thank me, but didn't want me to feel beholden. I thought it was a lovely gesture."

"Either that, or a lovely bit of bait," Ellie said thoughtfully. "I'm not well-off, either. I won this vacation in a random drawing. The letter said the island was an exclusive new resort they wanted to publicize. I had only a few weeks' notice and no choice of dates."

The more Ellie said, the more horrified Abby looked. "Are you suggesting we've all been lured here? By someone who's killed two people already and plans to kill us all?"

That was exactly what Ellie was suggesting, so they kept exchanging information in an effort to find some link that might have slated them both for death. Abby told Ellie she'd led a quiet life since her retirement. She loved to travel, providing she could find off-season bargains or motels with low enough rates. She'd been to the Berkshires in December, the Cape in February and New Hampshire in May.

The words *New Hampshire* set off a bell in Ellie's mind. She had been there at the same time as Abby. Both of them had vacationed at the same place, Oakwood Lake Cabins.

The accommodations consisted of isolated cottages scattered through the woods by a small lake.

Their being there at the same time could have been a coincidence, but Ellie doubted it. It was still cold in early May and a summer resort like Oakwood Lake Cabins would be relatively empty. Two complete strangers wouldn't have vacationed first in New Hampshire and then on Raven's Island. Then there was the fact that the cook had been working in New Hampshire at about the same time. It all had to tie together.

They finally had a promising lead but didn't know where to take it. They couldn't start questioning the other guests about who had been at Oakwood Cabins in early May. The murderer might guess they were on to him and strike before they had a chance to prove his guilt. They could only hope the cocktail hour would loosen a few tongues.

The parlor was empty when they walked inside. Ellie stuck with Perrier, but Abby fixed herself a bourbon. When Ellie teased that the drink might loosen *Abby's* tongue as well, Abby smiled weakly and took a long swallow. She had to be the most nervous woman Ellie had ever met.

Sister Mary came in next, followed by Lynette. Jed arrived last, entering the parlor with an air of great self-importance. "I have some bad news," he announced. "Scott worked on the radio all afternoon, with no success. I had a hand at it myself, but some of the parts had been removed. We tried to jury-rig replacements, but it was no use."

"Well, of course it was no use," Sister Mary scoffed. "You didn't expect us to believe your theories about the doctor and Marty, did you? One of us is a murderer—perhaps you, given how you keep insisting no murders have taken place. Any murderer worth his salt would make sure we can't communicate with the outside world."

Ellie walked to the bar to freshen her drink. "Sister Mary is right," she said. "The more you talk about people dying of illness or by accident, the more convinced I am that you killed them."

"And here I thought you had a devious mind." Jed helped himself to a Scotch. "If I'd killed them, I'd be the first to cry murder. It would look less suspicious that way." He smiled at her. "Perhaps that's what *you're* doing—insisting they were murdered so nobody will suspect you."

The atmosphere grew more and more heated as the cocktail hour progressed, with accusations being flung in every direction. Ellie kept badgering Jed about his theories, saying he was trying to cover up his guilt. Abby, who refilled her glass several times, hesitantly suggested that Lynette might have been his accomplice. After all, hadn't she discovered the poison?

Lynette dismissed the idea with an angry wave of her hand. She'd been mad about Marty, surely everyone had seen that. She wouldn't have killed him. Maybe the butler had done it.

Despite Lynette's denials, Ellie thought Abby had a point. Lynette might have pursued Marty to cover her murderous intentions. Still, Ellie's primary target was Jed, and she refused to let up on him even after dinner began. "Mr. Thorpe showed up amazingly quickly after Marty's body came flying down the cliff," she reminded everyone. "He's never really explained that."

"*I* showed up quickly?" he repeated incredulously. "You were the first one on the scene. What about you?"

"That's true," Abby agreed in a slurred voice, pointing a finger across the table at Ellie. "You *were* the first. I've never trusted you, Ellie White!"

Abby had so much bourbon in her by then that she was finally beginning to enjoy herself. "You never should have let it slip about the vacation you took last May," she continued, and then looked around the table. "We were at the same resort in New Hampshire, at exactly the same time. I say it's too much of a coincidence, especially with Marty being killed and *her* turning up right by the body. I say she should be locked up, for the safety of all of us.''

Ellie was making a silent toast to Abby's cleverness when Sister Mary chimed in, ''New Hampshire in May? Was the place called Oakwood Lake Cabins, by any chance?''

When Abby said that it was, Sister Mary went on, ''Good heavens, I was there, too! I was checking to see if the place might be suitable for one of our religious retreats.''

''This is incredible,'' Jed murmured. ''I was there also.''

''And I,'' Lynette said. She straightened, a stony look on her face. ''You know, it is a curious thing. Only a month ago I had never heard of this island. Then I received a letter from Mr. Tipton, saying he had seen me at a diplomatic reception with my papa and thought I was beautiful. He wanted me to visit Raven's Island, and if I liked it, I would become his spokeswoman. I thought, why not? It would be a lovely free vacation and perhaps I would become famous. Now I wonder—was the letter real? Or was I lured here to be killed?'' She paused, her gaze sweeping the room with hard contempt. ''I am not so easy to kill. If any of you plans to try it, you will find that out.''

Four different answers came back to her, almost at the same time. Everyone claimed to have either won the vacation in a contest or received it as a gift. If Lynette had been lured here, so had all the rest of them.

''So we come back to my original theory,'' Lynette said. ''We should be questioning Scott, Mr. Tipton's butler. Mr. Tipton must be behind this.''

''She's got a point,'' Jed agreed. ''Tipton was supposed to be here, but he never showed. It's a big island. Who's to say he's not hiding out somewhere, planning to pick us off one by one?''

For a man who had been accusing Ellie of murder all evening, Jed had fallen in with Lynette's hypothesis much too quickly. More suspicious than ever, Ellie reminded everyone that the murderer wasn't killing them just for the fun of it. "We have to remember the one thing we have in common—the vacation we took in May. Maybe something happened at Oakwood Cabins that we all know about. We just don't know that we know it."

Sister Mary gave a delighted chuckle. "A murder, you mean, committed by one of us in this house while all of us were at Oakwood Cabins last May. Now the murderer is killing off anyone who might have seen him."

"Exactly," Ellie said. She stared straight at Jed. "You're a very smooth talker, but I don't believe a word you say. I'll be watching you every minute from now on."

Jed lazed back in his chair, smiling his most lecherous smile. "You can watch me twenty-four hours a day if you like—including tonight in bed. I'm not afraid of you. Once I get your clothes off, you won't be able to conceal a weapon on that lovely body of yours."

Despite his confident drawl, Ellie sensed her warning had hit home. A plan began to take shape in her mind. People made mistakes when they were angry. She had a formidable weapon at her disposal—her skill at chess. She didn't know the particulars, but the general idea was to trick Jed into attacking her when he was too damn mad to be careful.

Her answering look was cool and amused. "I thought I'd made it clear that I only sleep with men who can beat me at chess. Would you care to have another try?"

Jed wanted to do more than *try*. That arrogant smile of Ellie's made him long to beat the tar out of her at chess and then haul her off to bed. He nodded and stood up. "After you, Miss White. I'll expect you to make good on your offer."

Ellie sat down in front of the black pieces, giving him the advantage of making the first move. If the gesture was meant to provoke him by demonstrating how easily she could win, it didn't work. He wasn't going to let her distract him. As he'd told her the night before, he didn't make the same mistake twice.

Neither did Ellie. She couldn't remember concentrating so hard on a game, even when she'd played competitively. She set Jed up with brilliant subtlety, leading him on, lulling him into a false sense of complacency, allowing him to believe he was gaining the advantage. She could sense the exact moment he tumbled into her trap. Another couple of moves and his rook could attack her queen. What he didn't realize—couldn't see—was that by sacrificing her pawn she would put herself in a position to seriously threaten his king. He was a good enough player to see several moves ahead, but Ellie could see even further.

She moved the pawn in question, then yawned and stood up. "I think I'll take a walk. Come find me when it's my turn again."

She didn't miss his quick frown. He was concentrating as hard as he could, and *she* was yawning and going for walks. Her arrogance was more than he could stomach. He wanted the victory so badly that his ego had gotten involved.

She had no particular plans about where to go. Her aim was to wage psychological warfare, not stretch her legs. It wasn't until she reached the hallway that she started thinking about that closetful of dummies. If Jed was going to attack her with a knife, she might as well even the odds.

She hurried up the staircase, turned into the narrow passageway and opened the door to the back steps. The kitchen, her final destination, was one flight down. She could hear somebody walking around behind the closed door when she reached the bottom step, so she had to wait. When the footfalls had finally died out, she gingerly opened the door and peeked around it. The kitchen was empty, at least for the moment.

A wooden knife rack was sitting on the counter, with eight handles protruding from the top. Ellie pulled out one after another, searching for the smallest knife. She'd barely yanked out a boning knife when the sound of approaching footsteps sent her scurrying back to the staircase. She closed the door as quietly as she could, stuck the knife in her purse, and hurried back upstairs.

She had one more stop to make, her room. She grabbed a sweater, threw it over her shoulders and headed back downstairs. Jed was coming out of the parlor when she reached the lower hall.

"I was wondering where you'd gone," he said. "It's your move."

"I was getting a sweater," Ellie said innocently. "It's a little cold in the living room, even with the fire."

The game resumed. Jed was still too absorbed in his own strategy to realize that disaster loomed ahead. After each move, he would study the board, but he always continued with his established plan of attack. Then Ellie swept a bishop halfway across the board and he laced his fingers together under his chin and stared even harder.

When he raised his eyes, they were stunned and disbelieving. "You've been playing me for a sucker, right from the beginning," he said. "You tempted me and manipulated me until I fell into your trap."

Ellie felt a little sorry for him, but that didn't stop her from provoking him. Give him an inch and he'd take a yard. Give him a yard and she'd be dead by morning. "You didn't do so badly," she said with a shrug. "You've got a good feel for the game, but you need more experience against skilled opponents."

"Are you offering me a rematch?" he asked in a clipped tone.

"You mean you're resigning?" Ellie gave him a condescending smile. "Believe me, Jed, your position isn't hopeless. I'll switch sides with you and show you how white can defend."

His reaction told Ellie he was furious. After staring at the board in coldly controlled disgust for several minutes, he finally stood up. "Fine, show me," he challenged. He knew he couldn't beat her with white, but he'd be damned if he was going to lose now that they'd switched sides. Black had the superior position—one he swore to hold onto.

She could feel the tension mounting with every move they made. Jed was right about chess—it was a very erotic game. She'd sensed it the night before, but the male-female battle was twice as intense now. She could feel the highly charged atmosphere in places she was embarrassed to think about. If she lost tonight, she wouldn't go upstairs alone. Jed wouldn't let her. She couldn't afford to lose.

He was simmering with frustration by the time it was over. Ellie had offered him a draw and he'd been forced to accept. The outcome was fine with Ellie, but to Jed, anything less than a victory had felt like a brutal defeat.

"You have to keep your emotions out of it," Ellie said. It was more than she'd been able to do, but she wasn't about to admit it. "You wanted the win too badly. It affected your ability to concentrate."

"*You* affected my ability to concentrate," he corrected ruefully. Ellie couldn't believe how quickly his mood had changed, from being frustrated and self-critical to resigned and self-deprecating. "I have trouble keeping my mind on chess when you're sitting across from me," he continued, "but hell, I might as well be honest with myself. I'd be lucky to beat you one time out of ten. You're too good for me." He suddenly smiled. "I'm a glutton for punishment. How about another game?"

Ellie barely trusted herself to answer, much less to play another game. When Jed turned on that sexy, coaxing smile, she forgot about chess and started thinking the kinds of thoughts that left her weak in the knees and light in the head. He was too handsome, too experienced, too appealing. Never mind losing at chess; when he turned on the charm she was in danger of losing both her virtue and her character's life.

Remember your original strategy! she thought, and then wondered how she could be expected to remember anything when she felt as if she were drowning. *He's probably the killer, dammit,* she told herself more firmly. *Something significant happened at Oakwood Cabins—probably a murder. You've got to think, Ellie!*

She frowned, suddenly wondering if Oakwood Lake was a real body of water. If so, where in New Hampshire was it located? Near the Maine border, where those body parts had washed up?

"Maybe tomorrow," she said to Jed. Her mind was finally back where it belonged—on the game. "I thought I'd go into the library." She paused, watching his reaction closely. "I want to spend a little time with an atlas. I was curious about the geography of Maine and New Hampshire."

Jed's expression remained the same—relaxed and smiling. If she'd scored a bull's-eye, it didn't show, but homicidal maniacs were probably accomplished liars as well. Ellie picked up her purse and left the room, sure she was on the right track.

She was looking around the library for an atlas when she remembered the map of Maine in the *National Geographic* she'd been reading the night before. Sure enough, the map included northern New Hampshire. Oakwood Lake was situated a few miles inland, just south of the Maine border. Those hacked up body parts had washed ashore near—where was it?—Kennebunkport. And Kennebunkport was only a short ways *north* of the border.

Everything fit into place. The killer had taken his original victim to Oakwood Cabins, counting on the isolation of the place to protect him. He had hacked the body to bits and thrown them into the sea, assuming that carnivores would dispose of the remains. But then something had gone drastically wrong. Evidence had washed up thirty miles to the north. If they could identify the victim, maybe they could trace the crime back to the killer. Anyone who might have seen him at Oakwood Lake Cabins would have to be eliminated.

Ellie could hardly contain her triumph when Jed showed up in the library. Obviously he was the murderer. He wanted to see how much she'd figured out, and the map she was holding wouldn't be reassuring. Her plans were going even better than she could have hoped.

"I came in to see if you would reconsider another game of chess," he said.

Ellie smiled and shook her head. Jed had fallen into one trap that night and now she was springing a second. "I'm afraid not. Have you noticed how clear it is tonight? I thought I'd go up to the observatory." She tossed the magazine onto the couch. "Good night, Mr. Thorpe. I'll see you in the morning."

She would see him long before the morning, if her suspicions were correct. She sauntered out of the room, thinking that the grief she'd given him at the chess board was nothing compared to what she had in store for him now.

Chapter Six

Abby and Sister Mary were playing chess when Jed got back to the living room, and Lynn was sitting in front of the fire. Jed found it amazing that three such different women had all been involved with the same man. Of course, they hadn't been the only ones. From what Jed had heard, Isidore Cludd had been mesmerizing women till the day he died.

Sister Mary moved one of her pawns and then looked over at Jed. "I thought you'd gone to bed. I hope we haven't stolen the chessboard from you and Ellie."

"No, not at all," he said. "Ellie was too tired to keep playing. She went upstairs. I thought I'd sit by the fire for a while."

Lynn twisted around to look at him. "So the flames can cauterize your wounds, darling?" Her smile was so broad she might as well have laughed herself silly and gotten it over with. She seemed to get a kick out of his defeats.

He was scowling as he made his way to the couch, silently warning her not to provoke him. He'd had enough of that from Ellie. She knew too much, he thought. Hadn't he seen the newspapers in her tote bag this afternoon? Hadn't she been looking at a map of Maine this evening? She'd come across the newspaper article about the hacked-up body parts. She'd checked the map to see if they'd washed up near Oakwood Lake. The answer was yes, and now she suspected Jed was the killer. There was no help for it. He would have to dispose of her tonight. The longer he waited, the harder it would be to catch her off guard.

Having decided that, he sat there wondering why she had mentioned going to the observatory. Was she trying to lure him there? Did she plan to set a trap? From what he'd seen of Ellie Landau, he didn't doubt she was capable of it. It was a far more plausible explanation than the other two possibilities—that she was either making idle conversation or hinting that she wanted to be alone with him.

His thoughts drifted back to their chess match. Ellie had dominated him with ego-shattering completeness, and he wasn't used to that in his life. His response had been so primitive that he wondered whether he was as civilized as he'd always supposed. He wanted to turn the tables on her. He wanted to arouse her into submission, to excite her until there was no question as to who had ultimately won. He'd occasionally felt a similar thirst for victory in his business dealings, but not in his private life. He was beginning to understand that Ellie had reached him in a very elemental, very personal way. The attraction wasn't only physical. The challenge she offered was hard to refuse.

Maybe Lynn was right. Maybe he was wasting his time on this island. Was there any reason to suspect Ellie more than the others? Sure, she winked at the rules, but so did Marty. Emerson had gotten sick at a very convenient time and Abby was impossibly nervous. Rosemary was as sharp as they came and hard-boiled enough to be Cludd's mistress for

twenty years. Any one of them could be guilty. Maybe it was
a coincidence that the sharp decline in Cludds's profits had
started when Ellie was hired. The logical course of action
was to use his connections in the banking field to check out
everyone's accounts for any unusually large deposits.

That took care of the future, but what about right now?
Suppose Ellie was anticipating an attack? He would have to
strike quickly, with silent and deadly efficiency. In order not
to tip off the others, he would have to wait till they went to
bed. He had his work cut out for him.

It was almost an hour before the three women retired.
Jed's knife, a switchblade modified with a rubber blade, was
locked inside his briefcase. He almost slipped it in his
pocket, but then he remembered the way Ellie had frisked
him on the beach, so he tucked it into his sock, under the
tongue of his right loafer. He wanted to be prepared for any
eventuality.

Ellie would have agreed. She wanted to be prepared for
any eventuality, which was why she was playing all the an-
gles—including the oldest angle in the book. She'd stopped
to change before going to the observatory, putting on a pair
of satin pajamas and a matching robe. She'd brushed out
her hair and dabbed on some perfume. She didn't see herself as a femme fatale, but if her appearance distracted Jed
even a little, so much the better.

Her knife was in the pocket of her robe, concealed in a
silk scarf. She'd taken some adhesive tape from the medicine chest and wrapped several layers around the blade so
nobody could get hurt. The moment Jed reached for his
knife, she would whip out her own knife and hold it to his
neck. She would have to be lightning quick, since the pen-
alty for hesitation would be death.

She was focusing one of the telescopes when the clatter-
ing of shoes on the metal steps made her stop and turn
around. She reached into her pocket, groping for the han-

dle of her knife. Her heart began to race. It was only a game, but she felt as if she were in real danger.

The only light in the room was coming from the three-quarter moon hanging high in the sky. The intruder staggered and cursed; Ellie tensed in anticipation. A few moments later she saw the beam of an approaching flashlight.

She stared at the top step, waiting to be attacked. Then the beam of the flashlight swept across her face and temporarily blinded her. Fighting down her panic, she blinked several times and tightened her grip on the knife. She could make out a man's head, but she couldn't tell who it was.

"Ellie?" he said. "Is that you?"

The voice belonged to Marty Robey. Relief mingled with exasperation. "What are *you* doing here?" Ellie demanded. "I thought you'd be long gone by now."

Marty climbed the last several steps and walked over to join her. "I could ask you the same thing. You're a sitting duck up here, don't you realize that?"

"Credit me with a little intelligence," Ellie said. "I have a knife in my pocket. And you still haven't told me what you're doing here."

He grinned at her. "Life imitates art, Ellie. They had a problem with the launch. By the time they fixed it, it was too dark to come out and get me. They're picking me up first thing in the morning."

Ellie knew a golden opportunity when she saw one. After all, who had been more casual about the rules than Marty? She smoothed the collar of his shirt and smiled flirtatiously. "It's sweet of you to worry about me. Wouldn't you like to tell me who killed you?"

"I'd love to," he answered, "but the killer would never forgive me. You'll have to figure it out on your own."

"At least tell me who you are, then. Otherwise I'll spend the rest of my life burning with curiosity." She paused. "You wouldn't want me to burn with curiosity, would you, Marty?"

"Of course not," he said. "I wouldn't want you to burn with anything, except possibly lust for yours truly."

"And here I thought your interests lay elsewhere!" Ellie's expression turned pleading. "Come on, Marty, put me out of my misery. Tell me who you are."

He laughed. "I'll call you when you get home."

"But how can I be sure?" Ellie asked.

"You'll have to trust me. Do you mind if I look at the moon? It's the reason I came up here."

Ellie didn't mind at all, especially after she noticed the wallet protruding from his back pocket. "I was having a little trouble focusing the telescope," she said. "Do you think you can do it?"

He bent over the lens and started fiddling with the knobs. Ellie slid a stealthy hand to his wallet, gave it a quick tug and took off across the room, laughing. By the time Marty realized what she'd done and came after her, she had clicked on the lights and was opening up his wallet. He made a lunge for her, but she scampered away before he could grab her.

His driver's license was in the first plastic sleeve. The name on it was Martin David Cludd. Ellie snapped the wallet shut and handed it back, a satisfied smile on her face.

"What a coincidence," she drawled. "You have the same last name as one of my clients—Cludds Haberdashers." James Emerson had mentioned that one of the owners was in Europe. Marty had grumbled about being dragged thousands of miles to take part in Death on Raven's Island. You didn't have to be a genius to figure out the connection.

When Marty didn't comment, Ellie prodded, "I. V. Cludd passed away about six months ago. He left two heirs. I know his widow was one of them. You must be the other—his grandson, I take it."

One look at Marty's face and Ellie knew she'd put her foot in her mouth. "I didn't mean to be so flip," she said quickly. "I realize it's only been a few months and I'm sorry—"

"You can save the apologies," he interrupted curtly. "He was my father, but we weren't close."

Judging by Marty's tone, they hadn't even been distant. He sounded like he'd despised the man. Cludd must have been well into his forties when he'd fathered Marty, and maybe there had been a mammoth generation gap. Ellie was curious about their relationship, but Marty looked as if he wanted to demolish the nearest inanimate object. She wasn't about to ask questions.

He clicked off the lights, walked back to the telescope and finished adjusting the lens. Much to Ellie's relief, staring at the moon seemed to improve his mood. By the time he invited Ellie to take a turn, the anger in his voice was gone. He even began to tease her about her fate, saying she would be dead within the hour. "I'll look forward to having your company on the trip back to the mainland," he added.

She ran her fingers over the handle of her knife, reassured by its smooth, hard presence. "The murderer can keep you company," she said. "He'll be the one to die tonight, not me."

"He?" Marty repeated. "Don't you mean she?" He winked at her and started toward the steps.

Jed hadn't expected the tower to be so dark. He didn't want to signal his approach by turning on the lights or using a flash, so he felt his way up the spiral staircase with only the moonlight for a guide. His night vision slowly improved as he climbed higher, so that by the time he saw someone coming from the opposite direction he was able to identify Marty at once. They met on the fourth-floor landing.

Taking him by the arm, Jed whispered, "How many times do I have to kill you?"

"Only once," Marty answered. "I've been up in the observatory, haunting Ellie Landau. A little friendly advice, though. I'd be careful if I were you."

"What's that supposed to mean?"

"Only that she's a menace to any red-blooded American male." Marty gave Jed a bracing pat on the shoulder, like a commander sending a soldier into battle. "Good luck, Jed."

Although Jed seldom took Marty seriously, he reevaluated his strategy as he continued up the steps. Maybe Ellie was lying in wait, planning to clobber him with a pair of binoculars. If so, his slashing surprise attack would backfire—fatally so. It would probably be safer to give her a full dose of Thorpe's egotistical chauvinism. Then, when she was too exasperated to think straight, he would strike.

He was confident as he climbed the stairs, but he never could have anticipated what awaited him in the observatory. Ellie was standing in the moonlight, a vision of filmy satin and flowing hair. With her delicate beauty and slender grace, she looked like she belonged in some sultan's harem. It was a toss-up as to which part of her body Jed would have liked to touch first. He swallowed hard and reminded himself why he'd come.

He swaggered up to her as if she'd been waiting her whole life to meet him. Looking her up and down with an insulting leer, he drawled, "I see you were expecting me. I approve of your choice of clothing."

If the sound of Jed's footsteps on the metal steps had twisted Ellie's stomach into knots, his actual presence had made it worse. She didn't believe Marty's talk about the murderer being a woman—she was sure it was Jed. She'd been hoping for a direct attack, but instead, he had swung into his Thorpe routine. If he thought he was going to aggravate her into dropping her guard, he had another think coming. She wouldn't be defeated that easily.

"I assure you," she said, "that the way I'm dressed has nothing to do with expecting you. I'm simply more comfortable this way. Am I supposed to change again just because *you* decided to barge in?"

"Why put on clothes that you'll only be removing?" He took a strand of her hair and let it slide through his fingers. A warm, possessive hand came to rest on her shoulder. Only a few unnerving inches separated their faces. "For me, that is. Up here. Now. Should I help you?"

Ellie's self-confidence took a nosedive. Jed was on the verge of killing her, and what was she thinking about? The warmth of his hand. The giddy danger of having him so close. The nerve-racking excitement of waiting and watching and wondering. She couldn't have said which was stronger—the need to have him touch her or the fear he might actually do it.

In the end her pride saved her. Jed had come up here to kill her, not to seduce her. She wasn't going to let him turn her head with husky propositions and provocative caresses. She had to turn the tables and put him on the defensive.

Their encounter at the beach suggested a way to do that. She tipped up her chin and gave him a knowing smile. "Gentlemen first," she purred. "If you don't take your clothes off, how can I be sure you don't have a knife?" She was going to die if he agreed.

Jed felt Ellie's smile in erogenous zones he hadn't known he possessed. The teasing challenge in her voice, the scent of her perfume, the firm, soft curves beneath her satin and lace negligee—they were turning his body into a giant exposed nerve, making him ache until he couldn't tell pain from pleasure. *Ease her suspicions,* he ordered himself. *A few more minutes and you'll have her where you want her.*

"You could always frisk me," he said. He hadn't forgotten the way she stiffened whenever he touched her. Given the sexual tension in the air, she wouldn't risk setting off a chain reaction by letting him get too close. At least he hoped she wouldn't.

Ellie forced herself to hold Jed's gaze. Good grief, what did she do now? Go ahead and frisk him? Surely she'd be wasting her time. He wouldn't have suggested it if his knife had been somewhere she could feel. Or would he? A man as sophisticated as Jed had to sense when a woman was reluctant to get too close. He was probably even counting on it.

She took a quick, steadying breath and told herself that even dying of embarrassment was better than having her throat slashed. "Put your hands on your head," she ordered. "If they move even an inch, I'll assume you're reaching for your knife. Believe me, I wasn't stupid enough to come up here without a weapon."

He complied smoothly, saying with a smile, "Take your time. I can't think of anything more enjoyable than having you search me, with the exception of what will happen when you're finished."

Ellie blushed, but she also began to frisk him. She couldn't let his words defeat her—it would have been utterly humiliating. Her eyes were on his hands as she probed beneath his jacket—she couldn't afford to lose sight of them. She couldn't afford to think of him as a man, either, despite the hard strength of his body and the intoxicating mixture of wool, after-shave and masculine heat that seemed to pervade the room. He was her opponent, nothing more.

As far as she could tell, there was nothing but warm, firm flesh under the crisp cotton of his shirt. He was taking deep, even breaths, but when her hand slid over his heart she realized it was racing. For a fraction of a second, her eyes dropped to his face. It was blank, like a robot's. Obviously he was nervous about what she might find.

She checked his inside jacket pocket. It was empty. Taking a step forward, she slid her arms around his back to frisk his neck and shoulders. The movement brought her flush against his body. Her nipples tingled responsively, aching with the desire to be touched. Then she made the mistake of making eye contact again, and saw a wicked half-smile flash across his face. He was enjoying this, damn him! She hastily looked away, her hands becoming clumsy as they patted their way down his back.

Enjoyable was the last word Jed would have used to describe the sensations that were slashing through his body. It only felt enjoyable if you thought torture felt enjoyable. All he had to do was grasp Ellie's hips and gently bring her forward and the tiny gap between them would be closed. All he had to do was take her chin in his hand and tip up her head and her mouth would be his for the taking. Everything he'd felt downstairs—the sting of defeat, the longing to conquer and possess—was magnified tenfold. He thought about reaching for his knife—anything to end the torture—but he'd noticed the bulge in her pocket. It was obviously the weapon she'd mentioned. One move of his hands and she would pull it out. Her pocket was closer than his sock. He couldn't take the chance.

She slid her hands under his belt and slowly brought them forward. He sucked in his breath when she reached his belly. Her eyes were fixed on his hands, which were clasped together so tightly by now that they were beginning to cramp. He stared at her mouth. She was biting her lip in concentration. The sensuality of the gesture made his gut ache. He didn't want to kill her anymore; he wanted to throw her down on the floor and make love to her.

He started to lecture himself about the reasons he couldn't do that. None of them cut much ice, but fortunately, it couldn't last much longer. He hadn't missed her reaction to his embarrassed smile. Obviously she knew what she was putting him through.

Ellie patted Jed's front pockets, felt various bulges and lumps, and realized she would have to check further. She didn't want to, not after what had happened on the beach that afternoon, but what choice did she have? One of those objects might be a knife. After all, what better place to hide it than where she'd be too chicken to search?

Her hands fumbled their way into his pockets. There were coins, a wallet and something that felt like a roll of Life Savers, but no knife. Her relief turned to despair when she realized he might have tucked the knife into his briefs. He could even have strapped it to his leg.

She removed her hands from his pockets and knelt down in front of him. She hesitated, then placed a hand on either side of his left knee. She had to be cool and methodical about this—as a policewoman would have been.

Jed went rigid when Ellie began to pat her way up his thigh. The higher she went, the less he could stand it, until the need to make love to her was a fiery, consuming ache. He thought it couldn't get any worse, but then she repeated the operation on his right leg and unwittingly brushed the most sensitive part of his body. When he realized she wasn't going to stop—that she was actually going to check whether he'd shoved a knife down his briefs—it was more than he could take. "Jesus, Ellie," he said, "do you have any idea what you're doing to me?"

Ellie didn't, except in the most abstract way. She was too much of a nervous wreck to feel much of anything, much less understand the havoc she was wreaking on Jed's equilibrium. "I'm sorry if I'm—if you're uncomfortable, but I have to protect myself." Despite the uncompromising words, her hands were suspended in front of Jed's legs. If he was reluctant, she was twice as much so. "Of course, if you promise me you don't have a knife there..." She looked him in the eye. "You, Jed, not your character."

"Dammit, Ellie, if you'd been dealing with my character he probably would have raped you by now. You have my word, okay? Now can you get on with it?"

Ellie couldn't believe how rattled he sounded. It had to be the moonlight and the lingerie—she wasn't that sexy. She stood up and resumed her search, working as quickly as she could. His jacket pockets—empty. His back pockets—empty as well. His arms—nothing but sinew and muscle up his sleeves.

She sank down on her knees again, still watching his hands. There was only one area left to check—his lower legs. She started with the left one.

Jed cursed himself for a fool. He'd assumed Ellie would be less thorough, but he should have known better. Somebody had once told him that no management consultant in town took more time with clients or probed their operations more deeply. Naturally, she would follow the same pattern in this idiotic game they were playing.

He had to stop her—and *now*. In one way, he only did what he'd been dying to do since the moment he'd entered the observatory. The sight of her on her knees in front of him, gazing upward, her body looking lithe and fragile in the moonlight, could have seduced a saint. At the same time, though, the rational part of him—the part that could still think straight—knew he couldn't let her get to his right shoe. She would find the knife. He was down beside her in a flash, pulling her into his arms.

At first, Ellie was too stunned to react. One moment she was frisking Jed's leg, and the next she was caught in his embrace. He twined his fingers into her hair and pulled back her head, baring her throat to his mouth. His lips settled against her neck, hot and urgent against the sensitive skin.

Waves of emotion washed over her, making it impossible to think. She only knew how she felt—confused, excited and frightened. A man like Jed could make a woman lose her head. She'd never experienced such feelings before. It was like being on a roller coaster and longing to crash.

She closed her eyes and tried to catch her breath. Her body seemed to be melting. Her lips softened and parted as he nuzzled his way toward her ear. When was he going to kiss her? Every second he waited was like an hour of delicious torture.

She swayed and clutched his waist. The room felt so hot that it was making her dizzy. His tongue flicked across her earlobe and then probed the inside of her ear. She shuddered and held him tighter. The world receded until his warmth and strength were the only existing realities.

Jed was in the same place as Ellie—lost in desire and emotion. Thorpe had completely disappeared. It never even occurred to him that he could have reached into his shoe, pulled out his knife and held it against Ellie's throat.

To the extent he could think at all, he was warning himself to go slowly. Maybe Ellie was skittish, but it wasn't anything personal. He knew that now. Some guy had probably hurt her, so she was afraid of getting involved again. He felt a hard-edged satisfaction when she moaned and pressed herself closer. She brought out the most conflicting feelings in him. Part of him wanted to conquer her, to pay her back for the challenges and defeats, and part of him wanted to coddle her. She was like tempered glass—tough on the outside but capable of being shattered into a million pieces by a man's carelessness.

He was aching to kiss her, but forced himself to wait. Let *her* take the initiative. Let her raise her lips and offer her mouth. Still, he couldn't stop his hand from moving to her waist and tugging at the sash that held her robe in place. She stiffened but didn't resist. His hand began to burn. He longed to slide it against her belly and savor the softness of her skin. A few seconds later he was doing exactly that. Then he was moving it higher...

Ellie went rigid as Jed's hand closed over her breast. A far-off voice told her to draw away, but when he started rubbing his palm back and forth across her nipples, the voice ceased to matter. He took a nipple between his thumb and forefinger and teased it until it was swollen with pleasure, then played with its twin until her body was on fire with excitement. She'd never been caressed that way before—with tenderness one moment and rough passion the next. She buried her lips against his neck and felt the sharp but gentle nip of his teeth in return.

She wasn't going to stop him. The realization hit her like a sharp slap on the face, momentarily shocking her. How could she be letting him touch her? She didn't even know his last name. She didn't know what kind of person he was. Maybe he was involved with somebody else. Maybe she was only a casual bit of fun to him.

And if she wasn't? If he was just as smitten as she was? That would be different. She still couldn't accept where they'd been headed, but if things went more slowly...

She needed to know the answer. She wanted to think this was real. She struggled to frame the words and get them out of her mouth.

"Jed, please." Her throat felt dry and tight. "I need to know what's happening here. Is this Thorpe and Ellie White or—or you and me? Two real people? If there's anyone else—Lynette or somebody—I can't cope with that."

Jed didn't know which was worse, Ellie's questions or the anxiety in her voice. He wasn't the kind for one-night stands and neither was she, so what had he been doing? How could he have forgotten the possible consequences?

He released her, sat back on his heels, and ran his hand through his hair. Everything was still foggy. He wanted to take her back in his arms and make love to her, but common sense prevailed. He took a deep breath and stood up. She did the same.

"Look, I'm really sorry about this," he said. "I'm not sure how it happened, except..." He hesitated, at a loss for words. Except that what? That he wanted her more than he'd ever wanted a woman in his life? That didn't excuse the fact that he'd acted like an irresponsible adolescent. She wouldn't have enjoyed herself if he'd taken her on a cold, hard floor, and even worse, he might have gotten her pregnant.

"I don't know," he said with a shake of his head. "Maybe it's the game. I've been hanging around Thorpe too much." She gave an appreciative smile and he suddenly felt less guilty. "I'm, uh, I'm not involved with anybody else—Lynn Cludd is just a friend—but I don't go in for casual sex. People should be friends before they're lovers."

Ellie had been telling herself how decent Jed was, thinking that some men wouldn't have stopped. A few well-chosen platitudes and who knows what she might have agreed to? But then he'd mentioned the name Lynn Cludd and her train of thought had abruptly derailed. Good God, *another Cludd*? Suddenly the only thing on her mind was the game and her work and how they fit together. Why were there so many people connected to Cludds on this island? Why choose people who knew each other, when complete strangers would provide a more accurate test of how the game would be played by a group of paying guests? Something else had to be going on.

"About Lynn," she said. "How is she related to Marty?"

Jed looked startled by her question. "She was married to his father. Technically, she's his stepmother."

Ellie was more confused than ever. "But she's so young—"

"There was a big difference in her and her husband's ages. It wasn't exactly a love match." He paused, visibly annoyed with her. "You don't need to hear about it from me. Lynn's your client—you'll probably know her life story before you're through."

"But who are *you*?" she asked. "Where do you fit in?"

He looked more offended than ever. "Does it matter?"

"It might be nice to know who's been trying to seduce me for the past five minutes," Ellie retorted. Why did he have to play things so close to the vest? Was the game that important to him?

"Look, I already apologized for that—"

"Did I ask you to apologize? All I want is your name."

Jed stood there glaring at her. He wasn't going to tell her his name. He wasn't going to tell her a damn thing. Although he never would have admitted it, his ego was badly bruised. He wasn't half out of his mind anymore, but he was still painfully aroused. The slightest sign from Ellie and he might have taken her downstairs and started in all over again. And what was she doing? Asking him a bunch of questions about who he was and who Lynn was and what their connection was! Didn't she ever forget business, even for a moment? Why was she so blasted analytical? Tempered glass, hell! She was more like cold, hard steel.

"My name is Jed Thorpe," he said. "I might be a killer. Doesn't that worry you?"

Ellie couldn't understand what Jed was so irritated about. Was he sore because she'd stopped him from killing her? Was the defeat really that devastating? "Not at all," she said. "I told you I had a weapon, remember?" She patted her pocket. "It's a knife, and I'll match it against yours any time you want."

"I'll bet you will," he muttered, and stalked to the steps. Ellie smiled at his stiff-necked retreat—she'd enjoyed getting the better of him. Then she walked to the telescope, thinking with a sigh that she might have enjoyed surrendering to him even more.

Chapter Seven

Jed knew he was being unreasonable. He didn't jump into bed with women he barely knew. He wasn't a Don Juan, needing to feel that every woman he met was his for the taking. So what was he so aggravated about? He didn't even trust Ellie, for God's sake.

He slowly descended the stairs, blaming his bad temper on how long a day it had been. Being a homicidal maniac was damn tiring, and the worst was yet to come. He still had a houseful of people to kill.

He should have disposed of Ellie when he'd had the chance. She hadn't been thinking about the game while he'd been making love to her, so why hadn't he finished her off? He shook his head, knowing the answer all too well. *He* hadn't been thinking about the game, either. Next time he'd do better.

He was halfway between the third and fourth stories of the tower when he picked up footfalls directly below him. Either Marty was still wandering where he didn't belong or another innocent lamb was making its way to the slaughter. He hurried down the last couple of steps, moving as quietly as he could, and ducked into the room beyond. A few seconds later, a wraithlike figure came into view. It was Abby Cludd, who of all the people playing the game was the least likely to creep around late at night. Jed wondered what emergency could have compelled her to abandon the safety of her room.

She was concentrating so hard on making it upstairs that she never even saw him waiting. He came up behind her as she paused to catch her breath, clapping one hand over her mouth and the other around her throat. Then he whispered in her ear, "Can we agree that you've just been strangled?"

She nodded, trembling in his arms. Jed was afraid she would scream if he let her go, so he kept his hand over her mouth as he led her into the hall. He closed the door and flicked on the lights. The sudden brightness made her squint, but it also seemed to reassure her. None of this was real.

"Don't talk. Just listen." He slowly removed his hand, prepared to clamp it over her mouth again if she got hysterical. "You'll be sleeping here on the third floor tonight. Marty is still on the island—there was a problem with the launch—so you'll be going back to the mainland together first thing in the morning. Your possessions will be returned to you on Monday. You can't go back to your room tonight, but Rebecca will get you whatever you need. Is that clear?"

She stared at him, looking more confused than frightened now. "I never thought it was you."

Jed took that as a compliment to his superior acting. "Thorpe pretends to be an arrogant jerk, but he's really both deadly and amoral. The rest is camouflage."

"But that's not why—I mean, naturally you threw me off the track." Jed was sure she'd started to say something else.

The near slip rattled her so much she began to babble. "Who would think a man like Thorpe would be able to plan all this out? The only one I trusted was Ellie. We were working together, I suppose you would say. I wanted to talk to her, but there was no answer when I knocked on her door. She's a light sleeper, you see. That's how she noticed James leaving the island this morning. So I knew she wasn't in her room. I couldn't find her anywhere, but I finally thought of the observatory. It was foolish of me to go up there alone, wasn't it? But everything was so quiet. I assumed everyone was in bed." A stricken look crossed her face. "Oh, dear, I suppose Ellie is dead! She was up there alone, wasn't she?"

Jed smiled at her. There was more here than met the eye and he intended to find out what it was. Maybe Abby would talk if he could calm her down and convince her he was trying to help.

"Yes, but she's very much alive," he said. "I noticed a knife in her pocket and decided not to attack her. She might have gotten me first." He put a hand on Abby's shoulder and coaxed a note of teasing intimacy into his voice. "Promise me you won't sneak upstairs and warn her. I'll never get her alone if she knows I'm definitely the killer."

"Of course I won't!" The words came out in a high-pitched rush.

"Good, good." Jed lowered his voice to a sympathetic murmur. "I can tell you didn't enjoy yourself and I'm sorry about that. I'm working very closely with Scott on the game and I know he'll want your input on how we can improve things. What did we do wrong?"

"You? You didn't do anything wrong. Really, it was me."

She reminded Jed of a trapped animal, which in a way she was. He was blocking the narrow hallway, preventing her from leaving. Since being the good guy hadn't worked, he decided to try the opposite.

"Exactly what made you so uncomfortable, Mrs. Cludd? The game itself—or the other people playing it?"

She was so shaken by the question that she staggered and almost fell. Jed's hand shot out to steady her. "How do you know my name?" she asked. "Who are you?"

"A friend of Lynn's. She happened to mention that you work for her." He dropped his hand and gave her a hard stare. "Do you have a reason to be afraid of someone on this island?"

The question started her babbling again. "I'm a hard worker. Ask anyone. Ask Mrs. Cludd." She meant Lynn. "There's so much to do. I should be at the office. That's why I didn't want to come. That's why I didn't enjoy myself."

Jed doubted she was telling the truth, but obviously she wasn't going to talk. He tried to figure out what she was so afraid of. She was the bookkeeper, so she must have noticed the decline in profits. Did she suspect someone of stealing—someone on the island, someone whom she feared? Or was *she* the thief, and terrified of being unmasked?

As curious as Jed was, the answers would have to wait. He couldn't do any investigating until Monday, when he was back in Boston.

Ellie stayed in the observatory for another ten minutes and then drew out her knife and started downstairs. She didn't trust Jed for a minute. In thinking about their latest skirmish, she'd realized he'd started kissing her before she could finish searching him. His passion had flared up with suspicious suddenness. She must have been only inches from discovering his knife.

She was satisfied that Jed was the murderer, but there was a second mystery to solve now. Why were so many of these people connected to Cludds? Why had somebody gone to the trouble of bringing them all here, even to the point of dragging Marty back from Europe? What else was going on?

She got into bed, hoping the darkness would relax her and help her think. But instead of sticking to Cludds, her mind kept jumping from subject to subject—Cludds, the game, the man who was trying to kill her. She was so keyed up she simply couldn't concentrate.

She fell into a restless sleep only to jerk awake with nerve-shattering abruptness. Somebody was inserting a key into her lock. Woozy and disoriented, she told herself it was probably Jed, making another attempt on her life. His key wasn't going to work so there was nothing to worry about.

A moment later she heard the click of the bolt disengaging. She frowned and pulled herself up. It wasn't fair to give Jed a passkey and let him slaughter them all in bed. He should have had to work harder than that.

She yawned and shook her head, trying to clear away the fog before Jed could get inside her room. As he opened her door, she slid her hand onto the night table and felt around for her knife. She'd left it by the lamp, but her eyes weren't used to the darkness and she couldn't see well enough to spot it.

The bed gave a creak as the intruder's hand slid through the partially open door, its fingers clasping the handle of a kitchen knife. The knife's long, sharp blade was revealed by a few beams of dappled moonlight. Then something, perhaps the creak of the bedsprings, halted the intruder's progress. Ellie could make out a dark-colored glove now, and a close-fitting sleeve. Staring at the now-still hand, she continued to search for her knife.

Her nerves got tauter as her body prepared for battle. As she groped around on the night table, the ring on her pinky slapped against the brass lamp, making a soft pinging sound. A moment later she finally found her knife, but the hand in the doorway was already withdrawing.

The door snapped shut as Ellie jumped out of bed. By the time she reached it, the intruder had relocked it from the outside. She turned on the lights and fetched her skeleton key, but she was too slow about unlocking the door. When she stepped into the hallway, it was silent and empty. Every single door was closed. That wasn't surprising, since Jed only had to cross the hall to reach the safety of his room. Ellie crept to his door and pressed her ear against it, but she couldn't hear a sound. Obviously he was back in bed.

She didn't take any chances once she'd returned to her room. Not only did she lock the door; she pushed a highboy in front of it. Come morning, she intended to keep a close eye on Jed. His next attempt at murder wouldn't go unwitnessed.

Ellie was the last one down to breakfast the following morning. Everyone was talking about the death of Abby Stone when she arrived, even Scott and Rebecca, who had joined the dwindling number of guests at the table. Sister Mary had discovered the body when she'd knocked on Abby's door on her way downstairs. When there was no answer, she had let herself into the room. The body had been lying on top of the bedclothes, its throat bruised with the evidence of a vicious strangling.

Ellie gave Jed a reproachful look, silently upbraiding him for killing a sweet old lady like Abby. "It isn't fair for the murderer to have a passkey," she said to Scott, who was pouring her a cup of coffee. "How clever do you have to be to attack someone who's fast asleep? Any idiot could manage it, especially with somebody like poor Abby. She was probably too terrified to fight back."

Scott put down the silver coffeepot and offered Ellie the creamer. "I agree," he replied. "However, as Sister Mary can tell you, it's unlikely that Mrs. Stone was strangled to death while in bed. She was wearing both a robe and her spectacles. Before you arrived, Sister Mary was speculating that Mrs. Stone might have gone looking for you, encountered the murderer, and been killed. The murderer then placed her body in bed."

Ellie shook her head. "Abby wouldn't have left her room. She was too timid."

"She was eager to talk to you," Sister Mary informed Ellie. "She told me so herself, after you went upstairs. Don't forget, she'd had quite a bit to drink. Alcohol has a way of making the meek bold."

"In that case, only one person could have committed the murder." Ellie raised her hand and pointed a dramatic finger at Jed. "Him! I went up to the observatory last night. He came up there to find me, obviously to kill me. He must have met Abby on the way back down." Before Jed could defend himself, Ellie was telling everyone about the body parts that had washed up near Kennebunkport and how she'd checked a map and learned that Oakwood Lake was near the Maine border. "He saw me in the library, looking at a map of Maine. He realized I was on to him so he came upstairs to kill me."

"Forgive me for pointing this out," Jed said, "but you seem to be very much alive."

"Obviously you noticed the knife in my pocket. You knew it would be dangerous to attack me, so you left." Ellie looked around the table, her expression entreating yet obstinate. "Believe me, Thorpe's the one we want. There's no other reason he would have come to find me."

Lynn gave a coy little laugh. "Really, Ellie, how can you be so naive? Jed has been chasing you from the moment he first saw you. Tell me, did he catch you?"

Jed answered the question before Ellie had a chance to. "I would have preferred to keep this private, but in the face of such an incredible accusation..." He sighed. "After all her empty protests, Ellie is naturally reluctant to acknowledge what actually happened. The truth is that she was waiting for me in her nightgown. We made love under the stars. Perhaps some of you heard her cry out my name in the heat of passion."

"Not only are you a liar, Mr. Thorpe; you overestimate your own sex appeal to an astonishing degree." Ellie hoped the disdain in her voice compensated for the blush on her cheeks. "There was no lovemaking and no crying out. Everything happened exactly as I've said."

He lazed back in his chair, smiling sardonically. "Why don't you show everyone your left ear? I'm sure my teeth marks are still visible."

Ellie felt like sinking through the floor. The man was a dirty fighter. He'd obviously realized that the fastest way to shut her up was to raise the subject she had the most trouble talking about—sex. But she couldn't afford to be silent.

She couldn't be sure there weren't teeth marks on her ear, either. As a result, her "Don't be ridiculous!" lacked the ring of real conviction. "Who else could have killed Abby? Everybody else was asleep."

"*You* weren't," Jed pointed out. "It's interesting that you always seem to be involved when a murder is committed. You've discovered two bodies so far, and now we learn that Abby was trying to find you when she was killed. By the way, what was that you said about having a knife in your pocket? Were you admitting you carry a weapon?"

"Only to protect myself from *you!*" Ellie retorted. She had the feeling she'd just been ambushed.

The feeling grew stronger over the next several minutes. Her every action was questioned, from her calmness upon finding the doctor dead in bed to her decision to work instead of searching for clues; from her uncharacteristic hysteria after Marty tumbled over the cliff to her willingness to be alone in the observatory when a murderer was on the loose. It didn't do any good to remind them who had figured out that murderer's motive. Jed insisted she'd only been trying to divert suspicion from herself.

Just when Ellie thought things couldn't get any worse, Scott chimed in with a polite but firm demand. "Miss White, I will have to insist that you return the two knives you stole from the kitchen. Even more important, there's the matter of the passkey." He held out his hand. "Please give everything back."

"I don't have the passkey; *he* has the passkey." Ellie glared at Jed and then turned back to Scott. "And I don't have two knives, either. I only have one, and I'm not giving it up. Anyone can see that the murderer has the other."

"Indeed," Jed drawled. "And since you're the murderer—"

"Don't push your luck," Ellie muttered. "At the rate you're going, your lies about me being a murderer are about to come true, at least as far as *you're* concerned."

Her remark was greeted by five horrified looks. Ellie swallowed her irritation and concentrated on eating something more digestible—her pancakes and sausage.

Jed, meanwhile, was having a wonderful time. He knew he'd gone a little too far with that crack about teeth marks, but something in him had delighted in getting under Ellie's skin. If her blushes were anything to go by, she'd enjoyed last night's lovemaking more than she was willing to admit.

He gave her a broad grin and teased her even more. "I've just realized what a narrow escape I had last night. If you hadn't been overcome with pleasure you probably would have slashed my throat. It's a good thing I'm so incredible in bed."

"Next time I'll try not to get so carried away." Much to Jed's amusement, Ellie stabbed a piece of sausage as if she wanted to kill it.

"You can murder the others," he said, "but you'll never be able to murder me. One kiss and all you'll be able to think about is taking me to bed." He shook his head and added in a pitying tone, "Give it up, Ellie. It's no use."

It took the greatest self-control for Ellie to sit there and continue eating. Before too long, the questions started in all over. She tried to answer calmly, but she was everybody's chief suspect now and anything she said only seemed to make it worse.

Ellie felt like a pariah. Nobody on the island would have anything to do with her. After an hour of being ignored while Scott and the guests played bridge, she gave up watching Jed and went upstairs to work. Jed and Lynn followed a little later. Ellie heard them laughing as they went into Jed's bedroom.

They came out around eleven. Ellie walked to her door and pressed her eye to the keyhole. If Jed and Lynn were leaving, she probably ought to follow. Jed might be getting ready to commit another murder.

Lynn smiled at him. "In all the months I've known you, I've never seen you so grumpy. On second thought, I'll take that walk alone. Talking about my problems seems to put you in a bad mood."

"I'm not in a bad mood," Jed replied. "I'm just distracted. I have a lot on my mind right now—a board meeting at the bank next week and the Tri-State Industries deal."

"Having a lot on your mind never made you snap at me before," Lynn said cheerfully.

Ellie swallowed back a laugh. It was no wonder Jed was irritable, given the fact that he still had a houseful of people to kill. A task like that would have exhausted even the best of men.

Lynn paused a moment, then added, "I'll bet your bad mood would disappear in a flash if Ellie showed up in your room. Your problem isn't suspicion—it's frustration."

"Is that what you think?" Jed sounded astonished.

"It's what I know. You're terrified of a new relationship so you find all kinds of reasons not to get involved in one."

"That's ridiculous. I never think about Kathryn anymore." Ellie didn't know who Kathryn was, but Jed sounded as if he thought about her all the time.

"All right, you never think about her. You don't even remember that she called you boring and priggish." Lynn put her arms around Jed's neck. "Don't look so cranky, darling. You're not either one of those things. You're simply a classic workaholic with an overly developed social conscience." She grinned at him. "In short, you and Ellie are perfect for each other. Why don't you stop fighting the inevitable and ask her out?"

"Dammit, Lynn, how many times do I have to tell you—"

"Until you're blue in the face, and even then you'd be wasting your breath. If you had any brains you would stop arguing and listen to me, but go on, go back to work. I know when to hold my fire. I'll see you at lunch."

Jed gave an aggravated shake of his head. "Fine. In the meantime, be careful. You never know who's going to sneak up behind you with a knife."

Lynn laughed and went on her way. Jed stared at Ellie's closed door for a long couple of moments and then returned to his room. He couldn't have seen Ellie watching, but she felt as though he had. A part of her wanted to march across the hall, knock on his door and find out if he was really interested in her, but she didn't. She didn't have the confidence to ask questions like that. She reluctantly went back to work, but her thoughts kept drifting to the conversation she'd overheard.

She left her room only when Jed did, to follow him down to the dining room about an hour and a half later. They were the first ones to arrive.

"I see the table is set for six," Jed remarked as Ellie walked into the room. "Are all of us still alive?"

"You would know that better than I would," she replied.

"So you're still trying to pretend you're not the murderer." He sighed in disbelief. "Next you'll be claiming you don't have the knives and the passkey."

Ellie had rarely felt so frustrated. Both of them knew he was lying, but he was never going to admit it. "I have one knife, period. Everything else is a figment of your imagination, including those teeth marks on my ear." She'd checked in the mirror, just to be sure. She preferred not to remember that there could have been a lot more than teeth marks if she hadn't come to her senses in time.

"Really?" he asked with a laugh. "Let me see."

His hands captured her head and held it where he wanted it. His thumbs, which were resting on her cheeks, slowly slid backward and tucked her hair behind her ears. He proceeded to inspect each lobe in turn, taking his time about it. Ellie chided herself for letting him unnerve her. Every time he got too close, her body went into its panic mode—heart rate skyrocketing, respiration quickening, temperature soaring.

"You're right," he said as he released her. "There are no teeth marks."

"And there was no cry of passion, either," Ellie insisted. "I never said your name."

"Right again," he agreed. "It was more like a helpless whimper." He pulled out her chair and she silently sat down. For all she knew, she *had* made a noise like that.

It wasn't long before everyone else came in, Scott and Rebecca joining the four guests at the table again. Ellie proposed that they review the evidence, a suggestion that was greeted by long-suffering acquiescence. She and Jed did most of the talking. By the time the meal was over, she felt she had shaken at least two opinions—Sister Mary's and Rebecca's. It wasn't so much that they trusted her, as that they had decided to trust nobody at all.

After lunch, Scott and Rebecca started clearing away the dishes and Sister Mary went off to the studio to paint. Lynn told Jed they needed to talk and led him toward the stairs. That left Ellie alone, as usual.

She knew she should follow Jed and Lynn, but she was too restless to wait around doing nothing until he made another move. She decided to take a walk instead, reasoning that he wouldn't try to kill anyone until late at night, when the house was quiet and everybody had retired.

She let herself outside and walked around to the woods. As she strolled through the tall evergreens, she struggled to do something constructive—think about the Cludds account. It was a puzzling picture. Every year for the past few years, things had gotten a little worse. The trend had grown more pronounced in the last eight or ten months, with the most recent figures, for April through June, the worst of all. Ellie was no expert on the garment industry, but she knew that the type of clothing Cludds made was popular on college campuses these days. The company should have been showing record profits.

She walked along, kicking at pine cones as she sifted through the facts. Maybe the old man's illness and death had caused the decline in profits. Maybe he'd refused to delegate authority. If he'd never trained anyone to carry on, his death could have plunged the company into disorder.

Interviews would help unravel what had happened. With Marty in the country and Lynn something less than grief-stricken, Ellie could begin in the next few weeks.

She was almost at the edge of the woods when a flash of green caught her eye. It wasn't the dark green of the trees or the washed-out color of the scrub, but a bright emerald.

She walked closer and bent down. There was a piece of fabric peeking through the leaves. She didn't realize what she was looking at until she was virtually on top of it. Needles and debris were mounded up over a long, narrow form, hiding everything but that one bit of clothing.

Ellie brushed away some of the debris, uncovering a head of blond hair. There was only one blonde on the island, Lynn Cludd, alias Lynette LaTour, who was scheduled to meet her doom in the same way as Ellie—on the wrong end of a knife. Working quickly, Ellie covered the dummy back up and hurried away. If the body was out in the woods, the murder would take place in the woods. Probably this afternoon.

Ellie was wearing white linen shorts and a red and white blouse. It wasn't the most inconspicuous of outfits, but if she was high enough up, in a thickly branched tree... She took a quick look around, searching for a tall, full evergreen, trying to judge which might be easiest to climb. Having grown up in Manhattan, she'd never climbed a tree in her life.

She selected a magnificent spruce, pulling herself from branch to branch without stopping until she was halfway to the top. Now that she knew where to look, it was easy to spot the dummy. Assuming Lynn would be attacked nearby, Ellie would be able to call out a warning and save her life.

She looked at her watch. Two-thirty. Two-forty. Two-forty-five. The wait might be a long one. Jed had all afternoon.

Ten minutes later, Ellie heard the sound of laughter—Lynn's laughter. She turned around and saw Jed pulling Lynn through the woods. They passed within only a few feet of her tree.

Jed took Lynn in his arms about ten feet short of the edge of the woods. The dummy wasn't more than fifteen feet away. "What's gotten into you?" Lynn asked with a giggle. "In all the time I've known you, you've never made a pass. Is your frustration finally getting the better of you?"

"I'm only doing what I should have done months ago," Jed answered. He took her by the shoulders and turned her around, so that her back was to his chest. "I love the back of your neck. Have I ever told you that?"

He wouldn't, Ellie thought. *Not while I'm up in this damn tree.* If push came to shove she would close her eyes. She couldn't climb down without being spotted, she couldn't shout a warning if making love was what Jed had in mind, and she certainly couldn't watch.

Lynn began to protest as he bent his lips to her neck. "Jed, I don't think—you have to stop doing that. You don't understand about Marty..." Her protests died out when Jed slid his arm around her waist and kept on kissing her. She finally sighed and rolled her head forward.

Ellie was turning away in embarrassment when, out of the corner of her eye, she noticed Jed's hand dart into his pocket and pull out a switchblade knife. A moment later he was drawing the blade across Lynn's throat. Everything happened so fast that Ellie never had a chance to open her mouth.

As Lynn's head jerked back in surprise, Jed drawled, "I'm afraid you've just been murdered, Miss LaTour. You can't trust anyone these days."

Lynn spun around, pouting and laughing at the same time. "What a skunk you are! How could you have sworn it was Scotty when it was you all the time?"

"Like I said, you can't trust anyone these days."

"You lured me out here to kill me," she accused. "That business about my neck was nothing but a line."

"No, it wasn't," he said with a smile. "I do love your neck. I love all of you." He pointed to a spot directly ahead of them. "Your body is over there, buried under some dirt and pine needles. The launch will be here later this afternoon to take you back to the mainland. In the meantime, you should wait on the third floor. Go into the house through the kitchen and use the back stairs. Find Scotty or Rebecca. They'll get you whatever you want to take home with you."

"I may never forgive you for this," Lynn said. "The least you could have done was kill me last."

"One has to take advantage of one's opportunities." Jed turned her around and gave her a gentle push. "The third floor, Lynn. I'm not about to hang around the scene of the crime."

"Of course not. You have all those other murders to commit." She stopped and looked back over her shoulder, a calculating look on her face. "Did I mention that I'm co-chairing the Heart Institute fund-raiser next fall?"

"Ah, blackmail! If I buy a whole table, will you keep your mouth shut?"

"Two tables, or I'll warn everyone on the island about you."

"Two tables, then," Jed agreed resignedly. Lynn gave a satisfied nod and strolled off toward the house.

Jed brushed some debris off the dummy and then headed toward the cliff. Ellie wondered what he was up to. Did he plan to climb down the steps to the beach and return to the house on the shoreline path? If so, he could find Sister Mary or Scott, say he'd been out for a walk, and ask if anyone had seen Lynn around. If Ellie walked into the house after Jed did, she would get blamed for Lynn's death. Jed would have tried to pin the crime on her in any event, but by going into the woods she had played right into his hands.

She didn't waste any more time in the tree. She had to beat him back to the house and make everyone aware of Lynn's disappearance. But in her haste to climb down, she missed her footing, fell to a lower branch and got a nasty scrape on her leg. Cursing impatiently, she dabbed at the blood with a tissue and waited for the pain to ease. She went more slowly after that, keeping her attention on the next branch down, the next handhold.

It wasn't until she'd almost reached the ground that she noticed the sound of someone running. She looked to her right, saw Jed near the edge of the woods, and froze. Her mind went blank. Obviously he had seen her in the tree. Obviously he was going to kill her.

She could climb back up the tree and scream for help, but they were halfway across the island. Maybe nobody would hear her. Even if someone did, even if someone ran outside to investigate, Jed could always claim he had caught her in the act of killing Lynn and trapped her up in the tree. They both had knives with them.

She needed more graphic proof of his guilt. Sister Mary was probably still in the studio. The room had a large picture window that faced the woods. If Ellie could make it that far, if Sister Mary saw Jed chase her past the window with a knife in his hand, there wouldn't be any question about who the real murderer was.

She scrambled the rest of the way to the ground and took off toward the house. She was running as hard as she could, zigzagging around trees that suddenly seemed to constitute a solid, lethal wall. Jed was somewhere behind her, his footsteps thundering in her ears, but she didn't dare turn around to see how big a lead she had. It could have cost her precious seconds. She gasped for air, feeling as if her chest was going to burst. Branches kept whipping against her skin, catching an arm here, a leg there, and even her neck and cheek.

She realized Jed was gaining on her. She could hear the sound of his breathing getting louder and closer with every passing second. She wasn't going to reach the window in time. Without breaking her stride, she fumbled with the clasp on her purse. Why wouldn't the damn thing open? She finally managed to unsnap it and reached inside for her knife. She groped for the handle, grasped it convulsively and pulled it out. She was trying to snap the purse shut again when a pair of hard hands closed around her hips. She staggered, struggling to keep her balance.

The rest of Jed's body hit her an instant later, his chest smacking into her back. He tightened his grip on her hips, twisted her sideways and brought her tumbling to the spongy, needle-cushioned ground. She landed half on top of him. The tackle wasn't hard enough to hurt her, but it did knock the wind out of her. The knife slipped out of her fingers as her hand hit the ground.

Her struggle was a pure, frantic instinct. Jed pushed her onto her back and scrambled on top of her, then reached for her wrists to pin them. She kicked and clawed and bucked like a trapped wildcat, but it didn't do any good. As he'd once boasted, he had an overwhelming physical advantage.

He forced her arms over her head and imprisoned her wrists in a single, unrelenting hand. Their eyes met and locked. Jed was breathing as hard as she was and looked every bit as dangerous as the character he was playing. She tried to twist free, but it was hopeless. Exhaustion was making her movements feeble and ineffectual.

She made a last-ditch effort to save herself, opening her mouth, gulping for air, praying that someone would hear her cry for help. She and Jed were a lot closer to the house now. If her scream was only loud enough—if she could only manage to hold Jed off until someone could come . . .

He stopped her hoarse, breathless cry a split second after it started, bringing his mouth down hard on her parted lips. She tried to twist away, but he grasped her chin with his free hand to keep her head from moving. There was nothing romantic about the kiss, at least not at first. He was trying to shut her up, not make love to her.

Then his lips grew gentler and his tongue began to seek out the taste and texture of her mouth. A wave of new sensations flooded through her. She could feel his muscled body pressing down on her own. His fingers were stroking her face while his mouth worked its magic on her resistance. The scent of evergreen was mingling with the musky aroma of raw male hunger and swamping her senses.

She fought her way back to reality, struggling against the coaxing intimacy of his kiss. He'd just murdered Lynn—Lynette LaTour. He intended to do the same to her. Only a fool would allow herself to forget that.

Say yes to free gifts worth over $20.00

Say yes to a rendezvous with romance, and you'll get 4 classic love stories—FREE! You'll get an elegant manicure set—FREE! And you'll get a delightful surprise—FREE! These gifts are worth over $20.00—but you can have them without spending even a penny!

MONEY-SAVING HOME DELIVERY!

Say yes to Silhouette romances and you'll enjoy the convenience of previewing brand-new books every month, delivered right to your home before they appear in stores. Each book is yours for only $1.95.—55¢ less than the retail price.

SPECIAL EXTRAS—FREE!

You'll get your free monthly newsletter, packed with news on your favorite writers, upcoming books, even recipes from your favorite authors.

Say yes to a Silhouette love affair. Complete, detach and mail your Free Offer Card today!

But his body... She wasn't exactly an expert, but surely a man couldn't fake all that pent-up tension. When a man wanted a woman, she could feel it. *Ellie* could feel it. Could a game really matter in the face of such passionate physical hunger?

His hand slid lower to caress her throat and then her shoulder. She wasn't fighting him anymore, at least not physically, but she wasn't responding to him, either. Although she was keenly aware of his teeth and tongue, of the way he'd begun to tease her by nibbling her lips and lightening the kiss, there were still those mental reservations.

She shuddered, finding it harder and harder to keep her mind in focus. Her mouth had a will of its own, softening under his expert touch and letting him do as he pleased. Her body had a will of its own, too. She could force herself to remember the way Jed had just hunted her down, intending to attack her, but it wasn't that frantic chase through the woods that had set her heart racing and made her internal thermostat go haywire. It was his mouth, which was suddenly demanding more than passive acquiescence. It was his fingers, which had covered her breast and were setting her flesh on fire with their sinuously erotic caresses.

The tension slowly drained from her body. He was giving her too much pleasure, exciting her until she no longer wanted to resist him. What had Lynn said in that hallway? That Jed was frustrated? That he wanted her but wouldn't admit it? Well, maybe he'd finally admitted it. He had to both want her and care for her, to make love to her with such an intoxicating mixture of tenderness and determination.

The thought gave her some badly needed confidence, but even so, her initial response was painfully tentative. She longed to arouse him as he'd aroused her, to sweetly torture him with her mouth and hands, but she'd never felt such desires before. Was a woman supposed to be so aggressive with a man?

She slid her tongue along his lips, heard his low grunt of pleasure and hesitantly kept exploring. He gave her a gentle nip and she nipped him back. Her tongue danced into his mouth and shyly withdrew. And then, hearing his quick intake of breath, feeling his body tauten with need, she finally began to understand that he was just as aroused as she was. Probably even more so.

Her inhibitions began to slip away. She teased him a little more with her tongue and teeth, then grew bolder. There was a heady sense of power in pulling away, denying him her mouth and then allowing him only a taste of what he craved.

At first he played along, content to coax rather than insist, but her provocation finally pushed him into retaliating. Playtime was over. He was going to kiss her deep and hard and she was going to reply in kind. He was going to release his body from the strict control he'd exerted and she was going to yield to his demanding thrusts—and answer with some demands of her own.

Ellie responded to his sudden conquest by giving him everything he asked for and more. She instinctively trusted him—trusted his gentleness, patience and playfulness, trusted the hunger and passion that had exploded into fierce possessiveness, trusted the emotion that seemed to vibrate in the air around them. When he released her hands to grasp her hips, she wound her arms around his neck and pressed herself as close as she could get. Wherever he led, she would follow. He'd taken her into a brand-new world, a world where surrender was a shattering pleasure.

Up until then, Jed had been firmly in control of his actions. His moves had been dictated by pure necessity. He'd heard Ellie slip and mutter to herself and looked around to see where she was. He'd spotted her in the tree and raced to intercept her. She'd tried to escape and he'd brought her to the ground. He'd anticipated her scream and cut it off in the quickest way possible, with his mouth. It was all very cut-and-dried.

He could have used his hand, but it had never even oc-curred to him. He didn't realize how much the chase and subsequent struggle had aroused him. He didn't under-stand that he'd used his mouth because, deep down, he was already half crazy to kiss her. So he'd done so, and the scent and taste of her had hit him with such a potent erotic punch that shutting her up was suddenly the last thing he wanted to do. He wanted her to feel the same way he did—just as hot, just as hungry.

The fact that she'd resisted at first hadn't bothered him a bit. He'd enjoyed coaxing a response out of her. Deep down, she'd obviously wanted to give it, and besides, each little concession along the way had felt so damn good.

He'd enjoyed it even more when she'd started to tease him. Any man would have. He knew he was the one in charge—after all, wasn't he pinning her down?—but her mouth offered the most exciting sort of challenge. How much could he take? What were his limits? If anyone could test them, she could.

And finally, when those limits had been reached and teasing had turned to torture... when he'd silently insisted that *he* would call the shots... when she'd so unmistakably surrendered... he'd enjoyed that best of all. Ellie Landau had been getting the better of him for two straight days now and he'd finally turned the tables. His male ego loved every moment of it.

But his sense of triumph hadn't lasted more than a few seconds. Ellie was too sweet, too eager. She wasn't holding anything back. The barriers he'd always sensed in Kathryn simply weren't there. He'd never experienced such open-ness in a woman, so much trust, and it left him badly con-fused.

He was still confused, but that didn't stop him from wedging his leg between her thighs to part them and set-tling himself intimately against her hips. She gave a low moan and rubbed herself against him like a pleasure-seeking little kitten. Her response inflamed him, but it also added to his confusion. Ellie had been alternately waspish and skittish all weekend, so where had the uninhibited passion come from? Who could have guessed that the cool, analytical Ellie Landau would turn into a raging bonfire after only five or ten minutes in his arms? She hadn't last night.

She hadn't last night. The realization came out of nowhere, smashing through the desire Jed felt. He had to get himself under control again. There were questions he needed to ask, important questions. Somehow he managed to do it.

Was any of this real? How far would Ellie go to defeat him? She had to know how much he wanted her. Would she let him take her if it meant escaping certain death?

If she was manipulating him with sex, he wasn't about to be suckered. He briefly wondered if she was as open and sweet as she seemed, but if she was, only a heel would have taken advantage of it. He had only one real option: to do what he should have done in the first place. He reached for his knife.

Ellie never sensed it coming. Between the passion of Jed's kisses and the throbbing eroticism of his movements, her excitement had built and built until she was sure she was going to explode. Half of her longed for release and the other half yearned to be teased until she collapsed.

When the rubber blade of Jed's knife snapped against her throat, her only response was a convulsive jerk. The object was alien, and it had startled her.

It was only when he drew away that her head began to clear. She realized what had touched her as she opened her eyes. Jed was staring down at her, smiling slightly.

"So much for Ellie White," he said, and slipped the knife back into his pocket. "I'm sorry to see her go. She was a worthy opponent."

Ellie had no idea what to say. Never mind coming up with a sassy retort; she couldn't even manage a trite one. Her emotions were ripping her to shreds. She'd taken Jed for a decent person. She'd allowed herself to believe Lynn was right—that he felt the same strong attraction she did. She'd never responded to a man the way she'd responded to him. My God, she'd practically bared her soul. She'd given everything she had to give. And what had he done with it? Manipulated her. Used sex to catch her off guard. She realized with a flush of humiliation that she'd set herself up for it only the night before.

She'd allowed him to see how much he could arouse her. Naturally he'd been apologetic at first; he'd been terrified she would take him seriously. So he'd put himself in the clear by stopping and backing off, and then, when it suited him, he'd used his sex appeal to arouse and distract her. He'd obviously enjoyed every minute of it, but he hadn't been nearly so carried away as she'd assumed. If she'd only been more experienced, she probably would have realized that. Lynn was right about at least one thing. Jed was an absolute skunk.

She stiffened and looked away. She wasn't going to smile the way Lynn had or joke about his victory. She wasn't even going to complain about his tactics. She'd offered him a way to beat her and he'd taken full advantage of it. Maybe he was a skunk, but at least he wasn't stupid. She was. She'd mistaken a game for reality.

He rolled off her and stood up. Ellie pointedly ignored the helping hand he offered. As she got to her feet and brushed off her blouse, she said coolly, "I already know the drill, so you don't have to repeat it. I should go to the third floor using the back staircase. Scotty or Rebecca will get me what I need. I'll be leaving the island with Lynn."

His smile got a little broader. "God, you're a sore loser. Do you react this way when you get beaten at chess?"

They hadn't been playing chess. As far as Ellie had known, they hadn't been playing any sort of game at all. She was suddenly so angry that logic and self-control flew out the window. Her hand shot up, came slashing across Jed's cheek and then jerked back to her side. A moment later she was running away. She was ashamed of her violent reaction, but too angry and upset to apologize.

Jed stood there, rubbing his cheek and trying to figure out what Ellie was so furious about. Could she really be so steamed about losing? It didn't make sense. Rational people didn't get so emotional about losing a game, and Ellie was nothing if not rational.

Was it something personal, then? Was she angry that he'd stopped? Was it more than her ego could bear? My God, didn't she realize how hard it had been for him to call a halt?

Maybe not. That openness he'd sensed—maybe it was real. Maybe she'd given more than she'd planned to and now she felt rejected. That was laughable given the state his body was in, and he was tempted to go after her and tell her so. He didn't mind admitting that he couldn't wait till both of them were back in Boston and could see each other again.

Boston. Cludds. Embezzlement. Jed shook his head and stayed where he was. He didn't want to think Ellie was guilty, but he knew it was a possibility. There was no sense getting involved with her until he'd ruled out that possibility. It would be too damn easy to fall in love with her.

Chapter Eight

Ellie had been bending the rules since her arrival on Raven's Island and saw no reason to stop just because her character was dead. She entered the house through the kitchen and used the back stairs, but she also made a discreet visit to her room. She only proceeded to the third floor once she'd collected her portable computer, the material on Cludds and her cosmetics and toiletries. The detour gave her a few minutes to catch her breath and calm herself down.

Scott was walking down the third-floor hallway when Ellie opened the door from the back staircase. When he started to scold her about being where she didn't belong, she drew a finger across her throat by way of explanation.

"I'm out of the game now," she said. "Jed knifed me down in the woods."

He looked surprised. "He's had a busy afternoon. I thought you would last longer. In fact, I told him he might not get you at all."

"He got me, all right," Ellie mumbled.

"You look a little upset. Is everything okay?"

"Let's just say I was played for a sucker." It was far too painful to talk about the specifics. "Where to, Scotty?"

"The parlor. Here, let me give you a hand." He took her computer and tote bag and started down the hall. "I see you've already stopped by your room. If you want anything else, let me or Rebecca get it. One of our staff members will drop the rest of your things by your house tomorrow evening."

He led her into the parlor, setting her computer and tote bag on the floor. Then, smiling slightly, he held out his hand. "The knives and passkey, Ellie?"

Ellie gave him her knife, but insisted Jed must have the key and the other knife. "I wasn't lying about stealing only the one knife," she added.

"In that case I'll check with Jed, but I doubt he's the one who took them. Like you said, the passkey would have given him an unfair advantage. As far as the knife is concerned, we gave him a switchblade to use on you and Lynn."

Ellie still thought he had the kitchen knife and key, but didn't bother arguing the point. She changed the subject to Lynn's whereabouts instead, and learned that Lynn was in Rebecca's room, napping. That was just as well, because Ellie was in no mood to socialize.

As soon as Scott left, she settled herself on the couch to work. After an hour with Cludds's records, she sighed and put them aside. The more she saw, the more she despaired of straightening the company out. Old family businesses could be a bear to deal with, especially when there was nobody clearly in charge. Tradition and loyalty took over, making it difficult to dismiss inefficient employees and to streamline and modernize operations. Ellie assumed that was the basic problem with Cludds.

Still, it was only an educated guess. She would need to do a thorough study of the company before she could make recommendations. First she wanted the figures on the printouts rechecked. Then she needed a look at the company's operations. Finally, there were those interviews she wanted to conduct. She never delivered a report until she had examined every aspect of a company's performance.

She killed the next hour and a half with a couple of fashion magazines. There was still no sign of Lynn, but Lucifer, the resident black cat, came into the room at about five and jumped onto her lap. Acting on impulse, she took out her appointment book and jotted down the phone number on his ID tag. If nothing else, she would satisfy her curiosity about who owned him.

Scott came to fetch her a few minutes later. Then they picked up Lynn, who was down in the kitchen with Rebecca, and quietly left the house. As soon as they were out of doors and out of earshot, Lynn asked Scott how the game would end. "Does everyone except Jed die?"

"Everyone but Thorpe and his mistress, Rebecca Hill, who escape to South America with their ill-gotten gains." The three of them stepped onto the jetty. "It's all in the newspapers," Scott continued, "but you have to read carefully. Thorpe is a gigolo who preys on wealthy women. When they start to get suspicious, he knocks them off. There were two deaths in addition to the murder at Oakwood Cabins, one from a drug overdose and the other in a car crash. Needless to say, neither was really an accident. If you put together the article about the cook with details from the accounts of those deaths..." He smiled, not bothering to state the obvious. Rebecca had always been somewhere close by when Thorpe's victims met their fate.

"And the absent Mr. Tipton?" Ellie asked.

"You mean Rebecca's current employer? Dead, I'm afraid, killed by Thorpe with Rebecca's help."

"I suppose she also helped Thorpe lure us all to the island," Ellie said, "by getting him her boss's stationery to use, for example."

"Exactly." Scott walked over to the waiting launch and shook hands with the skipper. "Two more, Doug. Stay by the phone."

Ellie hopped on board while Lynn said goodbye to Scott. Within five minutes, the boat was underway and the two women were seated together in the salon. Lynn introduced herself, then added, "I expect we'll be seeing a lot more of each other in the future."

Ellie didn't bother mentioning that she already knew who Lynn was. It was obvious from her lack of surprise. "I hope so. I've only taken a preliminary look at your company's records, but my initial impression is that you've got a real challenge on your hands."

"What a tactful way to put it!" Lynn gave a laugh. "I didn't expect that. I was told that you terrify people with your bluntness."

"Maybe I do, but I'd like to think I'm direct rather than blunt." Ellie assumed Lynn's information came from her attorney, James Emerson. Emerson had given Ellie's "growing reputation" as his reason for engaging her, and Ellie's directness was probably a part of that.

"You can call it whatever you want," Lynn said. "But blunt or direct, it's what I prefer." She took a pack of cigarettes and a book of matches out of her purse. As she lit a cigarette, she went on: "James Emerson, bless his chivalrous Yankee soul, insists on treating me like a fragile flower of womanhood. He told me you were horribly abrasive—so abrasive I would swoon and pass out if I had to deal with you myself. He even tried to talk me out of hiring you. I'm telling you this so you'll understand who you work for, Ellie. James told me you had other clients who would keep you busy at first, so I knew there was no point in my getting involved. But it's July now and I've been more than patient. I expect some fast results."

Ellie explained that her thoroughness could sometimes cause delays, but promised she would spend the bulk of her time on Lynn's problems. Even while she was talking, she realized that Lynn's statements hadn't tallied with what Emerson had told her. Treading carefully, she said, "Somehow I got the impression that Mr. Emerson had decided to hire me. Did I misunderstand him?"

Lynn took a drag on her cigarette. She looked amused. "I have no doubt James told you that. He likes to give the impression that he's in charge, especially when he's taking his orders from a woman. But the truth is that *I* decided to call in a consultant. James wasn't pleased by the idea. He thinks the company's problems should stay within the company and the family. Since his father was Cludd's attorney before he was, he considers himself a member of that illustrious fraternity."

Ellie had always liked Lynn Cludd. Despite her hard-edged sophistication, she was smart, frank and easy to talk to. If she meant to take control of Cludds, the company's future might be brighter than Ellie had feared.

"What made you choose me?" she asked.

"I asked a friend for recommendations. He gave me the names of four companies." Lynn listed the other three, all of them large and successful. "I know how the big boys work. They'll solicit your business by waving the names of their stars under your nose, but then, if you're a small company like Cludds, they'll foist you off on their junior-level analysts. I wasn't about to settle for trainees."

"So you selected me because you knew I would handle your case personally."

"And devote a major part of your time to my problems," Lynn said firmly. "What have you done so far?"

Ellie outlined her work to date and summarized her initial impressions. She also explained her general plans for the future, suggesting that they meet again in a couple of days to go over the specifics. Lynn kept smoking and nodding, allowing herself a smile when Ellie promised to question everyone from the janitor on up if that's what it took to determine why the company was performing so poorly.

"I can see I chose the right person," Lynn said when Ellie was finished. "Frankly, Ellie, I never intended to get involved in the business, even after Izzy died. Cludds was an old, established firm that seemed to run itself. I only got concerned when the size of my monthly checks began to drop. After the second month, I called my husband's son in Europe, told him what was happening, and asked for his advice. He owns the other half of Cludds."

"You mean Marty," Ellie said.

Lynn raised an eyebrow in surprise, then laughed. "I suppose he told you who he was. He's always had a big mouth."

"If you want the truth, I swiped his wallet and looked at his driver's license. Once I saw the name Cludd, I realized he must be the other owner."

"Nobody was more astonished by Izzy's will than Marty was," Lynn remarked. "They didn't get along. In any event, Marty suggested hiring a consultant and told me to contact an old prep-school friend of his for recommendations. Perhaps you know the man's name—J. L. Thornhill."

There was no "perhaps" about it. Everyone in the Boston business community knew the name Thornhill. The family was well-connected politically and controlled one of the area's leading banks, the First Pilgrim Trust Company. Cludds happened to have an account there, as did Ellie herself. The bank president's brother was a federal judge and his daughter was married to a congressman. J. L., the judge's only son and the family entrepreneur, controlled a fast-growing company called the Polestar Corporation. Ellie was flattered he'd even heard of her, much less recommended her to one of his friends.

"Naturally I know who J. L. Thornhill is," she said, "although from what I hear, he'll never need my services.

His company is supposed to be one of the best-managed firms in New England."

"I don't doubt it, given how hard he works." Lynn gave Ellie a coy smile. "But then, you know firsthand how single-minded he can be."

Firsthand? Far from knowing Thornhill firsthand, Ellie couldn't even recall having seen a picture of him. She was about to say as much when she remembered the conversation she'd overheard earlier that day. "A board meeting at the bank." First Pilgrim Trust, obviously. "The Tri-State Industries deal." Thornhill's newest target, probably. He was aggressive when it came to making acquisitions.

The realization that Jed Thorpe and J. L. Thornhill were one and the same person was as welcome as a bad case of flu. Dear God, she had slapped the man across the face. Not that she hadn't had good reason to lose her temper, but still, Thornhill was successful and influential. People went to him for advice. Impress him, and clients would be lined up on her doorstep. Antagonize him, and the damage might be irreparable. She'd really put her foot in it this time.

She didn't make a habit of flattering important people, but only a fool would have alienated J. L. Thornhill. The thought of apologizing made her gag, but business was business. It wouldn't kill her to pick up the phone and deliver a polite little speech about how much she appreciated his vote of confidence. She wouldn't have to mention anything personal. She could act as if they'd never met. It would be over in thirty seconds and she would never have to speak to him again.

Tuesday, she promised herself, and forced herself to smile. "If I'd known who Jed was, I wouldn't have poured my drink over his head. Now, about that meeting we need to have..." She took out her appointment book and suggested a date and time. The name J. L. Thornhill didn't come up again.

* * *

Ellie spent Sunday evening catching up on the local papers. She would have loved to put Jed Thornhill out of her mind, but fate was against her. The lead article on the social page of Sunday's *Times* featured a large picture of the woman she knew as Rebecca Hill and a headline reading, "Rebecca Sarah Thornhill Affianced to Playwright." The playwright in question, Bruce Scott, was also a writer for Skulduggery Enterprises. The bride-to-be, a *cordon bleu* chef whose French restaurant was scheduled to open in the fall, was the daughter of Judge and Mrs. John Thornhill—in other words, she was Jed's sister. Since Rebecca wasn't an employee of Skulduggery Enterprises, Ellie assumed Scotty had drafted her to help him with his latest creation.

Ellie went to bed early and got up early. Since she wouldn't need her car that day, she left it in her driveway and walked to work. Her office, located in a restored frame house about ten blocks from Harvard Square, was about a mile from her Cambridge apartment. She shared the building with an assortment of young professionals. The rent was exorbitant but the location had prestige. Appearances were important in Ellie's line of work.

She'd moved into the office building the previous winter, counting on money from her trust fund to pay the rent if her business should slacken off. Maybe the upscale surroundings had seduced her, because it wasn't long before she was looking for a nicer apartment, too. Then, of course, she'd needed new furniture—she'd blown a fortune on the place. Her final act of fiscal irresponsibility had been to buy herself a big American car. Ellie wasn't sure whether spending all her money reflected confidence in her own ability or sheer foolhardiness. She was inclined to blame it on the latter.

Ellie's assistant, Jan Potts, was already in the office when Ellie arrived. Jan answered the phones, kept the books, typed reports and helped with research. A former teacher with a bad case of burnout, she'd come to work for Ellie in the beginning of the summer. Jan, her husband and her teenage daughter lived in the same two-family house as Ellie, in the downstairs apartment. Within a week of meeting Jan, Ellie had realized what an asset she would be and had started coaxing her to change careers. Over the months they'd known each other, the two women had become good friends and were more partners than boss and employee now.

Jan welcomed Ellie home and gave her a stack of messages. "I saw your car in the driveway this morning but I didn't want to come upstairs. I thought you'd be sleeping late. How was your vacation?"

Ellie helped herself to some coffee and leaned against Jan's desk. She outlined the plot of Death on Raven's Island and mentioned the connection with Cludds, but she didn't go into the personal side of the weekend. Jan would have asked questions that Ellie didn't want to answer.

"Who do you suppose those two other women were?" Jan asked when Ellie was finished. "You said that most of the players seemed to know each other, so do you think they might be with Cludds?"

"Your guess is as good as mine." Ellie poured herself another cup of coffee. "It's fun to speculate, but I'd better get to work. I want to be well prepared when I meet with Lynn on Friday. I won't be able to give her any answers, so the least I can do is spell out my exact plans."

She settled herself at her desk and took out the Cludds printouts, but when it came right down to it, she couldn't keep her mind on her work. It was back on Raven's Island, asking the same questions Jan had just asked. Who were "Abby Stone" and "Sister Mary"?

She tried the most obvious approach first—she phoned Skulduggery Enterprises. But her request for the names of her fellow guests met with a firm refusal. They didn't give out that sort of information.

Ellie started dropping the names she did know, but it didn't do any good. The receptionist was apologetic but unmovable. The most she would agree to do was to forward any letters Ellie cared to write.

The setback only made Ellie more determined. She was too curious about Abby and Mary to write them care of Skulduggery Enterprises and wait for responses that might never come. Besides, she still had the phone number from Lucifer's collar. Maybe it would provide a lead.

She punched out the numbers, then sighed in frustration when a bored voice repeated those same numbers back at her. She'd reached a professional answering service.

"I'm calling about a lost cat," she said, and gave the operator a description of Lucifer. "This number was on his collar."

"I'll see if I can find out who owns him," the operator said. "Please hold, ma'am."

She didn't come back on the line until a good two minutes had passed. Ellie was fidgeting impatiently by then. "I'm sorry to keep you waiting, ma'am. If you give me your name and number, the owner will get back to you as soon as possible."

Another dead end. The cat wasn't really lost, so the owner would never get back to her. Ellie put a hard edge into her voice, pulling out all the stops. "Look, lady, I'm not that much of a cat lover. This animal came around last night and he's been bothering my poodle ever since. I can't even let Fifi into the backyard. Either somebody picks up that cat today or I take him to the Charles River and throw him in."

The operator told her to hold again. Ellie drummed her fingers on her desk, irritated with herself for not giving up. She should have been working, not playing detective. She'd had enough of that on Raven's Island.

"The cat's owner is out of town until tonight," the operator finally told her. "My supervisor asked me to find out if you would mind calling his office. She thinks his secretary might be able to pick up the cat.''

Ellie replied that she'd be happy to call his office and asked for the secretary's name and number. In the end, it wasn't necessary to speak to the woman directly. The receptionist told Ellie all she needed to know by the way she answered the phone: "Good morning, Polestar Corporation, Mr. Thornhill's office."

Ellie muttered something about a wrong number and hung up. So Lucifer was Thornhill's cat. What did that prove? That Scott, who lived on Thornhill's property and must have seen the cat around, thought he would make a good prop? That Thornhill was the indulgent owner of a spoiled feline that pouted if he was left alone for a few days? Who knew and who cared?

She'd reached another dead end, but maybe the names she already knew might help her. She picked up the phone again, punched out the number of one of the data bases she subscribed to, and placed the telephone handset in her computer modem.

A minute later she was typing out a list of names and instructing the computer to cross-check them with the index for the past twelve months of the Boston *Times. Lynn Cludd. Isidore Van Buren Cludd. Martin Cludd. Cludds Haberdashers. James Emerson. Bruce Scott. Rebecca Thornhill. J. L. Thornhill. Judge John Thornhill. The Polestar Corporation. Skulduggery Enterprises. First Pilgrim Trust Company.*

The computer began to screen every relevant article, working in chronological order. It was a time-consuming process to skim them all, but after three months of stories, Ellie found something interesting. The article was about a posh fund-raiser for Congressman Samuel Morgan's re-election campaign, held in the Beacon Hill home of Judge and Mrs. John Thornhill. The Thornhills were the uncle and aunt of the Congressman's wife. Reading further, Ellie found a reference to J. L. Thornhill, the wife's cousin and the campaign's finance chairman. Jed had attended the party with his fiancée, Kathryn Kent. The Kathryn who had labeled him priggish and boring? She had to be. Ellie instructed the computer to scan the index for Kathryn's name.

She went through another ten weeks of articles before she hit pay dirt. The story that caught her eye was on the social page, headlined, "Kathryn Lowell Kent Wed to Dieter Buckholtz." Buckholtz was described as "a member of Europe's most distinguished family of animal handlers." Ellie nearly burst out laughing when she realized that Thornhill's fiancée, a Boston blueblood with a mile-long pedigree, had thrown him over for a West German lion tamer. It must have been a crushing blow to his ego.

Heartbroken or not, he'd continued to make money. Ellie found items on a number of his acquisitions, the most recent of which had been made in April. That was when the Polestar Corporation had acquired Skulduggery Enterprises. Never mind Lucifer—Thornhill could have taken Buckholtz's entire circus to Raven's Island if he'd chosen to. He owned the place.

There were numerous other articles of interest—I. V. Cludd's obituary, some stories about one of James Emerson's cases, a feature on how well Cludds's two local shops were doing, an item in the sports section about Marty Cludd's racing career—but nothing that identified either Sister Mary or Abby Stone.

It was long past lunchtime by then and Ellie was starving. As she walked down the street to the local sandwich shop, she turned things over in her mind. Everyone on Raven's Island had been connected to Cludds in some way. She had to proceed on the assumption that the same was true of Mary and Abby.

She pulled out the Cludds file as soon as she returned to her office. The company owned a small shop downtown, a larger store in Newton where its administrative offices were also housed, and a factory in Worcester. The organizational chart Emerson had sent her listed about a dozen positions, but there were no first names given, only initials. One of the store managers had the first initial *M,* but the name that caught Ellie's eye was "R. McKay," who headed Cludds's manufacturing operation. She remembered how "Sister Mary" had first introduced herself.

She rang the appropriate office, crossed her fingers, and asked for Ms. McKay. "I'm afraid she's not in," the receptionist replied, "but you could leave a message if you want to, or try her again in the morning."

Ellie asked where she was and got the answer she expected: they couldn't give out that information. Obviously she was going to have to wheedle it out of the woman.

"This is a little hard to explain," she said, "but I think I met Ms. McKay over the weekend. I was at a place called Raven's Island, taking part in a mystery-adventure game. When I got home, I found a memo belonging to somebody named R. McKay in a magazine I'd inadvertently taken. I noticed this phone number in the memo and thought I might as well try it. The woman I met was about forty, with dark hair and brown eyes. She was playing a nun named Sister Mary, so I thought Mary might have been her real first name. Could it have been Ms. McKay?"

The receptionist went from guarded to garrulous in no time flat. "Rosemary was playing a nun? No wonder she wouldn't tell us about her character! She knew we'd never stop kidding her. About that memo—if it doesn't look too urgent, why don't you put it in the mail?" She gave Ellie the address.

Ellie promised to take care of it right away. Then, sensing she had a potential gold mine on the line, she continued: "I'm so glad I decided to call. You know, there was another woman playing the game who might have been with

Cludds." She described Abby Stone. "Does that sound like anyone you know?"

The receptionist chuckled. "That's Abby Cludd to a *T*. She's been here forever, keeping the books. She was married to the old man once, back during the war. I'll bet Rosemary was surprised to see her. Imagine them picking two people from the same company to play the game!"

"It's an amazing coincidence," Ellie agreed. "I got a letter out of the blue one day, asking me to take part. It looked like fun so I agreed. I guess the same thing happened with Rosemary."

"Then you don't know Rosemary. She isn't the type for games, so at first she said no. But then some guy called her up and sweet-talked her into changing her mind. She couldn't stop talking about what a salesman he was."

"What was his name?" Ellie asked.

"That's just it. He wouldn't say. He told Rosemary he would meet her on the island. I don't blame her for going. I answered the phone the first time he called and he had the most incredibly sexy voice."

Who had made the call? Not James Emerson—Rosemary would have known his voice. Not Marty Cludd—he'd been a reluctant recruit at best, and besides, he hadn't gotten in from Europe until very recently.

That left Scott and Thornhill. Scott was a good actor, but he didn't have a sexy voice. Thornhill had to have made the call. And Ellie knew full well how persuasive he could be.

She wrapped up the conversation and sat back to think. Thornhill's sister, Thornhill's cat, Thornhill's company, Thornhill's sweet talk. Six people connected to Cludds gathered together for a weekend that some would have preferred to skip, all of it apparently arranged by Jed Thornhill. He'd been playing a game with all of them, and it wasn't Death on Raven's Island.

Chapter Nine

It was raining hard when Ellie turned into the Newton branch of Cludds. The two-story building sat on its own parcel of land, looking as dated and faded as an elderly woman's well-worn Sunday best. The parking lot needed repaving and the building itself needed plastering and painting. The place had a lonely feel to it.

The only incongruous element in this picture of a business gone to seed was the crowd of people waiting in front for the doors to open. According to the article Ellie had read the previous Monday, the crowd was nothing unusual. Cludds's local retail outlets were doing very well. The company's financial records confirmed that profits were falling due to a downward slide in its wholesale and mail-order operations. Either its merchandise wasn't reaching people outside the Boston area or those people simply weren't interested.

Ellie drove around to the back, looking for the entrance to the administrative offices on the second floor. Cludds might have been in trouble, but some of the firm's employees seemed to be doing fine. She drove by a Cadillac and a BMW before pulling her month-old Oldsmobile into an empty space beside a flashy new Porsche.

The back entrance consisted of a metal door stenciled with washed-out letters reading Corporate Office. Ellie dashed through the rain, holding the hood of her raincoat over her head and clutching her briefcase. The door opened to reveal a musty-smelling stairwell housing a flight of worn wooden steps.

The corporate offices were no more prepossessing than the stairwell. The tile floor in the upstairs corridor was chipped and spotted and the walls were painted an institutional shade of green. There were doors in both directions, but the painted titles were so faded that Ellie couldn't make them out.

She had just started to her left when Sister Mary came striding out of the last office down the hall—or rather her real-life counterpart, Rosemary McKay, did. Rosemary was dressed in a skirt and blouse rather than a habit and was scowling in a way Sister Mary never had. For Ellie, meeting the woman out of costume and out of character was like meeting an imposter.

Rosemary's frown gave way to a smile when she spotted Ellie walking toward her. "Good heavens, what are you doing here? Don't tell me you're connected to Cludds, too!"

"Like everyone else on Raven's Island, you mean?"

Rosemary nodded. "That's exactly what I mean. Who are you, anyway? And did you call my office on Monday with some crazy story about taking one of my memos by mistake?"

Ellie admitted it. "It was the only way I could think of to get your receptionist to tell me if you'd been on Raven's Island. My name is Ellie Landau. I'm a management consultant. I'm doing some work for your company."

"Elaine Landau and Ellie White. I should have made the connection." Rosemary's smile got wider, her eyes sparkling in the way Ellie associated with Sister Mary. "The steel butterfly held a meeting here on Tuesday to tell us all about you. You should be honored, Ellie. It's the first staff meeting anybody's held in years. She put the fear of God into us about all the changes you're going to make."

The "steel butterfly" was obviously Lynn Cludd. Ellie only wished Lynn had held off on those comments about changes, because employee fear and resentment only made a management consultant's job harder. "I'm here to help, not to get anybody fired," she assured Rosemary. "Actually, I was hired a couple of months ago, but I've been tied up with other projects. The only thing I've done so far is look through some of your records. I haven't recommended any changes yet. It's much too soon for that."

"Well, Lynn's expecting great things from you," Rosemary said. "I suppose you've gotten to know each other very well by now."

Ellie shook her head. "As a matter of fact, we'd never even met till last weekend. My contact was James Emerson. You can't imagine how surprised I was to learn that Marty and Lynn Cludd were two of the other guests on Raven's Island. Then I began to wonder how many more of you were associated with Cludds."

"Everyone except the staff members and Jed Thornhill." Rosemary scowled again. "That's Thornhill as in corporate robber baron and noblesse oblige. Apparently he's a friend of Lynn's. I suppose she cooked up the weekend for fun and then asked him to help her arrange it. He owns Skulduggery Enterprises." She paused a moment, then complained, "He shot me in the back. Can you imagine shooting a nun in the back?"

Although Ellie saw a certain macabre humor in Jed's action, she knew she didn't dare say so. Rosemary looked grumpier than ever. "A warning, Ellie," she continued:

"Thornhill is just as arrogant in real life as he was when he was playing Thorpe. I've just come from a meeting in Lynn's office. From the way Thornhill acted, you'd think he was in charge around here. It makes me wonder why Lynn even bothered to hire you."

Ellie stifled a groan. Jed Thornhill was the last person she wanted to see. For three days now she'd been telling herself to call him and thank him. She'd even picked up the phone a couple of times, but she hadn't been able to bring herself to dial it. She was still smarting from her last encounter with the man, so much so that the thought of even talking to him sent her blood pressure into orbit.

It was beginning to look as if she'd have to do a lot more than talk to him—she'd have to insist that he stop interfering in the job she'd been hired to do. "Do you mean he was giving you a lot of orders?" she asked Rosemary.

"Not so much that as grilling me about everything under the sun, as though the company's problems were all my fault." Rosemary swept her hand from one end of the rundown corridor to the other. "Look at this place. It's old and tired, just like most of the employees. The company is stuck in the nineteenth century. I had to talk till I was blue in the face just to get them to computerize, and then what did they do? They messed it all up! If Lynn had any brains she would cut her losses and sell out."

"I hope it won't come to that," Ellie said. "Personally, I intend to do everything I can to turn Cludds around."

"Assuming Thornhill gives you the chance," Rosemary grumbled.

"Mr. Thornhill didn't hire me—Lynn Cludd did." Thornhill had obviously done a lot of damage here and Ellie moved to repair it. "I've never started a job I didn't finish. Neither Mr. Thornhill nor anybody else is going to stop me from making a thorough study of this company and figuring out what's wrong. When the dust settles, we'll need forward-thinking, experienced people to implement my recommendations. I hope you'll stay to help."

"Assuming you decide I'm worth keeping," Rosemary said. "Well, I am. I make a good salary but I could have done a lot better for myself. There's only one reason I've stayed all this time, and he's dead now." She looked at the floor, her eyes filling with tears. "God, I miss him."

Ellie couldn't keep the amazement out of her voice. "Are you talking about I. V. Cludd?"

"You wouldn't be so surprised if you'd met him when I did, over twenty years ago." Rosemary's expression grew wistful. "Izzy was irresistible. He had a way with women until the day he died. He was married six times, you know. His first wife was killed in an automobile accident but all the rest of them never stopped loving him. With Izzy there was no such thing as a messy divorce. His wives all adored him too much to argue with what he wanted—especially the second one."

I. V. Cludd's second wife could only be Abby Stone, alias Abby Cludd, the firm's longtime bookkeeper. Smiling slightly, Rosemary went on: "She's been here since the dawn of time—she couldn't bear to be too far away from him. Would you like to meet her?"

Ellie didn't want to spoil the surprise Rosemary planned to spring. "I'd love to," she said.

Abby's office was at the opposite end of the hall, behind a door marked J. Cludd, Controller. James Emerson had once mentioned that the controller, a cousin of I. V. Cludd's, was nothing but a figurehead at the company. Abby did all the real work.

They found her sitting in front of a computer, entering data from a stack of crumpled invoices. Her back was to the door and she didn't hear it open, so Rosemary got her attention with a booming, "I've brought you a visitor, Abby!"

Abby whirled around, startled to the point of panic. "Look who Ellie White turned out to be," Rosemary went on. "Elaine Landau, the management consultant Lynn was telling us about."

Instead of the smile Ellie expected, she got white-faced silence. The poor woman was so rattled she almost knocked over her coffee cup when she tried to pick it up. Did she think Ellie blamed her for Cludds's problems?

Ellie attempted to reassure her by talking about her plans. Corporations were complicated institutions, she said. Lots of things could go wrong. Her study of Cludds might take weeks or even months, but in the end she would track down the problems and find solutions. Once she did, there would always be a place for experienced, competent employees. Abby kept murmuring her agreement and nodding, but she didn't look reassured.

Ellie finally changed the subject to "Death on Raven's Island," hoping some casual chitchat might calm Abby down. It didn't. In the end, Ellie looked at her watch and said she had to be going. Her appointment wasn't for ten more minutes, but she didn't want to give the woman heart failure.

She said goodbye to Rosemary at the staircase and continued down the hall to Lynn's outer office. Lynn's secretary, who was as tired looking as everything else in the building, told Ellie to go ahead inside. Ellie plastered a smile on her face and reached for the door.

Lynn and Jed Thornhill were sitting on a nondescript tweed couch at the far end of the office. The wooden coffee table in front of them was littered with mail-order catalogs from both Cludds and its competitors. Thornhill stood up immediately while Lynn stayed seated. Ellie barely got out a polite "Good morning" before Thornhill was taking her briefcase and helping her with her coat. She stiffened and blushed at the same time. She didn't want Jed to touch her but couldn't help feeling the same old chemistry when his hands brushed her shoulders. He carried her coat to an old metal coat tree and hung it up.

All but gritting her teeth, Ellie forced herself to do what she should have done on Tuesday. She felt like a schoolgirl parroting an apology to her teacher. "Thank you for recommending me to Mrs. Cludd, Mr. Thornhill. From what I've heard, your company is a textbook example of good management. I'm flattered that you knew about my work."

He handed her briefcase back to her. She'd been too absorbed in her own reactions at first to notice the expression on his face, but now she saw the tight disapproval around his mouth and the coldness in his eyes. Her instinctive response was anger. What did *he* have to be so hostile about? Maybe she'd slapped his face, but she hadn't taken advantage of his naiveté and inexperience and made him feel like a fool. She wasn't trying to get in the way of how he did his job, either.

"You've made quite a reputation for yourself in the past year or two," he said. "I've been wondering if it's deserved. Have a seat and tell me your impressions of the situation here."

Ellie didn't miss his use of the word "me." Lynn could take her pick—Ellie's advice or Thornhill's—but she wasn't going to work her tail off only to have her recommendations brushed aside. "I'm beginning to feel a little superfluous," she said to Lynn as she sat down. "If Mr. Thornhill is giving you advice, perhaps you don't need me—and vice versa."

"If that's a polite way of telling me to get lost, forget it," Thornhill said. "Lynn doesn't have the experience to judge your presentation. I do."

Ellie struggled to keep her voice even. "Mrs. Cludd selected me, so I'm sure she has confidence in me. I would like to think my past successes prove something."

"They got you in the door," Thornhill drawled. "They gave you the opportunity to show me how much you know. If you would begin?"

Ellie closed her mouth and opened her briefcase. Compared to Thornhill, even Thorpe was beginning to look good. His hostile manner and subtle taunts made her long to reply in kind, but she couldn't afford the luxury of shooting off her mouth. He was too important, too powerful.

She explained her findings as crisply and concisely as she could, sticking to facts and refusing to speculate about causes. The bottom line was that Cludds was stagnating. Productivity was flat or declining. Sales, other than retail sales in the two local stores, were consistently disappointing. She concluded with a detailed explanation of her plans for the future, admitting it might be several months before she made her final report.

Thornhill jumped all over her the moment she was finished. He wanted her comments on a dozen different aspects of the company's performance. He demanded explanations and solutions to a slew of possible problems, some of them so unlikely that Ellie had never even considered them. She tried to explain that she didn't work that way—that she could only talk about causes and remedies after a thorough analysis of the firm's operations—but Thornhill kept pressing her. He couldn't seem to accept the fact that she couldn't pull answers out of a hat the way a magician pulls out rabbits. She needed complete information first.

The more he pressed her, the more her temper heated up. She started to forget about his power and influence. She wasn't a saint, for Pete's sake, capable of turning the other cheek no matter how great the provocation.

In the end she simply snapped. "Mr. Thornhill, we each have our own ways of doing things. I'm afraid I lack your brilliance and intuitiveness. I'm just a dull, plodding female, mucking along as best I can. I'll address Mrs. Cludd's problems when I have all the facts. Not before.''

He stood up, walked to the door, and pulled it open. "Please wait outside," he said. "I want to have a few words with Mrs. Cludd." It was an order, not a request. If Ellie had had a glass of Perrier in her hand, there was no telling what she might have done with it.

Jed closed the door and returned to the couch. He didn't know what he was feeling—only that he'd never felt that way before. It was hard to sit still. It was hard not to scream, much less keep his voice to a near whisper. He wanted to smash his fist through the nearest wall or run at top speed until he was too exhausted to think. The lack of a physical outlet was making his gut ache.

"*Now* are you convinced?" he said to Lynn. "If you don't know when you're being stalled, you shouldn't be trying to run this company."

Lynn was maddeningly calm. "I don't feel I've been stalled. Ellie told us she was busy with other cases when she first took the job. She's obviously done a lot of work during the past week and her plans for the future were logical and detailed.''

"Right," Jed snapped. "So detailed they'll take forever to carry out."

"But she has a spotless reputation," Lynn insisted. "Even you admit that. Why are you being so irrational about this?''

"Because your profits have almost disappeared since she took the job. Because a series of major deposits has been made to her bank account during the same period of time. Because anybody with half a brain can see that someone is robbing you blind, but Ellie never even mentioned the possibility—and God knows I gave her every opportunity.''

"So why didn't you confront her? Why didn't you toss out the idea of embezzlement or ask her about those deposits?"

Jed had to laugh at that. "Oh, sure! I'm going to tell her I used my position with the bank to personally examine her account activity over the past year. I can see the lawsuits if I'm wrong."

"If you're wrong?" Lynn looked thunderstruck. "My God, do you actually admit the possibility?"

Jed didn't have an answer for that. He knew he could be wrong. The case for embezzlement wasn't as rock solid as he'd pretended, and the evidence against Ellie was only circumstantial. It wasn't totally impossible that she had received a sudden windfall—a bonus from one of her clients, for example. But dammit, the money had been deposited directly into her personal account. It hadn't come through her business.

"You know what I think?" Lynn said. "I think you're in love with her."

"For God's sake, Lynn, don't start that again—"

Lynn continued talking as though Jed had never spoken. "You can't stand the idea that your judgment could be lousy enough to fall in love with a crook, so you refuse to admit how you feel and you overcompensate by trying to prove the worst. You know as well as I do that embezzlement is only one possible explanation for what's wrong here. You managed to keep your mouth shut during my meetings with Abby and Rosemary, and neither of them was exactly honest and forthcoming. So why the hatchet job on Ellie?"

The answer was simple. Abby and Rosemary hadn't deposited suspiciously large amounts to their bank accounts during the past several months. Ellie had.

Jed ran a tired hand through his hair and told himself it was pointless to argue. "Maybe I can trace the funds in Ellie's account back to their source," he said. "In the meantime, promise me you'll be careful about what you say to her. Remember, she has access to your computer system. She's easily good enough to crack the bank's security. It would be child's play for somebody with her skills to transfer money from Cludds's account to her own and then alter the records to cover it up."

"Which is why Abby is checking the data in the computer against the original paperwork. She hasn't found anything yet, remember?"

Lynn gave him a sly smile. Jed hated that smile. It said she could read him like an open book, and he didn't like to think of himself as that transparent. "Maybe you should mend your fences on the way out. Ellie was furious with you, and little wonder. You were horribly rude to her."

In Jed's opinion, Ellie should have done the fence-mending. He hadn't been rude so much as tough, and besides, she was in no position to alienate somebody as important as he was. Guilty or not, she shouldn't have been so evasive. She shouldn't have delivered that final, sarcastic lecture, either.

He grabbed his coat and walked to the door. He had every intention of walking straight through the reception area and out into the hall, but Ellie's reaction stopped him in his tracks. She was sitting on the couch, waiting, but the moment he opened the door, she pointedly turned her head, making a show of ignoring him. She looked as stiff and arrogant as an offended princess.

He had a sudden urge to march up to her, grab her by the shoulders and shake her until she told him the truth. Maybe there was an acceptable explanation for those deposits. If there was, he wanted to hear it. And if there wasn't? He wasn't about to get mixed up with a crook, but if she'd taken the money because she was in some kind of trouble...

Physical force wasn't going to get him anywhere, but psychological pressure might be a different story. If he got her alone and turned on the heat, maybe she would talk. He walked over to where she was sitting, then stood there staring down at her until she reluctantly met his eyes. She was trying not to show any emotion and failing completely. The tension and anger were practically sputtering out of her.

"I want to meet with you privately," he said, and pulled out his appointment book to check his schedule. "I'm busy for the rest of the day but I can meet with you this evening. We can talk during dinner."

She stood up, glancing around his shoulder at Lynn's secretary. The thought of making a scene seemed to bother her. "I'm afraid I'll be busy," she said.

"Then I can see you over the weekend."

"I'm afraid I'll be out of town." It was obvious she was lying.

"I can meet with you at four on Monday or see you after dinner." Jed's temper was beginning to simmer. He didn't like being put off, especially not by somebody he could make or break as easily as he snapped a twig.

"I'm afraid not, Mr. Thornhill. I don't have any free time next week, but I'll be happy to have my secretary call you if I have a cancellation. If you would excuse me . . ." She took a step to her right, trying to slip around him in order to get to Lynn's office.

Jed had taken all he planned to take. Catching her by the wrist, he said, "You're having dinner with me tonight, Ellie. If you really have another appointment, reschedule it. I'll pick you up at your house at five-thirty. It would be a bad idea not to show up. I'm not somebody you can afford to offend."

She reddened with anger, but her voice stayed perfectly even. "Is that a threat, Mr. Thornhill? Either I do what you want or you blacken my name throughout the entire Boston area?"

"Let's just say I didn't get where I am by being a Boy Scout." He released her wrist and walked away, but not before hearing her reply: "And I didn't get where *I* am by letting people push me around!"

As angry as Jed was, he still couldn't help smiling as he walked down the corridor. Ellie was as aggravating as hell, but she had spirit. He had to give her that.

Chapter Ten

Ellie wasn't the type to run away from fights, but she had no taste for suicide missions, either. She thought she could handle Jed Thornhill, but only if Lynn really wanted her to. Her position would be hopeless otherwise.

The smile on Lynn's face when Ellie walked back into her office told Ellie that Lynn had listened to every word of her argument with Jed. She wished she'd behaved more professionally, but dammit, the man had been infuriating.

"Have a seat and cool off," Lynn said, "and don't worry about Jed Thornhill. His bark is worse than his bite. About your presentation—Jed was so busy asking questions I hardly got a word in. He seems to have forgotten whose company it is. Can you stay and talk for a while?"

"Yes, of course." Ellie joined Lynn on the couch, grateful to her for making this so easy. Thornhill was a good friend of hers, and she might equally well have chewed Ellie out for being rude to him.

Their conversation went even better than Ellie had hoped. Lynn seemed completely satisfied, both with Ellie's progress to date and with her plans for the future. As she gathered up her papers to leave, Lynn told her she was leaving town that evening but would be back on Tuesday night.

"If there's any change in your plans for Monday and Tuesday, leave a message with my secretary and she'll notify the appropriate people," Lynn instructed. "Otherwise, I'll see you at the factory on Wednesday."

"Right. I hope you have a nice weekend." Ellie closed her briefcase and stood up. "If you're playing another mystery-adventure game, try not to get yourself killed."

"Once was enough, thank you," Lynn replied. "Actually, I'm going up to Maine. My late husband had a cabin up there, and I could use some time away. Marty doesn't know it yet, but he's coming with me."

"Please give him my regards." Ellie had been wondering how Marty fit into the picture. As half owner of Cludds, he would probably have an opinion as to how things should be run. "I imagine he'll have questions about the work I'm doing. Naturally I'll meet with him any time he's free."

"Marty would rather spend the day at the dentist than talk about Cludds. He has absolutely no interest in the business. He races cars for a living." Lynn paused a moment, then admitted, "The truth is that I'm taking him up to Maine to seduce him. He's a gorgeous man, don't you think?"

Ellie wasn't especially surprised—not after the way Lynn had chased Marty the previous weekend. "Both gorgeous and very nice," she agreed. Maybe even *too* nice for someone as hard as Lynn. Ellie hated to think of Marty getting hurt.

Her tone must have revealed more than she knew, because Lynn sighed and asked her if she would like to stay another couple of minutes. Ellie nodded and sat back down.

"Marty and I go way back," Lynn explained softly. "I was only nineteen when I first met him. I come from the kind of family they always describe as poor but proud, but let me tell you, there was nothing proud about us. I had five younger brothers and sisters and a mother who was old by the time she was thirty-five. I worked full-time as a secretary, gave every spare dime to my parents, and went to school at night. That's how I met Marty—in one of my classes. He had no money, either. His father had cut him off without a penny for refusing to enter the family business. He was working in construction during the daytime and putting himself through school at night. We'd been dating for about three months when he brought me to a family party. I realized right away that his father was interested in me, and all I could see was a meal ticket to a better life for me and my family. Izzy and I were married six months later. Marty refused to attend the wedding—he quit school and went off to Europe. The next time we saw each other was at the funeral. We reestablished contact, but it's been difficult. He's never forgiven me for what I did to him."

Ellie understood Marty's antipathy toward his father now, and also his coolness toward Lynn. What she *didn't* understand was why he'd agreed to come to the States when his feelings were still so raw. "I'm surprised he was willing to take part in Death on Raven's Island," she remarked.

"Jed talked him into it. Skulduggery Enterprises is one of his companies." Lynn hesitated, picking up a paper clip and fidgeting with it for a while. Finally she continued, "Jed wanted to test out one of the company's games on people who had some connection to each other, to see if it would still work in a situation like that. For some reason he insisted on including Marty. At first I objected, but things worked out for the best. The moment I saw Marty again, I realized I still felt something for him. And if he feels the same way..." She looked into her lap. "I'll let you in on a secret, Ellie. Deep down, I'm not nearly as tough as I pretend. Izzy wasn't the easiest man to live with, and when he died, all I wanted was to kick back and break loose. I've had a good time, but it's felt emptier than I ever dreamed it would. I need someone to share my life with, someone who's gentle, sweet and easygoing. High-powered types like Jed make me feel tense and unsure of myself. Really, I admire the way you stood up to him."

"It was either that or let him walk all over me," Ellie admitted. "I know he's a brilliant businessman with a million important connections, but he makes me so angry I forget to feel intimidated. If only he'd asked me politely, I would have been glad to meet with him, but I'm not going to let him order me around."

"Here, here!" Lynn teased, and laughed.

Ellie suddenly realized how silly she must have sounded. Who was she kidding? Not Lynn, and certainly not herself. "Okay, then, I shouldn't have lost my temper. I know I can't afford to make an enemy of Jed, but my emotions seem to bury my common sense where he's concerned. Eventually I'll have to give in to him, won't I?"

"Yes, but timing is everything." Lynn winked at her. "Jed enjoys challenges. Don't give in too fast, and when you do, smile at him and tease him when he tries to run his macho number on you. He'll forget about business in no time flat, believe me."

Having Jed forget about business was the last thing Ellie wanted. She was resigned to meeting with him, but she would do it in an office rather than a restaurant and there wouldn't be any smiling.

"I don't think I could do that," she said to Lynn. "I'm afraid I'm not the type."

"All women are the type," Lynn replied.

"Maybe you're right." Ellie was sure she wasn't, but all she wanted by then was to get out of Lynn's office. She smiled weakly and excused herself.

She'd barely closed the outer door before Abby Cludd peeked out of her office and gave a furtive look down the corridor. Seeing that it was empty, she slipped into the hall and scurried over to Ellie. They met near the door to the staircase.

"I have to speak to you," she hissed. Her eyes kept darting around, as though she was afraid of being overheard. "It's important."

"I could spend some time with you right now," Ellie offered.

Abby grabbed her by the arm and pulled her into the stairwell. "No, not here. I'll come to your office. I should be able to get away this afternoon. I'm not sure when."

Ellie assured her that she would be in her office all day, and then, bemused, watched her open the door and hurry back down the hall. What was all the mystery about? Was it something to do with the invoices Abby had been checking? Giving a shrug, Ellie started down the steps. She would find out soon enough.

It was raining even harder than before when she opened the outside door. She dashed to her car, noticing that both the Porsche and the BMW were gone. One of them obviously belonged to Jed, probably the BMW. The Porsche seemed a little showy for a conservative Yankee.

The side street in front of Cludds was about a quarter of a mile from the main road. Ellie had to stop to wait for a break in the traffic before she could turn onto the main road, and when she did, she noticed that her brake felt a little low. She cursed the American auto industry. The car was only a month old, and now she was going to have to take it into the shop. Between going back and forth and waiting around for the mechanic, she'd wind up killing half the day.

She stayed in the right-hand lane, driving cautiously. Boston drivers were maniacally aggressive, and her brake just didn't feel right. She shouldn't have had to press it down that far.

Not far ahead, a sports car came barreling down a back street and, ignoring the stop sign, zipped into the line of traffic. The car ahead of Ellie braked sharply. Ellie did the same. Her car decelerated for a split second, and then— nothing. The brake wasn't working. She repeatedly slammed on the pedal, but it was no use.

Time seemed to slow down. She was going to hit the car in front of her—she knew that—but everything seemed to be happening in slow motion. She looked to her left but there was no place to go. There was a solid line of traffic in the left-hand lane. She jerked her wheel to the right, desperately trying to steer the car onto the narrow shoulder. The car went into a skid, slipping on the rain-slick pavement like a skate on fresh ice. It spun around, miraculously missing the other cars, and wound up facing the wrong way, half on the shoulder and half on the grass, and still moving much too fast.

Ellie hit the emergency brake to try and stop it, but momentum and a downgrade kept it going. The last thing she saw was a large tree, looming dead ahead of her. She yanked the wheel to the right, trying to avoid both the tree and the ditch to the left of it. A couple of seconds later everything went black.

She felt dizzy and disoriented when she finally opened her eyes. No time seemed to have passed, but she hazily realized it must have. Her door was open to the extent the tree would permit and somebody was holding some gauze against her head. There was broken glass all over the place. There were bloodstains on her raincoat. Finally, there was pain, a stinging pain that seemed to be shattering half her face.

She instinctively tried to get up, but a large hand came down on her shoulder and gently pushed her back down.

"Just take it easy, ma'am. The ambulance will be here any minute, now."

She turned her head toward the voice, saw a policeman's uniform, and, reassured, closed her eyes again. After a few more moments, she was able to take over the task of holding the gauze against her forehead. The policeman began to clear away the broken glass. The pain eased, becoming a little more bearable.

Several more minutes went by. The policeman asked Ellie who she was and what had happened, and she was able to give him the answers. Despite the knock on the head she'd gotten, there was nothing wrong with her memory. In fact, she was more concerned about the Olds than about herself. It wasn't drivable, not with the left-front side smashed up and the windshield shattered.

The policeman couldn't have been nicer. He told her not to worry about her car—he would arrange to have it towed to the dealer where she'd bought it, for repairs. He commiserated with her about the way her brakes had failed, saying his late-model import was in and out of the shop all the time. Cars, he joked, were nothing but trouble.

Traffic, meanwhile, had slowed to a crawl. Nobody could pass the accident without craning his neck for a better view. As a result, the ambulance had to travel on the shoulder in order to get through.

It was nearly one o'clock before Ellie got to the hospital. Injured or not, she still had to fill out insurance forms and emergency releases before she was shown into a curtained-off examining room. An emergency-room physician finally came in to clean up her face, holding up a mirror afterward so she could examine the damage. All in all, she'd been lucky. Other than a nasty cut on her forehead, there were only minor scratches and knicks from the flying glass.

The ER doctor didn't want to stitch up her forehead himself—the cut was too jagged and too visible. He suggested calling in a plastic surgeon, and Ellie, not knowing one, asked him for a recommendation. The doctor he chose, Dan Goldsmith, was something of a local celebrity. Ellie had seen a show on public TV about his work with burn victims. She was relieved that somebody of his caliber would be repairing her forehead.

Her next stop was the X-ray room. Her chest was sore where the seat belt had crossed it, but the belt had also saved her from serious injury. Nothing, thank God, was broken. Her worst symptoms were a headache and mild dizziness— probably the results of the way her head had slammed into the side post behind the front-left window when the car had struck the tree.

Still, the doctor didn't like the idea that Ellie had lost consciousness. He wanted to admit her for overnight observation, but in her opinion, hospitals were the worst places to rest and recover. In the end, they compromised. She would have a CAT scan of her brain to check for internal bleeding, and if nothing showed up, she could go home.

By the time she got back to the ER, she felt like a slab of meat. There was still that cut on her forehead to deal with, but the plastic surgeon couldn't get to the hospital until four-thirty at the earliest. Ellie was so tired by then that she barely noticed the noise and activity on every side of her. The doctor left her lying on the examining table and went off to see his next patient.

Her thoughts drifted back to the accident, reliving it over and over. She should have stopped the moment she noticed the problem with her brakes. She should have swerved the other way, trying to go between the tree and the ditch. Now her whole day had been shot. She would have to work all weekend in order to catch up.

Thinking about work reminded her of Abby Cludd. Abby had probably shown up in Cambridge by then, only to find that Ellie had stood her up. The least she could do was phone the office and ask Jan to convey her apologies.

She slid off the table and went to look for a phone. Although she got some questioning looks from the staff, nobody had the time to worry about her. Jan, it turned out, was relieved to hear from her. Abby Cludd had come by the office at two, stayed for half an hour, and then left. Jan knew it wasn't like Ellie to make appointments and not keep them, and she'd been concerned about what could have happened.

She was even more concerned when Ellie told her about the accident. She wanted to drive out to the hospital to bring Ellie home, but Ellie told her not to bother. "You know how doctors are. The plastic surgeon said he'd try to get here at four-thirty, but he might get tied up with another case and not make it until five or six. I have no idea when I'll be finished, Jan. I may be woozy, but not so woozy that I've forgotten that you and your family have plans tonight. Enjoy your dinner and the concert, and I'll see you in the morning."

It took a little more persuading, but Jan finally agreed to let Ellie take a taxi home. Ellie decided to make one other call, as long as she was by the phone, to the repair shop where her car had been towed. She wanted to make sure it had actually gotten there.

She talked to the service manager, a man named Roger. He told her the estimate would be ready in the morning, adding that it would probably take until Wednesday or Thursday to complete the actual repairs.

"Make sure you take a good look at the brake system," Ellie said. "That's what caused all the trouble in the first place."

"I know. The policeman who helped you out told the tow-truck driver to be sure and tell us about that." There was a noticeable pause. "Look, Miss Landau, I don't know how to put this, but—maybe you need to have another talk with that policeman. The fact is, your brake-fluid line was cut."

Ellie didn't understand what he was talking about. "You mean during the accident?"

"Before the accident. It's hard to see how it could have happened as a result of crashing into a tree."

What Ellie knew about cars could have been engraved on one side of a postage stamp. "But the car was fine when I left the house this morning. I took it to an appointment and left it sitting in a parking lot. How could somebody have cut my brake-fluid line when it was out in the open that way?"

"It would take only a couple of seconds. The line is right under the car, near one of the front tires. Your brakes would have worked as long as there was fluid in the system, but they would have felt funny at first. When the fluid was gone, they would have failed completely. If that sounds like what happened, then the line was already cut when you got inside your car."

It was exactly what had happened. Ellie thanked him and hung up, feeling even shakier now than she had immediately after the accident. Why would somebody have vandalized her car? She didn't have any enemies. Was it some sort of vicious prank, then? She couldn't take it in.

She lay back down on the examining table, struggling to organize her thoughts. It was like fighting her way through a thick fog. It had been a long, difficult day and she wasn't in the best of shape.

Was it possible she wasn't a random target? That somebody had been after her particular car? That somebody had wanted to hurt her or even kill her?

Suppose the answer was yes. Only one logical motive came to mind. The damage to the car had to tie in with her work for Cludds. Maybe somebody was stealing from the company. It would explain those declining profits. If so, the thief might have cut her brake-fluid line because he—or she—was afraid of what Ellie might discover. She closed her eyes, unable to believe that such a thing could happen. Violence had never touched her life before—not real violence, anyway. The closest she'd come to death was during her stay on Raven's Island.

Raven's Island. She was suddenly back in the dining room at Tipton House, sitting at a table with Jed Thornhill and five people connected to Cludds. At least two of them, Rosemary McKay and Marty Cludd, wouldn't have come if Thornhill hadn't charmed or pressured them into it. According to Lynn, he'd arranged the weekend as some sort of special test, but was that his real motive? Why go to so much trouble when six employees from Polestar would have served the purpose equally well? It didn't make sense.

The plastic surgeon showed up a little past five o'clock. The radiologist who had done her CAT scan had stopped by to talk to her by then, assuring her that everything looked normal. She would be able to leave as soon as her face was taken care of.

She chatted with the surgeon about his work with burn victims as he stitched up her forehead. When he was finally finished, he told her to take it easy for the next several days and stop by his office in a week. Then, as an afterthought, he asked her if somebody was picking her up. "You shouldn't be driving," he said. "Not in this weather and not in your condition."

"I thought I was perfectly lucid," Ellie answered.

He smiled at her. "You wouldn't say that if you could hear yourself talk. Your speech is slurred."

"Well, don't worry." Ellie pointed to her forehead. "I smashed up my car when I did this. I'm going to take a cab home."

The doctor picked up the clipboard that was sitting on the table next to the bed. It contained personal and insurance information as well as medical reports. "You live on Vine Street in Cambridge? That's only fifteen minutes from me. I'll give you a ride home."

Dr. Dan Goldsmith was obviously a throwback to the days of dedicated family physicians who made house calls at one in the morning. Ellie said a grateful thank-you and accepted his offer. His Cadillac was so comfortable that she fell asleep within minutes of leaving the hospital.

They were a block from her house when she woke up again. The anaesthetic had begun to wear off by then and her head was starting to hurt. All she wanted to do was get inside her house, lock the door and take something for the pain. She needed to forget what had happened to her that day—at least, for the next several hours.

At first she didn't recognize the red Porsche that was parked in her driveway. Even after she placed it, she couldn't figure out what it was doing there. The right memory clicked into place when an angry-looking Jed Thornhill stalked out of the house and walked briskly toward the Cadillac. He wasn't the BMW type after all.

It was long past five-thirty, but Thornhill had evidently hung around waiting for her to get home. He expected her to have dinner with him. She sighed, thinking she should have spent the night in the hospital after all.

Chapter Eleven

When Jed made an appointment for five-thirty, he meant five-thirty. Not a quarter of six. Not six. And certainly not six-thirty, which was when he heard Ellie pull into her driveway. He hadn't believed she'd have the guts to stand him up and he'd been right. But she'd forced him to cool his heels for a solid hour. He wasn't happy about that.

He opened the foyer door and walked out into the rain. Then he stopped and frowned, because the Oldsmobile he'd expected to see was nowhere in sight. There was a Cadillac in the driveway instead, with a dark-haired man at the wheel. A boyfriend, maybe, recruited to run interference?

The driver opened his door, but Ellie remained in the right-front seat, not moving. Jed started toward the driver, who flashed a smile of recognition and extended his hand. A second later the recognition became mutual. *Danny Goldsmith*. Where did he fit into the picture?

Danny met him in the middle of the driveway. "Hey, Jed, how are you doing? We missed you at the game last weekend."

He was referring to a charity softball game that was held every year to raise money for a local hospital. Jed had skipped it this year in order to go to Raven's Island. "Next year," he promised. Danny's presence changed everything. Although he and Jed weren't close friends, they moved in the same social and charitable circles. He couldn't drag Ellie away if she had a date with someone he knew.

"We'll hold you to it," Danny answered. "If we'd had you in the lineup, maybe we would have won." He looked back toward the car. Ellie was still sitting there, her face and body obscured by the rain that was streaming down the windshield. "Obviously you're a friend of Ellie's. Was she expecting you?"

"We had some business to discuss, but it can wait." Jed was beginning to feel uncomfortable. It had never seriously occurred to him that Ellie was actually busy, but it should have. Women with her looks didn't sit home Friday nights. "I thought she was free tonight, but since she obviously isn't..."

Danny cut him off by laying a gentle hand on his shoulder. Jed recognized a doctor's professional bedside manner when he saw it, but couldn't figure out why he should be the recipient of it. "If you're not busy tonight, it would be a good idea to stick around," Danny said.

"Stick around?" Jed's heart started to pound. Was Danny here as Ellie's doctor, then, rather than as her friend? Jesus, the guy was a plastic surgeon. He took people who looked like hell and made them presentable. "Why?" he asked. "What happened to her? Where's her car?"

"Don't get excited—just listen." Danny gave Jed's shoulder a comforting squeeze. "Ellie lost control of her car and plowed into a tree. I stitched up a cut on her forehead for her, but I think it'll heal very well. She's got a concussion and a sore chest, but her CAT scan was normal and there aren't any broken bones. I'll write a prescription before I leave in case she needs something for pain. She's a lot woozier than she realizes, but that's only to be expected. It was a serious accident and it left her pretty shaken up. She was in the hospital all afternoon, getting tested and poked at. Naturally she's tired and disoriented.''

Jed stared at the car, wishing he could see something more than the rain-distorted outline of Ellie's face. His stomach was getting queasy. He could picture Ellie trapped inside the car, mangled, bleeding and helpless. Was this all his fault? Had he upset her so much that she'd plastered herself against a tree?

"How did it happen?" he asked. "Was another car involved?"

"She mentioned something about a problem with her brakes, but she didn't go into details. The subject seemed to agitate her so I dropped it. People talk about things when they're ready to.''

The accident had obviously traumatized her. Jed could understand that. It had to be one of the most terrifying feelings in the world to have your brakes suddenly fail.

He should have felt relieved that he wasn't responsible, but he didn't. Whatever emotion was tying his stomach into knots, it wasn't guilt. He was still just as shaken and nauseated. "I won't bring up anything that might upset her," he said to Danny. "Is there anything I should do? Anything I should watch for?"

"Bleeding, vomiting, loss of consciousness—anything that might indicate a more serious concussion. I wouldn't worry, though. The normal CAT scan is a very good sign. It doesn't guarantee that nothing will go wrong in the future, but the odds are heavily against it. Get Ellie comfortable, feed her if she's hungry and do what you can to relax her. She should take it easy for the next couple of days.''

The two men walked over to the Cadillac and Danny opened Ellie's door. Jed could see the jagged cut on her forehead now, under her bangs, and the series of neat, tiny stitches Danny had put in. Her coat was stained with blood and her face was unnaturally pale, probably from pain and fatigue. She also looked tense and wary, as though she expected him to start harassing her about Cludds. He didn't know which made him feel worse—the pain she was suffering or the fact that his presence was so clearly unwelcome.

He realized he would have to establish his authority immediately, before she had a chance to kick him out. Whether she liked it or not, he was going to stay. The need to look after her was so strong that his voice was tight with strain when he started to speak. "I'll lift her out of the car, Danny. Why don't you grab her briefcase and get her keys out of her purse? The outside door is open, but her apartment is locked."

Ellie might have felt exhausted, but she wasn't unconscious. And until she was, Thornhill wasn't going to carry her anywhere. It was bad enough he was here; now it looked like Goldsmith was an old friend of his. That ruled out the possibility of claiming she'd never set eyes on him before.

"I can manage on my own," she said. "I walked out of the hospital under my own steam and I can make it to my apartment the same way."

Given Jed's arrogance, she expected him to start firing orders. He didn't. "Okay, but at least let me help you get out," he said. The next thing Ellie knew, he was bending down beside her. He took hold of her legs and gently swung them out the door. Then he put an arm around her back to carefully lift her up.

Even with Jed supporting her, she was far from steady on her feet. She blamed that on hunger rather than tiredness. She hadn't eaten since breakfast.

They started toward the house. Jed's arm was around her waist and she was leaning against his shoulder. When it came right down to it, she probably couldn't have made it on her own. Besides, Jed was being tender and gentle—as different from the man she'd tangled with this morning as a teddy bear was from a grizzly. She didn't trust this softer side of him, but imagined he would stay in line as long as Goldsmith was around to watch.

Goldsmith unlocked her apartment and Jed walked her inside. He helped her off with her coat, his eyes fixed grimly on the bloodstains. Then he led her to the couch before he continued on to her bedroom. He was carrying a pillow and a blanket when he returned.

"I like your apartment," he said, and tucked the pillow behind her neck. "It's a nice mixture of modern and antique."

Even the antiques were recent purchases, but Ellie didn't go into how she'd blown some of her trust money on furniture. She didn't want to chat. Now that she was safe and sound, her only desire was to be alone.

"About that conversation you wanted to have," she began, "I really don't think I can handle it tonight."

Goldsmith scrawled something on a pad of paper, ripped off the top sheet and handed it to Jed. "Forget about business," Jed said as he shoved the paper in his pocket. "Danny told me you were in the hospital all afternoon. You must be hungry."

"I'll fix myself a sandwich later." Ellie looked at the doctor. "Dr. Goldsmith, I appreciate the lift home. I'll see you next Friday. And now, if you both don't mind, I'm tired and I'd like to sleep. Really, I'm not in the mood for company."

The two of them exchanged the kind of look men use to indicate that a woman is being difficult. Then they walked back to the entry hall to talk, keeping their voices too low for Ellie to hear. After a brief conference, Goldsmith shook Jed's hand and let himself out of the apartment.

He had left her keys on the table in the hallway; Jed picked them up and slipped them into his pocket. Obviously, he intended to stay.

"Danny wrote you a prescription for painkillers," he said, walking back to the living room. "I'll go get it filled for you. I can pick up something for us to eat at the same time, or I can cook something once I get back. What do you feel like having?"

Ellie took a deep breath, struggling to maintain her composure. Who did Jed think he was? He'd made her feel like a fool on Raven's Island and raked her over the coals in Lynn's office. Finally, to top it all off, he'd threatened her with professional ruin. Did he really think she wanted him around?

"Look, Mr. Thornhill—"

"Do you have to keep calling me that?" he asked.

"It's your name."

He sat down beside her on the couch, a teasing smile on his face. "Why don't you try Jed? It's easier. It only has one syllable." He stroked her hair, very gently. She should have been repelled by his touch, but wasn't. The accident had made her susceptible to any show of kindness or warmth. "You didn't have a problem calling me Jed on Raven's Island. If I remember correctly, during our last meeting you—"

"A meeting I'd prefer to forget," Ellie interrupted. She summoned up every last ounce of outrage. How could he bring that up? Didn't he remember how upset she'd been afterward? "The one I care about took place this morning. We were playing a scene from the Spanish Inquisition with you as Torquemada. Not long afterward, you ordered me to have dinner with you or kiss my career goodbye. Given the way you've treated me, can you think of any reason why I would willingly endure your company?"

"I can think of several," he answered blandly. "One, you're obviously in pain. Two, you're probably hungry.

And three, Danny said it would be better not to leave you alone. I happen to be here and I'd like to help."

"I didn't know you were such a humanitarian," Ellie retorted.

Jed's jaw clenched in irritation. Ellie steeled herself for a tirade about how ungrateful she was, but it never came. Instead, Jed put his arm around her and took her hand. She stiffened defensively, but a confusingly large part of her felt warm and protected. The urge to stop fighting him and put herself in his hands was very strong.

"You've had a horrible day," he said quietly. "I understand that this morning didn't help any, but I can't take back the things I said. Believe me, none of it was personal. I didn't want to argue with you." He paused. "Let's forget about this morning and call a truce, just for one evening. Later, when you're back in peak condition, we can go another eight rounds in the ring."

His gentle humor destroyed the little resistance Ellie had left. He was right about the pain and hunger. She could have used some medication, and the simple act of making herself something to eat seemed like a monumental undertaking. The need to be cared for and coddled was stronger than any competing emotion.

"All right," she said.

He slid his hand to the back of her neck and kneaded the tautened muscles there. She felt as if a pair of tightly coiled springs were slowly beginning to unwind. The pain in her head was still there, but it was receding into the distance. She closed her eyes and let her head droop forward.

"Danny said you need to relax," Jed murmured. "Does this help?"

"It feels wonderful," Ellie admitted.

His hands moved down to her shoulder blades. After a moment, his lips dropped to where his fingers had been and nuzzled the nape of her neck. She realized that it was the touch of a lover, not a sympathetic friend.

She felt as if she were floating. Instead of the fear and uncertainty she always experienced with Jed, there were only warmth and pleasure. Maybe she was too exhausted to feel threatened.

"I'd better get going." He reluctantly straightened. "Promise me you won't start brooding while I'm gone, either about what a louse I am or what happened to your new car." He pressed his lips to the back of her head, giving her a final, gentle kiss. He didn't seem to notice that she never answered him.

Jed told himself it was a good thing he had pills to pick up and dinner to buy. Another few minutes with Ellie and he would have wanted to do a lot more than kiss the nape of her neck. He wasn't sure whether that made him crazy or depraved, only that it was a bad idea.

She was in no shape for lovemaking. He should have known better than even to fantasize about it, especially given the suspicions he still had. He shook his head, not wanting to believe them. She was so defenseless, so sweet and responsive. He couldn't picture her coolly conning Cludds out of tens of thousands of dollars. His instincts said it was impossible.

He was beginning to realize that Lynn was right. He could tell himself over and over that he wasn't going to get mixed up with a crook, but he wanted to get mixed up with Ellie Landau in the worst way. Maybe it was time to forget about logic and listen to his emotions.

He double-parked in front of a drugstore, telling himself there had to be another explanation for those deposits. Maybe if he could get her to relax... Some pills for the pain, some food for the stomach, some music for the soul—maybe she would confide in him. He smiled at his train of thought. If he didn't watch himself, he would wind up spilling his guts about his suspicions. He couldn't afford to do that. If she was guilty, she would realize she was a suspect, and if she was innocent, she would realize he hadn't trusted her. He had to be careful about what he said. He had to be even more careful about what he permitted himself to do.

What happened to your new car. The words were pounding in Ellie's ears. How could she have forgotten about the accident, even for fifteen minutes? Her car hadn't skidded on its own. Somebody had cut the brake-fluid line. Somebody had wanted her dead.

How had Jed known she drove a new car? Why had he insisted that the people playing Death on Raven's Island should all be connected to Cludds? Why had he given her such a hard time this morning? Was there supposed to be a murder on Raven's Island? A real murder? She remembered a gloved hand stealing its way past her door, pointing a kitchen knife at her, and got light-headed with fear.

She began to tremble. My God, somebody on the island had searched her room earlier that same day. Maybe they had wanted a look at Cludds's records rather than at Ellie White's personal belongings. She had circled figures on the printouts to indicate where they didn't make sense, and she had written a pageful of questions and notes. It must have been obvious that she was onto something, even if she didn't know what it was. Was that why somebody had come after her with a knife?

Did Jed want to get rid of her—at any cost? On the face of it, the thought was preposterous. Jed had probably seen the Oldsmobile parked next to his Porsche and realized it had to be hers. Granted, he'd gone to a lot of trouble to arrange Death on Raven's Island, but the challenge had probably appealed to him. Why do something simple when you could have the satisfaction of arranging something complicated and difficult?

Besides, Jed didn't need to steal from Cludds. He was a millionaire. He was the one who had given her name to Lynn in the first place.

She pressed her fingers to her temples, struggling to think logically. Even millionaires could have financial problems. Sometimes the unlikeliest people found themselves short of cash. Financial empires that looked rock solid to outsiders could be built on foundations of quicksand. They could sink with staggering speed.

But *Jed's* empire? His family was loaded. They controlled a bank, for heaven's sake.

A bank, she argued back, where Cludds maintained an account. Given Jed's relationship with Lynn and his position at the bank, it would have been simple for him to transfer funds from Cludds's account to his own and alter both sets of records so the transaction would never be caught.

But then, why give Lynn the names of four respected management consultants? Did he think the first three were too big to delve deeply enough into Cludds's problems to uncover the fact that fraud was responsible? And did he think Ellie was too small or inexperienced?

On the other hand, Jed wasn't the only one who'd had the opportunity to cut her brake-fluid line. So had everyone else in the building—Lynn Cludd, Abby Cludd, and Rosemary McKay. It could even have been Marty, who had still been on the island when Ellie had been attacked with a knife. She had no way of knowing who might have been at Cludds that morning.

She knew only one thing. None of those other people had the keys to her apartment. None of them would be back at any time. And none of them intended to spend the evening with her. She was suddenly very, very frightened.

She sat there feeling nauseous and weak. Her headache was worse than ever and the cut on her forehead had begun to throb. She had to get out of the apartment. She couldn't wait here, a sitting duck for a murderer.

She stood up, then staggered and almost fell. She grabbed the arm of the couch to steady herself. She was dizzy from lack of food. Why hadn't she eaten at the hospital? She forced herself to go on, then froze in sheer panic at the sound of a key being inserted into her lock. Jed was back already.

The only thing she could think to do was dash into the kitchen and grab something to defend herself with. It was more of a drunken weave than a run, but she managed to get hold of a knife. Jed opened the door just as her fingers closed around the handle. A moment later, he called her name. She walked back into the entry hall with her arm extended and the knife grasped tightly in her hand.

Jed's hands were full with a sack of Chinese food and a smaller bag from the drugstore. He saw Ellie's knife at once, pointing at his chest, and almost shoved the packages onto the table in order to take it away. He stopped himself just in time. Ellie was high-strung to begin with and the day's events hadn't helped any. He didn't know what she was doing with the knife, but maybe she didn't either. It was best to ignore it—unless she tried to use it on either him or herself.

He smiled his most reassuring smile and started toward the dining room. Still, he was careful not to lose sight of her right hand. "I didn't know what you like, so I got a bunch of different things—shrimp with lobster sauce, mandarin chicken, beef with asparagus. There's also some wonton soup and a couple of different appetizers. I figured you could have the leftovers for lunch or dinner tomorrow."

She followed him into the dining room, not speaking. Once he'd set the sack of food on the table, he held out the bag from the drugstore. "Your pills."

Ellie looked at the bag the way a starving but abused dog looks at a strange human being who's holding out a slab of steak. She longed for the relief the pills offered but was afraid to take them. Then she noticed that the bag was stapled closed with the receipt attached to the outside. She knew that particular drugstore. They always closed their packages that way.

She snatched away the bag and hurried into the bathroom. Once she had locked the door, she examined the bag for signs that it might have been tampered with. There were none. The medicine, which was in a plastic bottle stuffed tightly with cotton, was in tablet form. It was hard to poison tablets. Besides, she desperately needed the relief they could give her. The recommended dosage was one or two, but she took three—from the bottom of the bottle.

By the time she returned to the dining room, Jed had set the table and unpacked the food. She sat down opposite him, placing the kitchen knife between her plate and the edge of the table. He gave it a furtive look and then picked up a ladle.

"How about some soup?" he said.

Ellie nodded. She watched him ladle out the soup, then realized he could have put poison in her bowl before he filled it up. She hadn't gotten a look inside. "Change bowls with me," she said. The look on Jed's face indicated that her deck was probably short a few aces, but he did as she'd asked.

Then it occurred to her that he might have anticipated her demand. "I have a thing about tasting new foods. I've never tried this particular restaurant. Taste the soup and tell me if it's any good." She pushed her bowl back across the table, indicating he should take his sample from *her* portion.

Without a word, he dipped his spoon into her soup. After a few sips he gave a shrug. "It's not great, but it's okay. They could have gone a little lighter on the salt."

Ellie was so hungry she could have swallowed the whole container, but she wasn't positive that the soup itself hadn't been doctored. She took the precaution of matching Jed sip for sip. If something was in there, he was damn well going to drink as much of it as she did.

She skipped the appetizers. She didn't trust something like an egg roll or a spare rib, where an individual piece of food could be poisoned. Jed coughed to cover his laughter when she mixed up the contents of each carton with tornadolike thoroughness, but he didn't make any comment. He even tasted each dish first, without her having to ask, but she noticed he was hard-pressed not to smile.

Both of them were very hungry. They ate quickly and silently, finishing about half the food. By the time Ellie pushed aside her plate, she felt a lot less tense. The pills she'd taken were probably responsible—they'd contained a narcotic—but that was okay. At least the pain was less awful. So was the fear. She couldn't concentrate on any one thing long enough to work up a feeling of panic.

Jed started to clear away the dishes and told her to lie down on the couch. She nodded and stood up, almost forgetting her knife. The feel of it in her hand reminded her that Jed might be dangerous. Now that he'd fed her, he had no further reason to stay. As far as the leftovers were concerned, she intended to throw every last bit of them out. Who knew what he would do to them in the kitchen?

Jed smiled to himself as Ellie wobbled away with her knife. Between the aftereffects of the accident and the pills, her mind was obviously playing tricks on her. Mentally, at least, she was back on Raven's Island, confusing Jed with the murderous character he'd portrayed. Her shenanigans with the food had been funny, but he couldn't say the same about the knife. Anything that sharp was inherently dangerous.

She was curled up on the couch when he returned to the living room. One look at him, and her hand closed over her knife. Jed winced, thinking he had to get the damn thing away from her before she stabbed herself.

He was about to sit down beside her when she thanked him for all he'd done and told him he could leave. Her speech was a little slurred, with the words spoken in a sing-song cadence. The pills had done their job better than he'd realized. He didn't dare leave her alone—she was too spaced out.

He knelt down beside her, willing himself to be gentle and patient. He had to get through to her. "This isn't Raven's Island, Ellie. I'm not Jed Thorpe anymore." He slipped off his jacket and laid it across her lap. "You can check the pockets." She immediately began to do so. "See? There are no knives or guns." Just to underscore the point, he emptied the pockets of his trousers onto her lap and turned them inside out. He was putting everything back when he remembered an incident from the game. Standing up, he slipped off his shoes and put a foot up on the couch. "Remember when you searched me in the observatory? The knife was in my sock." He raised a trouser leg. "See? No knife." He repeated the process with the other leg, then took back his jacket and laid it over the back of the couch. "You've had a bad day and the painkillers have left you a little doped up. You're confusing illusion with reality. I'm here to take care of you, not to harm you."

Ellie blinked at him, trying to focus her thoughts. It was getting harder and harder. Would Jed try so hard to reassure her if he were really a murderer? He might, if he was trying to catch her off guard.

She pointed to a chair on the other side of the coffee table. "Go sit over there. I don't trust you. I don't want you so close to me."

He went, but not without giving a frustrated sigh. Then, visibly forcing himself to be patient, he changed the subject to something innocuous. "The more time I spend in this room, the better I like it. Did you do it on your own or did a decorator help you?"

Ellie told herself she didn't mind making small talk as long as Jed kept his distance. A few more minutes alone with him wouldn't hurt her. "On my own, mostly. My older sister Carol came up for a few days and helped. She thought I was crazy, but she loves to shop." Ellie's thoughts jumped back a couple of months. She could see herself staring at the check, knowing she should save it but not wanting to. "It was funny about that check," she said, too woozy to realize Jed would have no idea what she was talking about. "I'd known it was coming for a long time, ever since my grandfather set up the trust fund. I was twenty-six in May. Every year for the next three years, at the end of May—that's when I get the money. And then there's the trust fund my grandmother set up. Not his widow—the other one. She did it the same way, only the date is more flexible. The assets are less liquid. Well, you know, for Carol it wasn't a problem. She's got three kids and everything she wants, so she puts away the money for their education. But I don't have any kids." Ellie giggled at the image of herself with children. Talk about pure fantasy! "Nope, no kids. It would have had to be an immaculate conception. You'd think three grandchildren would be enough for anyone, but all I ever hear from my parents is, 'Settle down, get married, have a family.' Do your parents ever nag you that way?"

Jed was doing his best to make sense of Ellie's ramblings. If he understood correctly, grandparents on both sides of her family had established trust funds for her and her sister. The money had come to each of them starting when they were twenty-six. It certainly explained those suspicious deposits—assuming she was telling the truth.

Hell, he thought, she's so out of it, how could she be doing anything else? She didn't have the presence of mind to pick up on his suspicions and offer explanations, all the while pretending they had slipped out in a drug-induced haze. Besides, her claim would be easy to check. She had to be telling the truth.

"Sometimes they do," he answered. "My younger sister plans to have children, but my parents have an obsession about carrying on the family name—as if there aren't enough Thornhills in Boston."

"At least you've been engaged." She sighed sadly. "I've never been engaged. I've never even gone steady. I'm sorry your fiancée ran off with a lion tamer. Did you love her very much?"

Although Jed wondered how Ellie knew about Kathryn, it wasn't a subject he cared to discuss. He ignored her question and went back to their original topic. "About your apartment—are you saying you used money from a trust fund to buy the furniture?"

"I blew the entire first payment on furniture and most of the second on a new car," she agreed, staring at her toes as she wiggled them under the blanket. "And you know what? I was going to invest it. It was supposed to be a cushion. I haven't taken a dime from my parents since I finished school. School cost a fortune. I went to school forever. It didn't seem fair to spend so much of their money." She jerked up her head, as if she'd suddenly remembered that Jed was in the room. "I've had some tough times. Six months ago I was living in a third-floor walk-up. In Allston. I shared it with a friend, but her boyfriend was always around and I got tired of sleeping on the couch. Then my business picked up, so I took better office space and moved into this place—because I knew I'd have the money in case things slowed down again. So what did I do? Logical, sensible Ellie? I blew the money on furniture and a fancy car!" She sobered abruptly. "I really loved that car. Do you love your Porsche?"

Jed assured her that he liked the Porsche very much. Lynn had talked him into buying it, saying it was part of learning to enjoy life. From the way Ellie talked, she was just as conventional as he was. Maybe even more so.

"It doesn't hurt to do crazy things once in a while," he said. "It keeps you from getting into a rut."

"Well, maybe. I only did one other crazy thing in my life, and I guess it turned out okay. I decided to become a management consultant instead of a math professor. In the beginning I was almost totally unqualified. Some nerve, huh?"

Her hand drifted back to the knife. Jed blanched when she ran a finger up and down the wrong side of the blade. She picked it up and held it in front of her face, then continued to trace its contours with her finger. "What have you done that's crazy?" she asked.

"I bought Skulduggery Enterprises because I thought it would be fun to own. I'm tying up money that would earn more of a return elsewhere." Jed stood up, unable to keep watching her with the knife. As he walked over to the couch, he continued, "I skipped an important business meeting to take Lynn to Paris last spring. We had dinner with Marty Cludd. Come to think of it, maybe that's why she wanted to go—to see Marty." He reached for the knife. "I wouldn't be surprised if the two of them got married. The chemistry is obviously right, and it would keep the family business together."

Ellie was so interested in what Jed was saying about Lynn and Marty that she almost let him have her knife. At the last minute her fingers tightened around the handle, though, and both of them pulled. She couldn't get any power into her grip—her fingers weren't working right. It was child's play for Jed to win the tug-of-war.

She stared at his hand, but the menace she knew she should feel was off in the distance somewhere, floating in a narcotic fog. She told Jed to give back the knife, that she needed to hold it, but he paid no attention to her. He placed the knife on the end table by her feet instead, then sat down beside her on the couch.

"At the rate you're going, you'll slice off one of your fingers." His tone was both amused and indulgent. "If it makes you feel safer to have the knife close by, fine; but no more picking it up and fiddling with it."

Ellie looked into his eyes, saw sternness along with the tenderness, and wondered if she was crazy not to fear him. He could pick up the knife and stab her. He could strangle her with his bare hands. Maybe she should have been screaming her head off and running for dear life, but those eyes... A man who could look at her so gently couldn't possibly want to harm her. Could he?

He ran his finger down her cheek and tilted up her chin. Then he lowered his mouth to her own. The touch of his lips was warm and reassuring rather than passionate. Ellie vaguely remembered what had happened the last time he'd kissed her—he'd slashed her throat immediately afterward—but the incident belonged to a different time and another world. Besides, the knife was out of his reach. She allowed him to put his arms around her and hold her close.

A warm pleasure suffused her body as his mouth moved lazily over hers. The fog swirling around her head made the world seem fluid and insubstantial. Nothing could penetrate it, not even the white-hot passion she'd always felt in Jed's arms.

She was responsive but unnaturally calm, as if Jed had roused her from a deep sleep to make love to her and she still hadn't fully awoken. When he ran his tongue along her lips she obediently parted them, willing to give him whatever he wanted. He pulled away for a moment, breathing a little too fast, but then he slipped his tongue inside her mouth and moved his hand to her breast.

She had the sense that time had slowed down. There was a languid sensuality about the way he kissed her, taking his time to explore and arouse. Somewhere along the line he started to undo the buttons on her blouse, but she wasn't aware of it until he deftly unsnapped her bra. She gave a sigh of pleasure as he moved his palm back and forth across her bare, taut nipples.

There was no frustration in her, no urgency. She was too woozy for that. There was only the tranquil enjoyment of being caressed and kissed. A kitten would have purred with contentment, but Ellie, being human, had to settle for throaty little moans.

Jed broke things off with bewildering abruptness. "That's enough, sweetheart. I should be letting you sleep, not making love to you." He pulled the two sides of her blouse together and started to button it up.

Ellie didn't follow that at all. "Why not? It was nice."

Jed thought it had been nice, too—too nice. It was bad enough that he'd kissed a woman who barely knew what planet she was on; even worse, he was picturing her in his bed, naked under the covers and shyly waiting for him to join her. Worst of all, he had made a second purchase at the drugstore in addition to the pills. Then, like a high-school kid hoping to score, he'd shoved the foil packets in his wallet in case he needed them.

He smoothed Ellie's hair and eased her out of his arms. What had she said about kids? Something about an immaculate conception? It sounded as if he'd gotten himself mixed up with a virgin. It was horribly chauvinistic of him, but he sort of liked the idea.

Those foil packets were going to come in handy eventually. The raw hunger he felt whenever he held her in his arms was going to get the better of him. She didn't seem inclined to stop him, and it was getting harder and harder to stop himself.

She smiled groggily and he felt a surge of raw possessiveness. "You never answered my question," she said.

"Your question? Oh, *that* question." He smiled back. "The truth is that my nerves are close to shot. You're very beautiful and very desirable. Those noises you make should be banned in Boston. Another minute of kissing you on

Raven's Island and I would have forgotten about the game. Another minute of kissing you here and I would have forgotten about your accident. As soon as you feel better I'm going to take you someplace romantic and isolated and make love to you until both of us collapse.''

Ellie couldn't believe the things Jed was saying to her. Men never spoke to her that way. Why did she feel safe when she should have been panicking? Why was the thought of having him seduce her so exciting? "Do I really affect you that way?" she asked.

"You don't know the half of it," he muttered.

"But what about Kathryn? Aren't you still in love with her? I mean, the way she left you . . .'' Her voice trailed off. Maybe she shouldn't have brought it up. It was really none of her business.

Jed was silent for so long that her thoughts began to wander. Her ability to concentrate was worse than ever. Then, out of the blue, he was telling her that he and Kathryn had gone together for years, finally become engaged, but they had always put off setting a date for the wedding. He admitted that he'd dragged his heels more than she had. He could only believe that he hadn't been sure of what he'd wanted, because otherwise he would have taken that final step instead of consistently shying away from it. He'd thought of himself as being in love with her, and yet the idea of marriage had terrified him.

He'd been hurt and embarrassed when she'd run off with somebody else, but he couldn't really blame her. Obviously she'd gotten tired of waiting. He'd missed her, but not as much as he should have. He'd still been able to work. He hadn't felt like dating, though. Still, he hadn't sat home all the time. He'd gone out with family and friends, most notably Lynn Cludd. She was lively and undemanding and they'd had a great time together.

Once he got started there was no stopping him. Ellie had trouble focusing on what he was saying, but she got the general idea. He had a problem making commitments. She was so tired that in the end she closed her eyes and drifted off to sleep.

Chapter Twelve

Jed had a self-deprecating smile on his face as he got up from the couch. *You're an exciting guy, Thornhill. The story of your life was so mesmerizing it put her straight to sleep.*

Why had he started spewing out words the way a volcano spews lava when only half an hour before he'd responded to her question about Kathryn by changing the subject? Because he was in love with Ellie Landau and he'd finally admitted it to himself. Her pain and vulnerability had taken what was left of his heart and totally conquered it.

He believed her story about the trust funds. Her only fault, assuming she had any at all, was a certain naiveté about why companies sometimes lost money. He was picturing a future with her, and when you pictured a future with a woman, you had to answer her honestly about your past. It didn't occur to him that in four years with Kathryn he'd never felt compelled to bare his soul that way.

He picked up the knife and took it into the kitchen. Then he made himself some coffee, helped himself to some magazines, and returned to the living room to read and relax. He figured he could carry Ellie into bed later and sleep on her couch. Then, tomorrow morning, they could make plans for the rest of the weekend.

He was in the middle of the latest *Newsweek* when the telephone rang. He dashed into the kitchen to answer it, hoping it hadn't woken Ellie up. Who in the hell was calling her at ten-thirty?

He recognized the woman's voice at once—it was Abby Cludd. When she asked to speak to Ellie, he told her Ellie had been in a serious auto accident and was sleeping. Then he identified himself and offered to take a message.

Abby was congenitally nervous—Jed knew that—but the news of Ellie's accident agitated her past anything he had anticipated. She started babbling about an appointment she'd made with Ellie, an appointment Ellie had never kept.

"I should have known it wasn't like her," she said. "I was afraid—if only we could have been alone—I wanted to warn her but I had myself to think about. And then I thought—but it doesn't matter. I left and I tried to forget but I couldn't. I should have called earlier but I was too selfish."

"Of course you weren't," Jed said soothingly, trying to calm her down. Ellie suddenly got up from the couch, and, zombielike, started toward the kitchen. He didn't want her to have to deal with a hysterical Abby Cludd. She was in no shape for that.

"I'll be glad to take a message," he repeated into the phone. His crisp tone of voice was meant to bring the conversation to a close.

"But don't you see?" Abby demanded. "It wasn't an accident. She has to give this up. Tell her she has to stop."

"I understand," Jed said, even though he didn't understand at all. What did she mean, "It wasn't an accident?" Was she saying somebody had tampered with Ellie's car?

"You don't!" Abby shrieked out the accusation. "If she doesn't stop she'll be killed. You, too. Everybody. You're all in danger. I can't say more. Promise me you'll let it alone."

Jed smiled and nodded. Ellie had just reached the kitchen and he'd be damned if he was going to let her take the phone. "Well, I'll certainly pass that on," he said to Abby. "Ellie will be back at work next week. She'll call you."

"No! You can't hang up! You have to listen." There was a brief pause, fraught with fear and indecision. "Meet me. I'll tell you all about it. I can't let it go any further, even if they send me to jail. Eleven-fifteen at Christopher's."

"Fine," Jed said. He knew the place she meant. It was a college hangout in Cambridge that stayed open till well past midnight. "I'll pass along your best wishes to Ellie. Good night."

"You'll be there?"

"Yes, that's right. Good night, Abby." Jed hung up the phone, relieved to be rid of the woman but shaken by what she'd said. If she was right and Ellie's brake problem hadn't been accidental—the implications were chilling. Somebody was stealing from Cludds all right, but it wasn't Ellie. On the contrary, the thief was so afraid of what Ellie might find out that he or she had decided to remove her from the picture—permanently.

Jed had no intention of frightening Ellie with something that might be either a figment of Abby's imagination or pure speculation. "That was Abby Cludd," he said. "She said she was sorry she missed you this afternoon. She wanted to show you some corrected printouts based on the invoices she'd been checking. She seemed to think you would accuse her of making the mistakes deliberately. I told her not to worry, that you would straighten it out next week."

Ellie had awoken with a start at the sound of the ringing telephone. She'd been disoriented at first, but the pills had started to wear off by then and her head was a lot more clear. Her first thought was that she'd fallen asleep with Jed in the apartment and might have been killed. She wondered how she could have been so stupid.

It hadn't taken long to remember his gentleness and his kisses, and to realize she was very much alive. Her fears had disappeared, but then she'd walked into the kitchen and heard him talking to Abby. He'd sounded too smooth, too calm. She was sure he was hiding something from her. His glib explanation about the reason for Abby's call just didn't add up. If that was all she'd wanted, why hadn't she phoned at a more reasonable time?

It was pointless to question him. He would only lie. "You don't need to stay here," she said. "I feel a lot better now." She would be safe once he left. She would also be able to call Abby back and find out what she'd really wanted.

"Okay, but let me get you into bed first," he answered. "I want to make sure you have everything you need."

More suspicious than ever, Ellie walked into the bedroom. Why was Jed so willing to leave when he'd previously refused to budge? She'd expected to have to fight him tooth and nail. She grabbed her pajamas and took them into the bathroom. Her covers were turned down when she returned to the bedroom, and a glass of water was sitting on her night table.

"You should wait another hour before you take any more of those," Jed said, looking at the bottle she'd carried in from the bathroom.

"I will." Ellie got into bed, thinking she would have to get herself a different glass of water. She wasn't taking any chances.

"I'll call you in the morning, then." He bent down and kissed her on the forehead. "Good night, darling."

The "darling" made her even more uneasy. They didn't know each other well enough for words like that. Was he trying to gain her confidence, and if so, why? She waited for the front door to close, then lay back in bed, confused but relieved. He was gone and she was safe. Nothing else mattered.

Reality set in with a sickening thud when she poured herself a fresh glass of water. She left it on the bathroom counter and rushed to the front door. Both locks were locked, but you needed a key to turn the top one from the outside. Jed had taken her keys, damn him! He hadn't argued about leaving because he planned on coming back.

There was a push-button lock on her bedroom door, but it wasn't very strong. Ellie could think of only one way to ensure her safety—by moving her dresser in front of the door. It was an antique and very heavy, and the effort left her exhausted. She collapsed onto her bed afterward, breathless and a little dizzy.

If Jed tried to break down the door, she would climb out the window onto the first-story roof and go down the rope ladder that served as a fire escape. Jan and her family would be home by midnight, so help would eventually be available. All she had to do was hang on a little longer.

She found an A. D. Cludd listed in the south suburban phone book, at an address in Quincy, and quickly dialed the number. Five seconds later, she hung up in disgust—she'd reached Abby's telephone answering machine. Abby must have turned it on just before going to bed. Ellie tried again fifteen minutes later, just to be sure, and reached the same recording. This time she left a message. Her head had begun to hurt again. She took another couple of pills, then turned off the lights and tried to sleep.

Christopher's was located on Massachusetts Avenue, not far from Harvard Square. The wet weather had made the congestion in the area even worse than usual, but Jed managed to find a parking space on a nearby side street when a VW pulled out ahead of him. He walked into the restaurant about five after eleven and sat down at a table to wait.

He ordered a cup of coffee and helped himself to somebody's discarded newspaper. Eleven-fifteen came and went, and then eleven-thirty. He started to grow impatient. Abby Cludd was so timid and paranoiac that you never knew *what* she was going to do. Maybe she was sitting in her car someplace, agonizing about whether to trust him. Maybe she had decided that her imagination had manufactured a crisis where none existed, and she wasn't going to come at all. How long was he supposed to wait?

After another ten minutes he decided to call her. The number he got from information turned out to be the correct one, but he reached an answering machine with the usual sort of recorded message. Either she'd gone out or she didn't want to be disturbed. He didn't put it past her to turn on the machine as a way of avoiding an irate call from him about why she'd stood him up.

He returned to his seat and ordered another cup of coffee. The minutes seemed to drag at a tenth their normal rate. He didn't know whether to leave or keep waiting. He eventually decided to give Abby until midnight.

When panic hit him, it was sudden, sharp and overwhelming. He was sitting here in Christopher's and Ellie was alone at home. How much did he really know about Abby Cludd? Lynn called her "the saint," but maybe she'd stuck around Cludds all these years in order to fleece the place out of a fortune.

She might have arranged Ellie's "accident." She might have called Ellie's house to check on the outcome, learned that Ellie was alive and able to continue working, and decided to finish what she'd started. She would have had to lure Jed out of the house first, something she'd accomplished with impressive efficiency. He slapped some money down on the table and ran out of the restaurant.

Ellie was too agitated to sleep soundly, but she wasn't exactly awake, either. The pills she'd taken made her feel as if she was floating in her own private movie theater while a series of short, surrealistic films played on some internal screen.

First, a romance. Jed was kissing her neck and ear.

She stirred at the sound of a car passing by. The students inside it were laughing and shouting.

Next, a mystery. She was on Raven's Island, searching the woods for clues.

The caterwauling of the neighborhood tomcat brought her back to reality.

Finally, a horror film. Somebody was chasing her down the alley behind her old apartment. She could hear his footsteps pounding behind her, coming closer and closer.

She opened her eyes with a start, but the only sound in the room was the wild beating of her own heart.

It began to rain again. She curled up under the covers and focused on the rhythmic slapping of the droplets against her windowpanes. Jan was due home any time now. Ellie closed her eyes, wondering if she would be able to hear the Pottses' car pull into the driveway. It was stupid to stay here alone when she could spend the rest of the night in their guest room.

A tiny squeak caught her attention. She rolled over, seeking the source of the noise, and realized that the wind must have rustled the screen in the window above her desk. A second, identical squeak followed a few seconds later, but she ignored it.

A ripping sound came next. It was so faint that Ellie barely heard it over the rain and wind, but some small part of her knew it didn't belong. More alert now, she struggled to sit up and then looked toward the window. It was too dark out to see anything. A little frightened now, she leaned closer to the sound and squinted into the blackness.

The window itself was locked, and the screen outside it was held in place from the inside, by means of a hook and eye. Ellie picked up some movement on the roof, and then, in a terrifying flash of lightning, she saw a dark, hulking form squatting behind the window. Her heart started pounding in her ears and her body grew taut with adrenaline.

A gloved hand reached through the hole in the screen and unlatched it. Ellie threw aside her covers. The screen was suddenly yanked free and thrown to the side. Ellie bolted out of bed, her knees buckling as her feet hit the ground. Looking back over her shoulder, she could see whoever was out there trying to force open the window.

She was staggering across the room when she heard the glass in one of the windowpanes shatter. All the intruder had to do was knock away the sharp shards of glass and reach inside, and the lock could be turned. The window tended to swell in the wet weather, but anyone with a reasonable amount of strength would be able to get it open.

Ellie fell against the chest she'd pushed across the door earlier that night and pressed as hard as she could. Nothing happened. She felt so weak. The chest was so heavy. Dear God, suppose she couldn't move it? Panic set in, giving her a strength she hadn't possessed before. She put her shoulder against the wood and pushed fiercely, and the chest began to edge to the side.

She was panting now, sweating with the effort it took to move the dresser. The window gave a grinding creak as it was slowly forced up. Shaking now, Ellie let out a convulsive, bloodcurdling shriek. She threw her body against the side of the chest with reckless disregard for her injuries.

Just as the chest finally cleared the door, Ellie heard someone scream out her name. She recognized Jed's voice, but he was somewhere far away, on the other side of the bedroom door. She clawed at the doorknob, yelling back to him. Directly behind her, the china lamp sitting on her desk was knocked to the floor and shattered with a loud crash. Ellie called Jed's name again and yanked open the door. He was running through the living room when she stumbled out of the bedroom. She burst into tears and flung herself into his arms.

For the first ten or fifteen seconds, she couldn't get out a word. She was shivering violently and choking back sobs. He led her into the dining room and took her back in his arms. "It's okay now," he murmured. "I'm here. I won't let anything happen to you."

Ellie heard him and believed him. He was the only bit of sanity in a world gone mad. "In the bedroom," she finally managed to tell him. "Somebody broke the window. Somebody is trying to kill me. Oh, God, Jed!" She began to sob again, overcome by a day full of tension and terror.

Jed was almost as shaken as Ellie. His memories were like waking nightmares. The nameless dread as he'd run to his car and sped to Ellie's house...the dry-mouthed fear as he'd dashed up the steps and heard her piercing scream...the moments of heart-stopping panic before she'd finally reached his side... He never wanted to live through anything like that again.

He kept his eyes on the archway between the living and dining rooms, but nobody came out of the bedroom. Leading Ellie to a chair, he said, "Sit here and wait while I check out the apartment." She gave him a glassy-eyed nod and implored him to be careful.

He grabbed a knife from the kitchen and walked back into the living room. His search was slow and methodical, starting with the entry-hall closet. He'd never been so scared in his life, or so fully alert. He turned on every light, checked out every possible hiding place. The living room— empty. The bathroom—empty. The bedroom—empty. The roof outside the window—empty as well. The attacker must have been afraid to take on two people at once.

When he returned to the dining room, Ellie was still huddled on the chair, motionless and waiting. He lifted her into his arms and carried her to the couch, settling her on his lap so he could hold her while they talked. "We'll need to call the police. Maybe there are fingerprints."

Ellie recognized the logic of what he was saying, but couldn't face the prospect of cold-eyed detectives asking endless questions. "Please, let it wait till tomorrow. I want to get out of this house. Take me home with you, Jed." Her voice grew hoarse with emotion. "You have no idea what I've been through today."

"The accident—"

"Wasn't an accident. Somebody cut my brake-fluid line. God help me, but I thought it was you. You were so awful to me this morning, and I knew you'd gone to a lot of trouble to arrange the weekend on Raven's Island. You seemed to be up to something suspicious. Then, after the accident, I realized that something was very wrong at Cludds—it looked more like embezzlement than mismanagement. I got it into my head you must have stolen the money and wanted me out of the way before I caught you."

Saying the words aloud brought home the absurdity of the idea. "I don't know how I could have been so stupid. The amount involved is a lot of money to someone like me, but to you—it's small change." She shook her head. "I feel so guilty about not trusting you. You've been so wonderful to me tonight, and here I thought you were trying to kill me."

"*You* feel guilty!" Jed gave her a sheepish smile, then admitted he'd reached the same conclusions about Cludds as she had, but suspected *her* of being the cause. After all, there were those large deposits to her personal bank account to explain.

Under other circumstances Ellie might have complained about how Jed had abused his position at the bank and violated her privacy, but none of that seemed important now. They were alive, they were together, and they were finally straightening out the misunderstandings of the past.

Far from being angry, she was grateful she'd even met him. He'd probably saved her life. Of course, their meeting hadn't been accidental. "Why were we on Raven's Island?" she asked. "What did you hope to accomplish?"

"Call it my personal version of *To Catch a Thief*," he answered. "I had the crazy idea that if I got the most likely suspects together and watched them closely enough, I would be able to pick out the embezzler. You were the most obvious candidate. A month after Lynn hired you, her profits took a nosedive, and then there was the way you played the game. You violated the rules without a second's hesitation if you thought you could get away with it." He kissed her on the nose. "You're obviously a sociopathic personality, sweetheart. Come on, let's get out of here. We can deal with the police tomorrow."

Ellie threw some clothes into a suitcase and scrawled a note to Jan. Jed sealed up the broken windowpane with cardboard and mailing tape and hammered a couple of nails into the frame so the window couldn't be opened. By the time they were settled in his car and on their way to Lexington, the day's traumatic events had begun to take on an unreal quality. Ellie was an ordinary person. How could such things have happened to her?

It wasn't until she was walking into Jed's house that she thought to ask him where he'd gone and why he'd come back. He explained about his conversation with Abby, saying that she'd never shown up. "I think she was the person outside your window. I think she lured me away from the apartment in order to get you alone."

Ellie couldn't believe it. "Abby was an elderly woman. She would have had to come up the rope ladder at the side of the house, and it isn't easy to climb even in good weather. Besides, she was having a horrible time with the new computer. She didn't have the skill to shift around funds and then cover it up."

"You're taking her at face value," Jed pointed out. "She was smart enough to be the controller of the company in everything but name for thirty or forty years. Everything about her—her frailty, her constant fear, her confusion about the computer—it could have been an expert act. For all we know, she's been stealing from Cludds for years.''

"But what if she wasn't? What if something is really wrong? I left a message on her answering machine but she never called me back.''

Jed put his arm around Ellie's shoulders. As far as he was concerned, Abby was either a psychopath, a coward or a nut case. He didn't much care which. His only concern was for Ellie.

"Nothing's happened to her," he said. "Assuming she didn't try to kill you, she's still mixed up in something she thinks could send her to jail. She probably decided her own neck was more important than yours. She must have turned on the answering machine to avoid having to speak to either one of us. We can talk about it in the morning, but right now you're going to bed.''

Ellie followed him into the guest room. She was almost too tired to think, much less argue with somebody as forceful as Jed was. She curled up under the covers and waited for exhaustion to overtake her.

Instead, her mind kept flashing back to the day's traumatic events—her car skidding out of control, the service manager telling her somebody had tried to kill her, the desperate struggle to move her chest and get out of her room. She started to tremble and couldn't stop. Rationally she knew she was safe here, but she didn't feel safe. Suppose they had followed Jed's car? They could break into his house, murder her while she lay sleeping in bed, and Jed, whose room was down the hall, would never know she was dead until he found her mutilated body in the morning.

She tried to calm herself by breathing deeply and evenly, but only succeeded in hyperventilating. Panic is an insidious thing. The more she tried to control it, the worse it got, until every shadow and sound belonged to the maniac who had tried to kill her.

Finally, she couldn't stand it a moment longer. She jumped out of bed and ran out of the room. The hall was dark except for a single strip of light shining out from under one of the doors. She ran up to it, pushed it open and then stood there clutching the doorknob, staring into the room beyond.

Jed was lying in bed reading, with Lucifer, his cat, sleeping by his feet. The covers were pulled to his waist, but not so far that Ellie couldn't see a glimpse of bare hip in addition to his chest. A glass of wine was sitting on the night table and half a dozen folders were scattered across his lap.

He gathered up the folders and set them aside, started to get up, and then hesitated. A moment later he shrugged and tossed aside the covers. Ellie blushed and looked away as he crossed the room to the closet. She heard the door open and close and then a soft laugh. "It's okay. I put a robe on."

Although the robe covered him from neck to calf, the image of his naked body had been burned into her mind. She felt a mixture of fascination and fear. Part of her wanted to touch him, part of her wanted to stare, and part of her wanted to run as fast as possible in the opposite direction.

"I guess this was the last straw," he said as he walked over to her. "After all you've been through, some big, hairy guy jumps out of bed and comes charging past you."

"You're not that hairy," Ellie mumbled. She couldn't bring herself to meet his eyes so she was staring at his waist instead. It was a mistake. He wanted her and it showed.

"You're supposed to tell me you like me the way I am." He put a finger under her chin to lift it up. "What's the matter, honey? Is the pain keeping you awake?"

"It's not that bad. The pills keep it under control." Ellie felt a mixture of nervousness, embarrassment and excitement. Jed's hand had been warm and tender against her face. It brought back memories of more intimate caresses.

"I guess my imagination got the better of me," she added. "I was afraid to stay by myself—afraid of being attacked."

"I can't imagine why!" Jed took her hand and led her to his bed. "Come on, spend the night with me. I shouldn't have left you alone."

"I won't disturb you?"

"You won't disturb me." Jed was lying through his teeth. Ellie disturbed him just by standing there, but he wasn't going to admit it. She needed protection and reassurance, not a confession about how hard it was to keep his hands off her.

"I guess it's okay, then," she said. "I'll stay on my own side of the bed and I won't hog the covers. Keep working if you want to. The light doesn't bother me."

Jed assured her he was ready to go to sleep and switched off the lamp. Then he lay there, wide awake, thinking about how badly he wanted to hold her. Not make love to her, just hold her, although he couldn't deny he would have liked to do both. He said good-night and turned his back to her.

Ellie was too tense to sleep. She might have been inexperienced about men but she wasn't deaf and blind. She knew what Jed was thinking. He wasn't the type to touch her after everything that had happened to her that day, but he would have liked to. She'd seen it in his body and heard it in his voice.

And what would she have liked? Not to lie there all night, isolated and frightened. She needed some human contact. She needed some human warmth. She needed to relax or she would never fall asleep.

She touched his shoulder. "Jed? Could I ask you a question?"

He rolled onto his back. "Hmm?"

"Would it bother you to hold me? I mean, I know you, uh, you feel—you want . . ." Her voice trailed off. How was she supposed to put this?

He took a deep breath and held out his arms. "Don't worry about me. I want to take care of you. Come on, I'll rub your back till you're sleepy."

Ellie edged closer and laid her head on his chest. He was the sweetest man in the world. How could she ever have distrusted him?

As she snuggled against his shoulder, the fabric of his robe scratched against the cut on her forehead. She winced with pain. "Can I get on the other side? Your robe was rubbing against my forehead . . ."

"Sure." He grasped her hips and gently lifted her up. "Just swing over me—that's it—let me give you some more room . . ."

Ellie's thighs brushed him intimately as she crossed over his body. She felt a hot tingling where her flesh had touched his. She wasn't so much frightened as confused. She would have said she was too tense and beaten up to feel sensations like that.

He slid his hand under her pajama top and started to massage her back. She sighed in contentment and nestled into the crook of his neck. Everything he did felt wonderful. Yawning, she curled her hand into a fist and burrowed it under his robe. His skin was smooth and a little damp. She enjoyed touching him. For the first time in her life, she felt that a man belonged to her—that she could give and take without having to ask permission or offer explanations.

His hand traveled from her neck to her scalp. "That's nice," she murmured. It was even better than the pills. She nuzzled his collarbone and slid her hand over to his arm, gently kneading his biceps. Her caresses were a way of saying thank-you, of telling him she was glad they were together.

He smoothed her hair and went to work on her shoulders. Ellie felt cherished and secure. Her trust in him was complete, even after his palm slipped under the waistband of her pajama bottoms. He massaged her buttocks and then reached lower, rubbing the backs of her legs. She moaned in appreciation. His touch was clinical and unthreatening, like a professional masseur's, but the local health club didn't provide the same sort of warm pleasure.

Thoroughly relaxed now, she ran her lips back and forth against his neck. "Your hand must be getting tired. You don't have to keep doing that."

"I'll stop when you're asleep." He slid his palm between her shoulder blades, stroking rather than rubbing now.

Ellie nodded and yawned. She doubted she would be able to sleep. She felt a disturbing warmth between her legs, and her breasts were swelling with the need to be touched. She recognized her stirring desire, but only in the haziest way. Her hand floated upward to stroke Jed's face. His lips were so soft. Her finger stole into his mouth and slipped between his teeth.

He inhaled sharply and forced her hand back down. "None of that. Go to sleep."

"None of what?" she asked groggily. She knew exactly what he meant, so she wasn't surprised when he didn't answer. She was pleased that she affected him that way. It made her feel feminine and desirable. "Was I turning you on?" she teased.

"Go to sleep," he repeated. Ellie couldn't tell whether he was genuinely annoyed or only trying to sound firm.

She didn't want to go to sleep. She wanted to be kissed. The more she thought about it, the more she wanted it, until it was impossible simply to lie there. She crept closer and raised her lips. When Jed ignored her invitation, she grasped his chin and turned his head toward her mouth, holding it only inches away from her own. She could feel his warm breath on her face.

Jed was fighting temptation for all he was worth and slowly but inexorably losing. Lovemaking was out of the question—he knew that—but when Ellie started running her finger back and forth across his lips, he told himself a few kisses wouldn't hurt anything. After all, he wasn't a kid anymore; he would keep things under control.

He remembered reading an article about desire being a normal human response to danger. Ellie had been through a lot and she needed a physical outlet. A little necking and she'd be ready to go to sleep. It was the least he could do for her.

He put his hand behind her head and turned onto his side. He was about to kiss her when she said his name in a smoky voice that was even sexier than the husky moans she was always making. This was going to be tougher than he'd thought.

Ellie parted her lips and waited. She felt the flick of Jed's tongue, the brush of his lips, and then, finally, the gentle possessiveness of his mouth. The slow, sweet kiss they shared deepened and grew hotter as the seconds ticked by. When the kiss was no longer enough, their arms went around each other's bodies and they strained to get as close to each other as they could. Ellie was content for a little while longer. It was enough to feel Jed's hard strength molding her softness, and to drown in the pleasure of his mouth.

She gradually began to need more. He wasn't touching her and she didn't know how to ask him to, so she pushed up her pajama top and shoved aside his robe. He buried his lips against her neck and, breathing hard, pulled back for a moment. Then he gave her what she wanted, covering her breast with his hand and roughly caressing the nipple.

She shuddered as he rolled her onto her back. He unbuttoned her pajama top and bent his mouth to her breasts. Pleasure had turned to raw excitement by then. She thought she wanted him as much as it was possible for a woman to want a man, but learned differently as soon as he slid her pajama bottoms down over her hips and slipped his hand between her legs. A few gentle caresses and she was burning up. He knew exactly where to touch her and how to tease her.

She knew she had to stop him. Too much more of it and she would explode. When her "No, don't..." had no effect on him, she pushed away his hand. "That's enough. I won't be able to wait."

His mouth returned to her lips. "Let me. I want to make you happy."

It took her a moment to understand his intention. "Only me? But what about you?"

"Another time," he said.

Ellie didn't want that at all. She wasn't that selfish, and besides, she wanted to become a part of him. She wanted him as close as it was possible to get. His body represented safety and security, and perhaps even a sort of oblivion.

"Now," she insisted. "I want you to make love to me. I want to know what it's like to feel you inside of me."

Jed couldn't believe what he was hearing—not from shy, inexperienced Ellie. He put it down to trauma, exhaustion and too many pills. Determined to be a gentleman about it, he said, "I promise you'll find out, but not tonight."

"But I want you to," she answered doggedly.

He realized he would have to be more specific. "Listen to me, darling. You're hurting enough already and I don't want to add to it. The first time you make love..." He paused, feeling uncharacteristically awkward. He'd never been in this particular situation before. "It might be painful. Trust me, okay? I know what I'm doing."

"You sure do," she said with a giggle.

"So let me keep doing it." He caressed her breast, felt the nipple harden against his palm, and fought down the ache in his loins. "It'll relax you. You'll see." As his hand moved lower, he made both of them a husky promise. "In a week or so, when you're feeling better, we can talk about this again." It wouldn't kill him to wait a week—not unless they kept sharing the same bed.

The idea of waiting a week struck Ellie as hysterically funny. Even the feel of Jed's hand stroking the inside of her thigh couldn't cut off the thought that popped into her head. "A week? I'll probably be dead in a week. I mean, how much longer can my luck hold out? First my car, then my house—somebody will probably plant a bomb in my office next."

"Don't talk like that," Jed muttered. "I'm not going to let anything happen to you."

Ellie scarcely heard him. She was thinking that she'd finally met a man she wanted to sleep with and it was crazy to wait. What good was virginity when you were six feet under? "Everyone should make love at least once before they die. If you're not interested, all you have to do is say so." She knew darn well he was interested. "If you're not going to make love to me, I'll go back to my apartment for the night."

Jed began to realize he was dealing with a deranged mind. Ellie had gotten it into her head that they should make love, and she wasn't going to change her mind, no matter what he said or did. How was he supposed to handle her?

The answer came flying back. Was there really any harm in giving her what she wanted? He'd be as careful as he could. If he inadvertently hurt her, he would stop. He was in love with her, for God's sake, and he fully intended to marry her. Deranged or not, she wouldn't have propositioned just anyone who happened to be handy. Obviously she had to care for him. He kissed her on the mouth, very gently, and told her he would be right back.

Jed was naked when he got into bed again. Ellie didn't know why he'd gone away, but his kiss had told her it wasn't for lack of interest. She'd taken off her pajamas and waited, a satisfied smile on her face.

She understood the reason for his absence once he'd taken her into his arms again. It wasn't as funny as that business about waiting a week, but it was close. "You don't have to worry about getting me pregnant," she said with a giggle. "I've already told you, I'll be dead—"

"I know. By next weekend at the latest." He sounded flustered. "If you don't mind, I'd rather not count on it. Now, do you think you could stop laughing long enough to let me make love to you?"

"Only if you stop saying funny things."

He shut her up by taking her lips. Her giddiness disappeared after a single, demanding kiss. He was the expert here, not she, and she was eager for the next lesson. His earlier lovemaking had taught her what to expect, but familiarity had only heightened her anticipation.

He teased her until she was white-hot with urgency, then suddenly stopped. She waited tensely as he fumbled in the night-table drawer. His fingers were cold and slick when they began to stroke her again, but the ice had turned into fire by the time he slipped them inside of her to mimic the act of love.

Then, finally, he moved on top of her and parted her thighs. She clutched his hips and moaned his name. There were no doubts or fears. He'd aroused her past the point of feeling anything but a desperate need for release. If there was pain she scarcely cared. After his first few careful thrusts, she was writhing underneath him, silently begging him to hurry his pace.

The playful touch of his fingers pushed her over the edge. The waves of pleasure went on and on until she was too spent to move. Jed stayed inside her while both of them caught their breath, and then rolled onto his back and settled her against his chest. Her ribs were a little sore and her forehead hurt, but it didn't matter. She'd never felt so at peace in her life. The last thing she heard before she drifted off to sleep was his soft, "I love you."

Chapter Thirteen

Ellie felt something tickle her cheek, opened her eyes and came face to face with Lucifer's whiskers. The cat let out a howl as Ellie looked at the clock. It was almost nine-thirty. She never slept this late.

The events of the previous day came rushing back. She felt as if she'd lived through a twenty-four-hour nightmare, but nightmares didn't leave you with stitches and sore ribs.

They didn't deposit you in strange beds, either. Ellie remembered exactly how she'd gotten there and exactly what had happened afterward. If she'd needed any reminders, her naked body and the bloodstained sheets would have provided them. Dear lord, how could she have done it? Had she been out of her mind last night? What had possessed her to throw herself at a man she'd known for a grand total of only eight days?

At least he wasn't in the bedroom. He had brought in her suitcase, though, and left it on the dresser. Ellie picked it up and carried it into the bathroom. If she had to face him, at least it would be with fresh clothing and clean hair.

She covered up her stitches with an oversized Band-Aid and turned on the shower. The hot water felt soothing on her back but painful against her face. She thought about taking another couple of painkillers but decided not to. They didn't help when it came to keeping a clear head.

She dried her hair with Jed's drier, thinking about having breakfast. Nervous or not, she was famished. That was probably a good sign.

Jed was standing in the middle of the bedroom when she walked out of the bathroom. Her eyes swept the room, avoiding him. She'd counted on having more time. He'd made up the bed and brought up some breakfast. The tray was sitting on the table by the window. Her heart began to race. How was she supposed to begin?

Jed forced back a smile, thinking that Ellie was the quintessence of morning-after regret. It wasn't very kind of him, but he was glad they'd made love. It would be harder for her to run away now, harder to pretend there was nothing between them.

He walked over to her and put his hands on her waist. She dropped her eyes but didn't move. Encouraged that she hadn't bolted out the door, he bent his head and pressed his lips to her neck. The clean, fresh scent of her made his senses reel. His physical response to her seemed to get stronger all the time. He felt her shudder and breathe in sharply.

"Good morning," he murmured. "I love you."

Ellie didn't know how she'd expected Jed to behave, but it wasn't like a bridegroom on the morning after his wedding night. Surely he had done this before. Did he think he had to cloak it in hearts and flowers?

"You don't have to say that." The way he was kissing her made her weak in the knees. He was so handsome she could almost forgive herself for what had happened the night before. "I'm not going to have hysterics because I'm not a virgin anymore," she said.

He smiled down at her. "Good. It's hard to propose to a woman who's having hysterics. Do you want to get married this afternoon? We could have the judge waive the waiting period."

"Get married?" Ellie was utterly astonished. It was a long couple of moments before she managed a response. "Jed, this is the twentieth century. You don't have to marry me just because we—just because you were the first one to sleep with me."

"I don't?" The smile turned into a wicked grin. "That's a hell of a deal. In that case, can we do it again sometime?"

Ellie felt herself redden. "I wish you'd be serious about this. Last night was—it was what happens when two people go through a lot together. One thing leads to another. You can't base a marriage on that. We hardly know each other."

"I know you well enough not to be surprised by what I'm hearing," Jed retorted. "Just for the record, I happen to be in love with you. As far as last night goes, I want you to look me in the eye and tell me the same thing would have happened with any other man you know. Suppose Marty had been waiting for you when Danny brought you home? Would you have wound up in *his* bed, handing him that line about wanting to feel him inside of you?"

Ellie wasn't just blushing now—she was scarlet with embarrassment. "How can you bring that up? You know I didn't—that I never would have said it except that—"

He cut her off. "I can bring it up because it was *me* you needed to be with last night, not just anyone. I'll accept the fact that you're confused, but don't stand there blaming everything on how rough a day you had. Not after twenty-six years of saying no to every guy who asked."

Ellie knew he was right—she did feel something special for him. She could remember their lovemaking with astonishing clarity—the intoxicating physical pleasure of his every caress and the deep emotional peace she'd felt afterward. "I know it was more than that," she admitted. "It's just— when I first saw you this morning it was like looking at a stranger. It must have been the same for you; so how can you talk about love and marriage? For heaven's sake, Jed, you went with Kathryn for years and you never could bring yourself to marry her. To propose to me after only a week— it's either misplaced chivalry or temporary insanity. You can't be ready for that sort of commitment."

"Wrong again. I never loved Kathryn the way I love you. Not after a week and not after a year. If I had, I would have married her." He gave Ellie's hand a hard squeeze. "Now I understand what was missing. Come on, let's eat. You don't have to answer me right away. I can see that you need some time."

Jed walked over to the table and pulled out a chair. Ellie sat down, thinking that for all his patience and understanding, he was used to getting his way. How long would it take before he started pressing her?

She screwed up her courage as he served the bacon and eggs. She wanted to be honest with both of them. Otherwise there was no point in talking. "I've never been attracted to a man the way I'm attracted to you," she said softly. "When I think about leaving you, my whole body gets clammy. But don't you see why I can't trust that? You took care of me last night, you saved my life, and then, when I was most vulnerable, you made love to me in a way that—that..." She looked at her plate. "It was incredible. I've never felt that way before. Now I can't separate the real you from the man who charged into my life on a white steed and rescued me."

"Who says there's a difference?" he teased.

"Of course there's a difference. You were horrible to me yesterday morning. I wanted to strangle you. Nobody is a hero one hundred percent of the time."

He smiled. "Ah, so you *can* separate the real me from the guy on the white horse."

Ellie was more confused than ever. "In my head I can, but not in my heart. I know you didn't get to be a successful businessman by being a nice guy all the time, but I look at you and I forget that. I can't be realistic."

"Lovers are never realistic." He winked at her, then stabbed a forkful of her scrambled eggs. "I'll taste this for you. I know how you feel about new restaurants."

Ellie resigned herself to being teased. He sampled her eggs and bacon, and then reached for her juice. A single sip and he was clutching his chest and gasping for breath. "Poison," he moaned, and slumped back in his chair. "Call the paramedics."

"Very funny," Ellie grumbled, but it *was* funny.

Jed opened his eyes, saw the smile on her face, and burst out laughing. Ellie did the same. Their laughter broke the ice, making her realize that they didn't have to settle the rest of their lives in the next ten minutes.

They discussed the day's plans over breakfast. First they would have to deal with last night's break-in, and then they would have to check on Ellie's car. She needed to tell the police why the brakes had failed. Finally, she wanted to talk to Abby Cludd.

She sat down with the phone while Jed cleared away the dishes. Her first call was to Jan, to assure her everything was all right, and her second was to Abby Cludd, to set up a meeting for later that day. She was listening to the same old recording when Jed returned to the room.

"Abby's answering machine is still on," she said as she hung up the phone. "That bothers me, Jed. She should have turned it off by now."

"She's probably still avoiding us," he said. "Or maybe she skipped town."

"I think something is wrong. I want to drive out to her house. I can go to my apartment afterward."

Jed decided to humor her. Quincy was forty-odd miles from Lexington and neither of them knew the area well, but Ellie found Abby's street on one of the maps in his glove compartment. The house was at the end of a short driveway.

It was large for only one person to live in and sat on a sizable parcel of land. Nobody seemed to be home. The inside lights were off and the front door was locked. As they walked past the garage on their way around to the back, Jed gave the garage-door handle an absent tug. Much to Ellie's surprise, the door began to roll open.

The Cadillac inside, a model from the sixties, was in mint condition, but she only noticed that later. The first thing she saw was the rubber hose leading from the tailpipe to the front window and the second was the woman's body in the front seat. She turned into Jed's arms as they backed away from the exhaust-laden air. She didn't want to believe what she'd seen. Where was this going to end?

"I'll take you back to the car," Jed said. "There's no reason for you to deal with this."

"No." Ellie took a deep breath and squared her shoulders. "I'll be okay. It was just such a shock that she would kill herself that way."

"Maybe she gave up after what happened last night. She knew we were on to her. The thought of going to jail for attempted murder must have been too much for her."

Ellie hung back a little as Jed opened the door of the Cadillac and examined Abby's body. She was wearing a tan raincoat and had a silk scarf over her hair. Her purse was on the seat beside her and a key chain containing about a dozen keys was dangling from the ignition. The car had run out of gas.

Jed switched off the engine and removed the keys. Ellie noticed him glance at Abby's face as he backed out of the car, then stop and begin to stare. She took a step forward as he pushed aside the collar of Abby's coat.

"What is it?" she asked. "What are you looking at?"

He straightened out of the car. "There was a bruise on her neck. Maybe this isn't what it looks like."

Ellie felt the blood drain from her face. "Are you saying she might have been murdered?"

It was exactly what Jed was saying. He was also remembering snatches of his conversation with Abby the previous night and feeling more and more guilty. "I should have listened to you last night and come here right away. She sounded terrified on the phone. Obviously she knew who the embezzler was. She knew who had tampered with your car. Oh, God, why didn't I take her more seriously?"

Ellie was sick with horror at the thought of what Abby must have suffered, but she was also worried about Jed. She hated to see him blame himself for Abby's death. Abby had *always* sounded terrified, so why should he have taken her seriously? Besides, he'd been worried about Ellie at the time.

She turned away from the car and put her arm around his waist. "You're saying she might have been strangled to death and put in the car afterward—that the murderer wanted it to look like a suicide. She might have been leaving the house to meet you when she was attacked."

"Maybe." Jed ran a hand through his hair, a grim look on his face. "Let's go inside and call the police."

He set Abby's keys on the counter and reached for the phone. Ellie picked them up and studied them. Each key was labeled with stick-on embossed tape from a hand-held label maker—obviously the work of the meticulous bookkeeper in Abby. While Jed talked to a detective, Ellie removed three keys from the key chain. They were labeled C-BLDG., C-OFFICE and C-FILES. Abby's murderer was going to pay for what he'd done. Ellie intended to track him down, even if it meant examining Cludds's records under a microscope.

A couple of hours later, she was a fraction less determined. She and Jed had told their story three times by then, first to the police in Quincy, then to the ones in Cambridge, and finally, by phone, to an officer in Newton, where her accident had occurred. With three different jurisdictions involved, it was going to be a complicated investigation. Ellie had her doubts about how fast things were going to move, because her statements about murder and attempted murder had met with a fair amount of skepticism. Not surprisingly, the police preferred to withhold judgment until they had received the autopsy report on Abby and examined Ellie's car for themselves.

Between the aftereffects of the accident and chasing around three different counties, Ellie was beginning to wilt. She was also hungry, so they stopped into a seafood place for lunch. The nautical decor made her think of Raven's Island, where everything had begun. Even the attempts on her life had begun there.

"Remember when you accused me of stealing two knives and a passkey last weekend, when we were on Raven's Island?" she said to Jed.

Jed remembered it very well. He remembered everything Ellie had ever said or done, especially what she'd done last night. The other knives and passkey, he told her, had turned up in the library. "Are you saying you didn't put them there?" he asked.

"No. I thought *you* had them. Somebody searched my room on Saturday, even though I'd locked the door. And then, in the middle of the night, somebody unlocked my door and started to come in. He was holding a kitchen knife. I guess I made too much noise while I was feeling around for my own knife, because he backed away after a few seconds and closed the door. He was gone by the time I got out of bed and looked into the hall."

"Did you pick up any details? Whether it was a man or a woman, for example?"

Ellie shook her head. "All I saw was a gloved hand holding a knife. Even last night—I think the person on my roof was either a small man or a larger woman, but I was too frightened to notice very much." Now that it was over, she could have kicked herself for not looking.

Jed wished Ellie would drop the whole topic. She was only upsetting herself—and him. Still, he could understand her reaction. Somebody had tried to kill her, or at least to scare her. She wouldn't be able to get on with her life until she knew who it was.

"Let's back up and look at this logically," he said. "The man or woman with the knife and the one who broke in last night must have been the same person. That narrows it down to somebody who was on Raven's Island last Saturday. James Emerson had left by then. Abby is dead now. Scotty and my sister have no connection to Cludds. That leaves Lynn, Marty and Rosemary McKay. Lynn hired you in the first place and Marty has nothing to do with the business. Besides, they had already left for Maine by last night. Rosemary looks like the most obvious possibility."

Ellie wasn't certain about that. "How can we be sure that Emerson was really sick? Maybe it was an act. Maybe he came back to the island later that day. And how do we know that Lynn and Marty really went to Maine? Maybe they're in this together. After all, you went to a lot of trouble to drag Marty back from Europe. You must have considered him a suspect."

Jed explained that Lynn had made up the list, including Marty because she'd wanted to see him again. Besides, he couldn't picture them embezzling from their own company. "You have a point about Emerson, though," he added. "In fact, anybody in the world could have slipped onto the island. I feel as if we're going around in circles."

Ellie opened her purse and took out a bunch of keys. Jed couldn't figure out what she was doing until he noticed the blue labels on them. They had come from Abby's key chain. He'd never even noticed they were gone.

"You filched those?" he said.

She smiled at him. "How else are we going to get into Abby's office on a Saturday?"

Jed could think of a dozen reasons why they should go straight home instead. Ellie was obviously tired. She was still recovering from the accident. The police should be handling this, not a pair of civilians. How much could the files really tell them, anyway?

One look at the determination on Ellie's face and his arguments died unspoken. Either he accompanied her to Cludds or she would get there on her own. As much as he loved her, she was the most stubborn woman he'd ever known.

He dawdled over his lunch so she would have a chance to rest, but he could stall for only so long. An hour later they were pulling into Cludds's parking lot. Although the store itself was busy, the area in back was deserted. Jed insisted that Ellie follow along behind him as they walked inside the building. The office looked empty, but somebody might be lying in wait.

The moment Ellie sat down at the computer, the tiredness that had dogged her all day seemed to disappear. She decided to go back five years and see what trends she could pick up. The most noticeable one was an increase in the cost of raw materials—fabric, notions, and so on. The total climb, although great, was surprisingly uneven. The same was true for the increase in the amount of wages paid to factory workers. It would stay the same for months, then suddenly jump.

Jed tried to track down the causes. Most of the original paperwork had been destroyed or filed elsewhere, but he managed to find invoices for the previous fiscal year as well as for the past six months. He jotted down the names of some of Cludds's suppliers, planning to call them on Monday and ask about their prices.

He was refiling the invoices when Ellie turned away from the computer. "I. V. Cludd sure gave a lot to charity." She handed him a list of year-by-year figures. "Lynn was apparently less generous. Her donations run about a quarter of his."

"Can we get a breakdown on these numbers?" Jed asked. "I'd be curious to know who was getting the money."

"I'll have to look at the check-by-check records."

Jed pulled up a chair to watch the screen as Ellie punched out the appropriate code, requesting the records from five years ago. "Beth Israel Hospital, $500," he read aloud. "Harvard University, $250...American Cancer Society, $100...NAACP, $200..." They were on August already. "That's peanuts. Where are the big contributions?"

"Let's go back. Maybe we missed something," Ellie said.

They read through the list of checks again, moving more slowly now. Midway through the month of February, Ellie pointed to the screen. "Look at this one: 'The Charles River Corporation, $3,000.' Who are they? A supplier?"

"I didn't come across the name on any invoices," Jed said. "Let's keep going."

By December, Cludds had paid $11,000 to the Charles River Corporation. The same was true over the next several years, with the final payment coming in the month of I. V. Cludd's death. A little addition showed that the payments to Charles River had been included in the total figure for charitable contributions, but Jed had never heard of the outfit. That was odd, because there wasn't a charity in town that didn't hit him up for money with tiresome regularity.

When the organization wasn't listed in the phone book, Jed started hunting around the office for cancelled checks. Only the past eighteen months' worth were in the files, but that was enough. He pulled out a check made out to the Charles River Corporation and looked at the bank stamp on the back.

"I have a friend there," he said, and picked up the phone.

"On a Saturday?" Ellie asked.

He smiled. "What are friends for?"

Ellie wasn't surprised when his friend turned out to be the president of the bank. The man seemed happy to do Jed a favor, even on a Saturday and even right away. Jed asked him to phone the house when he had some answers.

Ellie didn't miss the stern look on Jed's face as he hung up the phone. "If you're thinking about arguing with me about leaving, forget it," he said. "You've done enough for one day. Some dinner, a game or two of chess, and you're going to bed."

"And if I refuse?" Ellie was only teasing him. She was as tired as he'd claimed.

"I'll tie you up, carry you out of here over my shoulder, and force-feed you dinner." He folded his arms across his chest, waiting for her answer.

"In that case, I'll go quietly." She picked up her purse, and, smiling, headed for the door.

There was no question of returning home for the night. Jed had invited her to stay at his house and she'd accepted. She'd picked up some additional clothing when they'd stopped by her apartment. The only undecided issue concerned the sleeping arrangements.

The problem had been in the back of her mind all day. For as long as she could remember, she'd had a certain set of principles. No sex without commitment. Love and marriage came first, then physical intimacy. It was easy to say no to men who wanted the opposite, but Jed had complicated everything by proposing. As hard as it was to refuse him, she really had no choice. She needed to be sure of her feelings.

No sooner had they sat down to dinner than she launched into a speech about her values. Jed listened patiently for the first minute or so, then cut her off with a wave of his hand. "Let's get to the bottom line here. What am I allowed to do? Kiss you? Touch your breasts? Take off your clothes?" A smile tugged at the corners of his mouth. "Rub up against you and whisper compliments into your ear? Caress your beautiful body until you tell me you want to feel me inside of you?"

"I suppose you'll never let me live that down," Ellie muttered.

"Probably not," he agreed cheerfully. "So what's the verdict? How far do I get to go?"

Ellie knew what would happen the moment he began to touch her. She would want more and more, and Jed, who wasn't about to make a crusade out of being honorable, would generously let her have it. "We need to keep things platonic for now. Just friendship, Jed."

He managed to look crushed, but Ellie suspected he was secretly laughing at her. "Not even a kiss good-night? Nothing?"

"Maybe a handshake," Ellie conceded.

"If that's the way you want it." He turned his attention to his steak, acting as if he hadn't a care in the world.

Ellie didn't trust his casual attitude. "I'm serious about this," she insisted.

"Sure you are. We're going to keep things platonic. The only physical contact permitted will be—" He was interrupted by the ring of the telephone. "I'd better go grab that. Finish your dinner."

Ellie sat there brooding while he spoke on the phone. He was taking her dictum too well. Maybe he planned to sneak into her room when she was half asleep and do his best to seduce her. He would probably succeed.

He looked angry and a little distracted when he returned to the table. "That was Mike, from the bank. He tracked down the paperwork on the Charles River Corporation. The president and treasurer is James Emerson, Jr. The secretary is Matilda Emerson—probably his wife. If the outfit is a legitimate charity, I'm the King of Spain. The whole thing stinks of extortion."

"You mean Emerson was blackmailing I. V. Cludd?"

"It looks that way. The payments weren't for legal services and they weren't to a legitimate charity, so what else could they have been?" Jed started drumming his fingers on the table. "Only one thing bothers me. None of this ties in with Cludds's drop in profits. The real plunge only started *after* the last payment to Emerson. Obviously it has something to do with increases in the cost of labor and raw materials, but I've been working on the assumption that those increases weren't legitimate, that somehow the money was going elsewhere—into the embezzler's pocket."

Ellie agreed completely. "We need to have a talk with Mr. Emerson. Even if he has an alibi for last night, he's still mixed up in something suspicious. He's been connected with Cludds for a long time and he obviously knows where the bodies are buried. Maybe we can scare him into talking."

Jed didn't have to be told what Ellie had in mind. She wanted to drive to Emerson's house immediately, but that was out of the question. Emerson was almost certainly a blackmailer and might have been a murderer as well. Jed wasn't letting Ellie within a mile of the man.

That left the phone. Without a word, Jed got up from the table and walked back to the kitchen. Ellie followed, asking what he planned to do. He pulled a piece of paper out of his pocket and showed it to her.

"Call him," he said. "Mike gave me the address and phone number from the bank's records. Let's find out if he used his home phone for the Charles River account."

The phone was answered by a woman, who told him that Emerson wasn't at home. Jed then identified himself as J. L. Thornhill of the Polestar Corporation, giving her the impression it was a business call and something of an emergency. The woman became a little flustered, saying her husband was in the hospital but would probably be released next week. If it was really urgent—her tone said she knew how important J. L. Thornhill was—he could be reached in his hospital room.

When Jed asked for the details of Emerson's illness, it was like opening the spillway on a dam. Matilda Emerson went on and on, explaining how a cold had turned into flu and flu had become pneumonia. Her husband had been in intensive care for two days, practically since the moment he'd returned from Raven's Island. He'd been working from dawn to dusk, she complained, and the dank salt air had been the last straw. Jed finally cut her off by asking what hospital he was in.

He repeated the conversation to Ellie as soon as he'd hung up the phone. "Emerson seems to have an airtight alibi," he pointed out.

Ellie looked at her watch. "It's only eight o'clock. We still have time to see him."

"Now? At the hospital?" Jed had to restrain himself from yelling at her. "Be reasonable, honey. You've been chasing around all day. This is no time to confront Emerson about what he's been up to."

She lifted her chin in a way that spelled trouble. "I'll take a cab. What hospital did you say he was in?"

Jed hadn't mentioned the name, but it didn't matter. Ellie was perfectly capable of phoning every hospital in Bostin until she tracked Emerson down. Short of locking her in the nearest closet, he couldn't stop her from leaving.

Having no choice, he reluctantly agreed to take her. She rewarded him with a glowing smile that did unprintable things to his system. The woman was turning him into a marshmallow—a toasted marshmallow. If he hadn't been sure he'd have his way where it really counted, he would have had a tough time accepting what a patsy he was becoming.

Ellie had enormous confidence in Jed's abilities as an interrogator. After all, she'd once been on the wrong end of them. True to her expectations, he attacked James Emerson like an F-16 bomber—crisp, hard and precise. After summarizing the attempts on Ellie's life, he reeled off the history of Cludds's payments to the Charles River Corporation. Then, in an icy voice, he accused Emerson of blackmailing I. V. Cludd and then attacking Ellie and murdering Abby in a desperate effort to avoid detection. The last couple of charges were strictly for show, of course. Jed knew Emerson couldn't have killed anyone.

Emerson was too experienced an attorney to be stampeded into incriminating himself. Still, he was a sick man whose resistance was down, and the news of Abby's death had shaken him up. His stony denials were less convincing than he would have liked them to be.

"I'm willing to make a deal," Jed finally told him. "Let's lay our cards on the table. I'll concede that you didn't kill Abby or try to kill Ellie. Your illness gives you an alibi. But you did blackmail I. V. Cludd. I want to know why, Emerson. If you don't tell me what you know, I'll see that the Charles River Corporation is subject to the most stringent investigation that's ever been conducted in this state. If you think your reputation and your license to practice law can survive that, you're sicker than you look." He paused. "My only concern is Ellie's safety. I'm not averse to sweeping a little blackmail under the rug if I can get some satisfactory answers in return."

Emerson had become noticeably paler, but there was still no sign of panic on his face. It was utterly blank. "You understand that I'll deny everything if you come after me," he said coolly.

"Naturally," Jed replied.

Emerson took a sip of water and stared at the wall in front of his bed. "My father was Cludds's attorney before he died. He was also I. V. Cludd's closest friend. Izzy fell in love with Abby Devon during the war—madly in love with her. She'd come to work as a maid in his house. I'm told she was beautiful at the time." He gave a thin smile. "Beautiful and scared of her own shadow. Sound familiar?"

Jed ignored the question. "So he married her."

"Eventually, yes. But first there was an inconvenient first wife to dispose of. Jeanine wasn't the type to let him go without a scandal and an expensive divorce, and he knew it. He'd had affairs in the past and she'd made an unholy stink about them. Izzy took the only possible way out. He decided to kill her."

"But I thought she died in an automobile accident," Ellie said. That was what Rosemary had told her.

"She was dead before they put her in the car. Slow poison. Izzy used to mix it into her scrambled eggs before Abby brought up her tray. He got drunk one night years later and told my father about it. My father eventually told me."

"And you took full advantage of the knowledge," Jed said.

Emerson shrugged. "You're welcome to reach your own conclusions."

"Abby obviously knew you were blackmailing Cludd," Jed said, more to himself than to Emerson. "After all, she was the bookkeeper. She also must have known that somebody was embezzling from the company."

"Embezzling?" Emerson looked surprised. "Are you saying that embezzlement was at the root of the company's financial problems?"

"That's exactly what I'm saying." Jed was beginning to see the connections here. "The embezzler must have known how Jeanine really died. He—or she—used that knowledge to frighten Abby into keeping her mouth shut. No wonder the woman was terrified. She was being blackmailed over a murder she'd helped to commit years before. After Ellie's accident she finally decided to talk, and got murdered for her troubles." He paused. "Who else might have known how Jeanine really died?"

"Nobody," Emerson said. "Izzy wasn't that stupid."

"Obviously he was," Jed corrected, "at least when he wasn't sober. It all fits together. Who could have known? Who was he close enough to drink with?"

Emerson hesitated, then listed the possibilities. Besides his late father, there had been Cludd's mistress, Rosemary McKay; his son Marty, at least before their estrangement; and his various wives, especially the last of them, Lynn Cludd. In short, all the people they had already considered.

Jed had heard enough. In his own mind, the strongest suspect was Rosemary McKay. He didn't know how she'd stolen the money, but as soon as he figured it out he was going to call the police with the details and insist that they make an arrest.

Chapter Fourteen

For once, Ellie agreed with Jed about how to proceed. As much as she would have liked to go after Rosemary with both guns blazing, she realized it was impossible. It was late. She was tired. And they had no proof.

Exactly what had Rosemary done? Between the two of them, they came up with a number of possibilities, but none seemed more plausible than the next. Ellie could have spent the whole night speculating about it, but she could see that Jed was sick of the subject. He'd been a human Rock of Gibraltar for the past day and a half—not to mention an absolute sweetheart—so she tactfully shut her mouth. He suggested a game of chess and she agreed. He'd taken her everyplace she'd wanted to go that day, and the least she could do to thank him was spend the evening the way he wanted.

But the game was barely a few moves old when her attention began to wander. Part of her mind was on Cludds and part was on how attractive Jed was, which didn't leave much room for chess. Every few minutes she would have to scold herself into concentrating a little harder.

· Her thoughts drifted back to Cludds as she waited for Jed to make a move. Phony invoices, phony checks, high-tech scams with the computer—which was responsible for their problems? She chewed on her bottom lip. Embezzlement or not, the company should have been doing better. Their business in New England was strong. Why weren't their clothes selling as strongly elsewhere?

Was there greater competition elsewhere? Was somebody knocking off their designs? The question brought her up short. She could hardly wait until Jed had moved to tell him her newest theory.

"About Cludds," she began, and then ignored the long-suffering look on his face. "Rosemary ran their manufacturing operation. She was apparently given a lot of autonomy. Suppose some of the goods they produced never made it to market under the Cludds label? Suppose she stole the clothing and sold it herself? Cludds paid the costs of labor and materials and Rosemary kept the profits."

"It's possible," Jed said, sounding decidedly uninterested. "In case you haven't noticed, you're losing the game. Do you want to resign?"

Ellie studied the board, realized he was right, and grinned. "Resign, my foot. I'm going to beat you. Excuse me for a minute, would you? I need to make a phone call."

"For God's sake, Ellie, what now?" he asked. "Can't you forget business for even a minute?"

"As soon as I call Carol," she promised.

"Carol as in your sister?"

She nodded. "Carol is one of the all-time great shoppers. Department stores, boutiques, discount places—you name it, Carol knows it. I want to ask her if anybody in the New York area is selling clothing exactly like Cludds's."

"You know where the phone is," Jed said with a sigh.

Carol and her husband were at a play in the city, so Ellie left a message with the babysitter that Carol should call her at Jed's house first thing in the morning. She was so satisfied with her theory about stolen clothing that she was finally able to forget about Cludds and concentrate on chess.

Half an hour went by. Jed was playing well—better than he ever had before. After one especially creative move, he lazed back in his chair with an air of self-satisfaction and looked her up and down in a way that made her blush. "I seem to remember something about you sleeping with men who can beat you at chess. You're going to have to put out, darling."

"That was Ellie White, not me," Ellie corrected, "and besides, who says you're going to win?"

"I do," he replied. "Try to make it up those stairs without giving me what I've earned and see how far you get."

Alarm bells went off in Ellie's head. She couldn't tell if he was serious. "You agreed we'd keep things platonic. You can't go back on your word."

"I wouldn't think of it," he drawled. "I was talking about a handshake."

Ellie had her doubts about that, but the quickest way to spike his guns was to beat him. She was confident at first, but she hadn't counted on having to deal with the seed he'd planted. She would look at him, picture the two of them together, and ask herself questions she couldn't answer. Would he grab her before she could leave the room? Kiss her senseless? Undress her? Throw her down on the rug in front of the fireplace and make love to her?

They said the brain was the most erotic organ in the body, and they were right. The images kept coming until the room felt like a sauna. Ellie couldn't concentrate on chess. She would escape a trap with what she thought was an excellent move only to have Jed squeeze her even harder a few moves later. As the game wore on, she began to sense it was hopeless. He was playing far too well for her.

In the end she placed her king on its side and gave him a wary look. "We might as well stop playing. It's only a question of time before you mate me."

He picked up her queen and sensuously stroked it. The symbolism of the act was anything but subtle. "Smart lady. I was wondering when you would figure that out."

"I was talking about chess." Ellie fumbled for a snappy follow-up and came up empty. "Good night, Jed. I'll see you in the morning." She started to get up.

His hand shot out to circle her wrist. "You owe me a handshake first."

"*Just* a handshake," she reminded him.

"Right." Still holding her wrist, he got up from the table and slowly pulled her toward him until their bodies were almost touching. Then his fingers slid down to grasp her hand and shake it. The contact was electrifying. Ellie was torn between throwing herself into his arms and running away.

His hands settled on her hips to keep her where she was. "Don't you think my victory deserves more than a handshake?"

"No." Ellie looked at the floor. "I've already told you what I think."

"That we should keep things platonic."

"Yes."

He let his hands drop to his sides. "Okay, you win. If you want me, I'll be taking a shower—a *cold* shower." He stalked out of the room, leaving a shell-shocked Ellie to stare at his retreating back.

She tried to pull herself together as she put away the chess set. She'd stuck to her principles and that was all that counted. Damn Jed, anyway. He knew how he affected her. He didn't play fair, touching her that way. Now she was tense all over again, and frustrated into the bargain.

She took a long, hot shower and got into bed. The room felt empty and lonely. Every noise—an animal, scurrying through the attic, the oil burner clicking on, a door opening and closing—made her flinch. She huddled under the covers, fighting the same old fears. She was safe here, she told herself. Nothing was going to happen. If she repeated it over and over again, surely she would eventually believe it.

She wasn't conscious of deciding to leave. One moment she was shivering in bed and the next she was hurrying down the hall. Jed looked up from his magazine when she appeared in his doorway, but he didn't say a word. She got into bed with him, keeping as close to the opposite edge as she could.

She closed her eyes. Jed was so very close. Fear wasn't the only thing that had brought her here. Her desire for him was equally as much to blame. It was an endless torment to lie there in silence while the ache between her legs grew hotter and more distracting. It was scalding her blood and making her tremble. Without a single word or touch, her memories and her imagination were bringing her to flash point. Principles were hard to stick to when they collided with human weaknesses.

Jed put aside his magazine and turned off the light. He knew Ellie was upset. He knew he should offer to hold her. Her and her crazy ideas! Platonic friendship, hell! What did she think he was, a saint?

He began to lecture himself. It was his own damn fault for suggesting the chess game. He'd thought he was being clever, but his well-laid plans for seduction had blown up in his face. Winning had made him feel that he had proprietary rights to Ellie's body. He didn't. She'd made that crystal clear. Maybe a one-night stand was all they would ever share.

He angrily rejected the idea. Where was his self-confidence? She had to feel the same way he did. A woman like Ellie didn't climb into bed with a man she didn't love— not two nights in a row. Of course she loved him.

He was lying there, wrestling with the kinds of doubts that only a rejected lover can feel, when Ellie began to edge closer. He tensed, knowing she wanted comfort rather than sex. The satin of her pajamas brushed against his thigh, and her hand settled on his bare chest. He took a deep breath, shaking now. Christ, he had it bad. After last night, he shouldn't have been burning up this way.

When her hand moved lower to caress his belly, he was so startled he almost went through the ceiling. She couldn't be making a pass. It wasn't possible. She'd been responsive the night before, but *he'd* done all the touching. He hadn't expected anything different, given how inexperienced she'd been; but in time . . .

He flinched as her hand moved lower still, and discovered for itself how much he wanted her. The way she was stroking him—where had she learned to do that? Her mouth came down on his lips and he stopped wondering. Lying there and letting her arouse him clouded his mind and crystalized his senses. Surely he'd died and gone to heaven.

Ellie was groping her way in the darkness, touching and experimenting to learn what Jed liked. She'd wanted him so much that in the end she couldn't stop herself from taking him, but she'd never dreamed that touching him would be so arousing. She loved the feel of his skin. The urgency of his mouth when she kissed him told her how excited he was, and she loved that, too. She even loved the passive way he was lying there. Sooner or later he would lose control. How long would it take to make him do that? How much teasing could he take?

The moment arrived with shattering abruptness. He shoved away her fingers, pushed her onto her back, and made love to her with a passion-roughened intensity that might have stunned her if she hadn't been as excited as he was.

He didn't go as slowly as the night before, but he took the same care to protect and ready her. She felt a surge of love and gratitude as they joined together. Then gentleness gave way to need, and everything in the world disappeared except the demanding thrusts of his body and her own reckless response.

She remembered every second of it even before she opened her eyes the next morning. She'd done it again. *This* time she'd baldly seduced him. This time he was still in bed with her, cuddled up behind her with his arm thrown possessively around her waist. This time her mind had been clear, not fogged by drugs or terror. There were no excuses, no rationalizations.

She wriggled onto her back to see if he was awake. He was, and smiling the most arrogantly triumphant smile she'd ever seen. She couldn't blame him. She'd given herself body and soul last night. Actions spoke louder than words.

"Good morning," he murmured, and brushed his lips across her mouth. Ellie took the kiss for a casual greeting, but it was actually the exact opposite. Without another word, he started making love to her—kissing her deeply and passionately, caressing her with possessive, restless hands, holding her close and using his body to tease her. She felt like one of Pavlov's dogs—conditioned to respond. She was shocked by how quickly she caught fire and even more shocked by the things she allowed him to do.

She'd read her share of books, but nothing could have prepared her for the writhing pleasure he gave her with his tongue and teeth. She was desperate for release by the time he came inside her. She wanted to wait for him to catch up, but couldn't. Half a dozen thrusts and she was lost.

The most incredible feeling of tenderness took hold of her afterward. He'd stopped for a moment to let her catch her breath, but his body was still tense with need. She began to move her hips, slowly and seductively. Her fingers skittered down his back to seek out the places that would give him the most pleasure. The more intimate her caresses, the less his self-control, until he gave himself up to the moment and blindly took what he wanted.

A few moments later, holding her in his arms, he smiled the same self-satisfied smile as before. "I love your definition of platonic," he drawled.

"I suppose you'll be insufferable now," Ellie grumbled, and then mimicked what she expected him to say: "Why don't you admit you can't keep your hands off me? You wouldn't have done this with any other man. Doesn't that tell you something about the way you feel?"

"I couldn't have put it better myself," he said. "Go on, darling, answer your own questions."

Ellie forced herself to be honest. She'd seen a new side of herself during the past few days and it would have been cowardly to pretend it didn't exist. "All right, then. I can't keep my hands off you. I wouldn't have done it with any other man. I'm crazy about you. But love—I don't know about love."

He laughed at that. "There's a difference?"

"Of course there is. Love is forever. What we have now— it's like being on a roller-coaster ride. Everything's happening too fast. Sooner or later we'll have to slow down, and that's when I'll know if it's real."

"How long before that happens? A week? A month? A year?" He was still smiling at her, but very tenderly now. "I hope we'll be young enough to have children. I like the idea of having kids with you."

Few women could have resisted a statement like that, and Ellie was no exception. Even so, she wasn't going to be pushed into something she wasn't ready for. Jed didn't seem to realize how impulsive he was being. One of them had to be sensible.

"It's not something I can put a time limit on," she said. "When I'm sure of what I feel, I'll tell you. Who knows? Maybe you'll have changed your mind by then."

"Not a chance," he replied.

Ellie didn't want to quarrel with him. She felt wonderful at that moment—happy, relaxed and almost shamelessly satisfied. "Look at the bright side," she teased. "At least I'm not arguing about sleeping with you anymore." She traced a slow circle around his navel. "Your methods of persuasion were very effective. Keep using them and there's no telling how much you'll get out of me."

Jed privately told himself it was the other way around. Ellie had him wrapped around her little finger. He couldn't deny her a thing, especially after last night. God only knew what she'd talk him into next.

They decided to shower together and then fix breakfast, but neither was ready to get out of bed yet. They were lying in each other's arms, half dozing and half cuddling, when the telephone rang.

Jed picked it up, listened for a moment, and then said groggily, "She's right here. I'll put her on."

"Your sister," he added as he handed Ellie the phone.

Ellie barely had time to say hello before Carol started throwing questions at her. "You're right *where*? And who is this Jed person, anyhow?"

"A friend." Ellie smiled to herself. "A very special friend, okay? It's a long story, but the reason I called—"

"Special as in your lover?" Carol demanded.

"Yes, but what I need to know—"

Her sister gave a shriek. "You're kidding! I don't believe it! Well, actually I do believe it, and I want the details. How old is he? Has he ever been married? How did you meet him? What does he do for a living? When are we going to meet him?"

"Never, unless you quiet down for a minute," Ellie answered. "I need some information first."

"And then you'll tell me everything?"

"Within reason. Listen, Carol, do you know a company called Cludds Haberdashers? They sell classically styled clothing, on the preppy side, fairly expensive but it wears like iron.''

"Do I know Cludds?" Carol gave a disbelieving snort. "Is the Pope a Catholic? Of course I know Cludds, but why should I pay their prices when I can get almost the same clothing at two-thirds the price?"

Ellie asked Carol for some details and got chapter and verse in reply. The clothing in question was different in minor ways from Cludds's—buttons, thread colors, decorative touches—all of which Carol enumerated. She had come across the brand, Back Bay Fashions, in a number of different discount outlets, but had never seen it in any of the major department stores. In fact, she'd bought a skirt only a couple of days before and hadn't removed the tags yet. Did Ellie want her to check them out for further information? Ellie did. She was hoping the company's address would be listed, but there was only a city—Worcester, Massachusetts. It was probably no coincidence that Cludds's factory was in the same city.

Having satisfied Ellie's curiosity, Carol insisted on satisfying her own. Jed lay there with an amused look on his face while Ellie tried to come up with suitable answers. Carol was a worrier and Ellie didn't want to alarm her, but it was hard to explain about Jed and how they'd gotten together so fast without touching on little details like accidents that weren't really accidents and suicides that weren't really suicides. Faced with her sister's growing hysteria, Ellie finally gave up and handed the phone to Jed. He calmed Carol down by promising they would let the police handle everything from that point on.

Later, over breakfast, Ellie pointed out that the police wouldn't handle anything because they had nothing concrete to go on. She'd already told him about Back Bay Fashions and now she moved in for the kill. "We have to tie the company to Rosemary McKay. We have to prove she was taking garments that belonged to Cludds and selling them through Back Bay. The police aren't going to do anything unless we can give them some solid evidence.''

Ellie detected a distinct lack of enthusiasm in the answer Jed gave. "What do you want to do? Storm her house and confront her with your suspicions?''

"Of course not,'' Ellie said innocently. "I was thinking of something a little more subtle, like tracking down the company's address and officers.''

"It's a Sunday,'' Jed pointed out.

She dismissed that with a reproving smile. "Now, darling, I'm sure you know someone who could help us. It won't be that much trouble to check through the list of corporations registered with the secretary of state and jot down the information we want.''

"No trouble at all,'' he agreed with a sigh. He knew several people who might be able to help, including the secretary of the commonwealth himself. "And then what?''

"Then we'll go take a look. Nobody will be there on a Sunday. If there are windows, we'll be able to get an idea of what Rosemary's been up to.''

Jed sat there, thinking it over. He wasn't crazy about the idea of snooping around Rosemary's office, but if there were people around they could leave. He would have to keep Ellie on a short leash, that was all. "All right,'' he said. "I'll find out what you want to know, and I'll even drive you to Worcester, but that's it. Don't even ask me if I know how to jimmy locks. Breaking and entering is out of the question.''

Ellie laughed and said the thought had never occurred to her. Both of them knew she was lying.

Back Bay Fashions was a duly registered corporation that had filed all the proper forms with the Commonwealth of Massachusetts. It came as no surprise to Ellie that Rosemary McKay was the company's president. In fact, Ellie had to admire the woman's audacity. The corporation was fourteen years old, so obviously she'd been cheating Cludds for years. The situation might have continued on indefinitely if she hadn't gotten greedy and started stealing such large amounts.

It was late afternoon by the time Jed's friend had phoned back and they could leave for Worcester. They had passed the time with chess, conversation and the Red Sox game. They had also made love, with Jed slowing Ellie down and stretching things out until she was half out of her mind with frustration. He claimed he was only killing time, but Ellie knew better. Afterward, taking in his smile, she told him if his ego got any bigger, it would outgrow the bedroom.

It took less than an hour to get to Worcester, but finding Rosemary's office was a different story. Lacking a map, they stopped at a gas station for directions. Nobody had heard of Rosemary's street. They went through several more gas stations and fast-food places before somebody was able to help them. Then they wondered if the directions they'd gotten could be correct, because they were heading out of town, into an area where there were no office buildings and only an occasional house.

They finally came to the proper street, an isolated back road. Ellie was beginning to think neither the address nor the office existed when they spotted a mailbox with the proper number on it. Jed turned into the driveway, a narrow, rutted dirt road. There was a house on the left, beyond a stand of trees, but it looked as if it belonged in a horror movie. The paint was dirty and chipped and some of the shutters were askew or missing. The chimney was crumbling and several upstairs windows were boarded up. The yard was overgrown with weeds and scattered with rocks.

Jed made a U-turn and drew to a halt. "It looks like we can add violating health and safety regulations to the list of Rosemary's crimes," he said as they got out of the car. "This place makes a sweatshop look good."

They walked to the front door. It was locked, but probably not securely. Nothing about this place looked secure.

The shades on the first-story windows were cracked and yellowed with age. Although they were pulled down, Ellie was able to peek around them for a glimpse inside. The room on the right contained some industrial sewing machines and a portable heater. It was littered with scraps of fabric. The room on the left contained two large tables, one of them with a phone on it, and numerous stacks of flattened cartons. It looked as if Rosemary had taken unassembled garments from Cludds to this house, hired people to sew them and add distinctive finishing touches, and then shipped them to discount stores everywhere but New England. Ellie remarked to Jed that she must have used illegal aliens, because regular workers would never have tolerated such conditions.

They continued around to the side, passing a run-down bathroom and a filthy kitchen. The back door, which had no doorknob, was nailed shut. All of the windows had been locked up to that point, but the one next to the door was boarded up from the outside.

"I'll bet we could pull that off," Ellie said, referring to the slab of plywood.

Jed grabbed her hand before she could try it. "Why bother? Haven't you seen enough?"

"Maybe there are records inside. She had to keep track of her accounts." Ellie couldn't see what harm a quick look inside would do. The place was so ramshackle that the Big Bad Wolf could have disposed of it with a single puff. They weren't really breaking in. "Aren't you curious?" she asked.

"Not *that* curious," Jed said. "Come on, let's get out of here."

Having failed to move him by appealing to his curiosity, Ellie tried a more physical means of persuasion. She put her arms around his neck and nuzzled his lips. "Just five minutes, darling. Nobody's going to come."

Jed wondered how he could make love to Ellie three times in less than twenty-four hours and still feel as if lightning was slashing through his body just because she'd kissed him. He'd created a monster here, a brazen temptress who could turn him inside out with a single look or touch. Only a wimp would have let her get away with it.

"Forget it," he said aloud. "You're not going to manipulate me with sex. We're leaving."

"Spoilsport," she pouted. "Next time I need to solve a mystery, I'm leaving you at home."

"There's not going to be a next time, even if I have to lock you in the house." He removed her hands from his neck. "Do you walk or do I carry you?"

She raised herself to her full height and glared at him. Jed knew an outraged feminist when he saw one. "I'm not a child, Jed. I can make my own decisions. If you don't agree with them, fine; but don't try to tell me what to do."

Something inside Jed snapped. He'd gone along with every crazy demand from the woman—even against his better judgment—but enough was enough. "Dammit, Ellie, we're dealing with a psychopath here. For all we know, she's booby-trapped the house to blow up if anybody tries to break in. It's not male chauvinism to insist on a little common sense. I happen to love you. I don't want you to get hurt."

Ellie thought he was being ridiculous. They'd looked into most of the windows and hadn't seen any wires or plastic explosives. She said as much, then announced that she was going into the house—with him or without him.

"And I'm going to the car," he said, furious with her now. "If you care about me at all—if our relationship means anything to you—you'll come along. This whole business has turned into an obsession with you. It's not worth risking your life over." He turned around and walked away, his body stiff with anger.

Ellie watched him until he'd disappeared around the corner of the house, then stared at the boarded-up window. She gave the board a halfhearted tug, but it was stronger than it looked. Maybe Jed was right. The police wouldn't ignore this sort of evidence, especially not from a Thornhill. There was no need to go inside—not if it was going to give Jed fits.

She stood there for another couple of seconds before finally deciding to leave. But just as she turned around, a chill skittered down her back. She'd never experienced anything like it. An icy, inexplicable fear had taken hold of her, making the hairs on the back of her neck bristle.

Then she heard the voice—Rosemary's voice, addressing Jed. "Where's your little friend, Thornhill?"

There was menace in her tone, and bitter sarcasm. Ellie froze. Jed and Rosemary were at the side of the house, or maybe even in front of it. What did she do now?

"I don't know what you're talking about," Jed answered.

"I'm talking about Ellie Landau. I know you two are together. I saw your car in her driveway on Friday night. You wouldn't have left her alone. Get her out here—*now*!"

Rosemary obviously had a weapon, because otherwise Jed could have overpowered her. Ellie went from frightened to terrified when Jed ignored Rosemary's order and said instead, "Friday night? You mean after you killed Abby Cludd?"

"The stupid bitch deserved it. She had the nerve to call me and threaten me. Now stop wasting my time and get Ellie out of that house. I want her where I can see her."

Ellie started in the opposite direction from the way Jed had gone, toward the other side of the house. She'd just turned the corner when she heard him call to her. "We have to leave, darling. Come on out and let's get going."

There was a short silence while they waited for Ellie to appear. Then Rosemary said something about the front door. Ellie couldn't make out every word, but it sounded as if she was ordering Jed forward, so she could watch both him and the door at the same time.

Ellie had nearly reached the front corner of the house when Rosemary told Jed to call her again. "Tell her you're going to leave without her," she added, her voice chillingly close by.

The next voice Ellie heard was Jed's. "Come on, honey. Get a move on. I can't afford to wait around anymore."

Ellie steeled herself not to shake and peeked around the corner of the house. Rosemary was about fifteen feet away, standing with her back to Ellie and her side to the front door. She was pointing a gun at Jed's chest. If he saw Ellie's head dart around the corner, he gave no sign of it.

Instead, playing for time, he said to Rosemary, "You were running a brilliant operation here. You must have made a fortune over the years."

"You bet I did," she replied. "Izzy wouldn't marry me—I wasn't a virgin like his precious wives all were—but I paid him back." For all its venom, her voice had a hysterical edge to it. Ellie picked up a medium-sized rock and took a deep breath. "I'll be first in line when the bank opens tomorrow. As soon as I get the rest of my money, I'm leaving this stinking—" She cut herself off, as if she'd realized she was babbling. "Call her, damn you! Where is she?"

Ellie charged around the corner, holding the rock above her head. Rosemary heard her footfalls and jerked around, but Ellie was already heaving the rock at Rosemary's head and throwing herself to the ground. A shot exploded in her ear as Jed flung himself on Rosemary's back and knocked her down. There was a second shot as they struggled for the gun. Ellie somehow managed to scramble to her feet and pick up the rock she'd just thrown. A few seconds later she was bringing it down hard on Rosemary's head. A bloody gash appeared.

Everything had happened so fast that it wasn't until Rosemary was out cold and Jed had stood up that Ellie began to shake with reaction. This was real life, not a mystery novel, and she'd almost gotten Jed killed. The thought was even more horrifying than her own recent brushes with death.

"I'm sorry," she said. "This was all my fault. If I'd listened to you, none of this would have happened."

Jed had taken Rosemary's gun out of her hand and was carefully removing the ammunition cartridge. His face was deathly pale, as if he were going to faint. "I can't leave. I have to watch her." He took a deep breath. "Your shoulder—is it all right?"

Ellie had no idea what he was talking about until she looked at her left shoulder and saw the slowly spreading bloodstain on her shirt. She was suddenly aware of a throbbing pain. She pushed the shirt aside to examine her bare skin. There was blood all over, but no hole that she could see.

She started toward him. "It must have just grazed me. I didn't even feel it at first."

He put an arm around her, and, still watching the unconscious Rosemary, gave her a fierce hug. He was shaking as much as she was. "There's a first-aid kit in my trunk." He dug into his pocket. "Here, take my keys. Get a bandage on that."

"But Rosemary—shouldn't we call the police?"

"See if you can find her keys. We can try the phone inside."

Ellie wasn't so shaken that she didn't remember Jed's earlier warning. "Do you think it's safe to go in there?"

"It has to be," he answered. "That's where she thought you were. Until I saw you by the side of the house I thought she might be right. I was hoping you'd realize I sounded too friendly for something not to be wrong." He looked away for a second. "I shouldn't have lost my temper with you, but I was so damn frustrated and worried—"

"No, you were right. I never went inside. I was just start-ing toward your car when I heard Rosemary's voice."

She walked over to the Porsche and unlocked the trunk. After taking out the first-aid kit, she continued on to Rose-mary's station wagon. She had left her purse on the front seat. Her keys were inside, along with an airplane ticket to Rio de Janeiro. The rear seat was down and the back was filled with luggage. There were also two plastic containers of the type used to hold gasoline.

Ellie told Jed what she'd seen as she handed him Rose-mary's keys. She was still lying motionless on the ground, breathing regularly but showing no signs of coming to. The gash on her head was still oozing blood.

"I think she was packed to leave for good," Ellie said. "Maybe she was stopping here to burn the place down—to make it harder to trace her activities—before she left the country." She knelt down with the first-aid kit and took out some gauze pads and tape.

Jed knelt down beside her. "Maybe. She said something about getting the *rest* of her money out of the bank. She probably has a nest egg stashed away in a numbered ac-count somewhere—in Switzerland or the Caribbean. Here, let me help you with that."

As soon as he'd bandaged her shoulder, he nodded to-ward the house. "I'll see if the phone works. Watch her. If she moves even an inch, I want you to call me."

But Rosemary remained motionless, even after Jed came out to say that the police and an ambulance were on their way. He had found about a dozen cartons in the left-front room and opened one up to discover invoices and corre-spondence inside. The police would have plenty of evi-dence to work with.

The two of them stood and waited, both of them lost in thought. Ellie still blamed herself for what had happened, and Jed was only just recovering from the shock of realiz-ing Ellie had been shot. Each thought the other was incredibly brave—Ellie because Jed had faced down Rosemary so coolly, and Jed because Ellie had kept her head and managed what might have been a lifesaving attack with the rock.

Rosemary regained consciousness shortly before the ambulance arrived, but the glazed look in her eyes said she neither knew where she was nor realized what had happened. The police began to question Ellie and Jed even before the ambulance had pulled away. The session was shorter than Ellie had anticipated, perhaps because of her injury and perhaps because the physical evidence supported their story. Besides, the policemen knew the name Thornhill.

Somebody would be calling them in the morning to arrange for a more complete interview, but for now they were free to go. Ellie sighed and closed her eyes as Jed drove down the driveway. "I'm so sorry," she said, scarcely aware that she had already told him that. "You were right. I was being obsessive. If anything had happened to you..." Her throat was too tight to continue.

"Stop thinking about it. It's over and both of us are okay." He stroked her hair. "You were magnificent. You saved my life. I guess she didn't want to fire the gun because you might have heard it and gotten away, but I could tell she was starting to unravel. Another minute and she might have shot me. You didn't have to risk your life to save mine—you could have run away, but you stayed."

"Of course I stayed. I wouldn't have wanted to keep living if anything had happened to you." Ellie's eyes filled with tears. "I love you. I never want to be without you."

Jed pulled over to the side of the road and took her in his arms. Later, when the nightmare had faded a little, he would probably admit to her that the sight of her bloodstained shirt had brought him as close as he'd ever come to losing his last meal out of naked fear. What if the bullet had struck her head or heart? Thinking about it made his blood run cold, even now.

He told himself to think about her last few words instead. Did she really mean them, or was it the trauma of the past hour doing the talking? "You love me? Is that love as in you're crazy about me or love as in forever?"

"Love as in forever." Ellie didn't even have to think about it. "I told you that when *I* knew, you would know. Well, I know now and I'm telling you."

"Just like that?"

"Just like that." Snuggled against his chest this way, she hadn't a doubt in the world. She only knew that the idea of being without him was unthinkable.

He kissed her very gently, and she parted her lips for more. The embrace they shared was pure, raw emotion. Intensely passionate on the surface, it was really a way of saying to each other, "I need you. Don't ever leave me. Don't ever stop loving me."

When they drew apart, Ellie looked into Jed's eyes and saw that he still wasn't sure of her. He was afraid she would change her mind when morning came and the danger was merely a memory.

Her instincts told her that drama and tears were never going to reassure him. If ever two people had needed to smile together, it was Ellie and Jed at that particular moment.

She ran a teasing finger across his lips and gave him the coyest look she could manage. "Did I ever mention that I only marry men who can beat me at chess?"

He smiled, but only for a moment. "I beat you last night."

"That doesn't count. You distracted me with your incredible sex appeal." She paused, pretending to think the problem over. "We'll play again tonight. You have to promise to be dull and unappealing. If you win, I'll marry you."

"And if I lose?"

"Do you really need to ask?" She put her arms around him and gave him a smile that lit up the whole car.

Jed was about to say yes when he realized that the answer was no. He didn't need to ask. Ellie was calm and rational, and her feelings were written all over her face. She knew what she wanted—him—and she'd never hesitated to take what she wanted. He was going to win that chess match tonight, even if she had to play the worst game of her life.

COMING NEXT MONTH

FORGIVE AND FORGET—Tracy Sinclair
Rand worked for the one man Dani hated—her grandfather. And though Dani knew it was just Rand's job to entertain her, she found herself falling in love with him.

HONEYMOON FOR ONE—Carole Halston
Jack Adams was more than willing to do the imitation bridegroom act, but he didn't want to stop with an imitation, and Rita wasn't willing to comply. She wanted someone serious and stable, and Jack was anything but.

A MATCH FOR ALWAYS—Maralys Wills
Jon was a player without a coach; Lindy was a coach without a player. They made an unbeatable team so it was only natural they would find each other. Suddenly tennis wasn't the only game they were playing.

ONE MAN'S LOVE—Lisa Jackson
When Stacey agreed to help Nathan Sloan with his daughter, she didn't realize that the father would be the biggest puzzle—and cause the most problems.

SOMETHING WORTH KEEPING—Kathleen Eagle
Brenna was unsure about returning to the Black Hills, but nonetheless she was excited to compete against Cord O'Brien. She was confident she could win the horse race, but she might lose her heart in the process.

BETWEEN THE RAINDROPS—Mary Lynn Baxter
Cole Weston was hired to prove that Beth Loring was an unfit mother. But how could he build a case against this woman when he found himself falling head over heels in love with her?

AVAILABLE THIS MONTH:

DOUBLE JEOPARDY
Brooke Hastings

SHADOWS IN THE NIGHT
Linda Turner

WILDCATTER'S PROMISE
Margaret Ripy

JUST A KISS AWAY
Natalie Bishop

OUT OF A DREAM
Diana Stuart

WHIMS OF FATE
Ruth Langan

Silhouette Desire

**Available
January 1987**

NEVADA
SILVER

The third book in the exciting
Desire Trilogy by Joan Hohl.

The Sharp brothers are back, along with
sister Kit...and Logan McKittrick.

Kit's loved Logan all her life and, with a little
help from the silver glow of a Nevada night,
she must convince the stubborn rancher that
she's a woman who needs a man's love—not
the protection of another brother.

Don't miss *Nevada Silver*—Kit and
Logan's story and the conclusion
of Joan Hohl's acclaimed
Desire Trilogy.

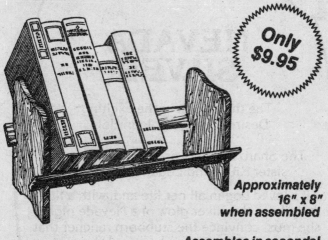